# STUPIT
# PEOPLE

# STUPIT PEOPLE

Tales of Corporate
Stupidity in a Business
World Gone Mad

## STEVE EATTS

A catalogue record for this book is available from the National Library of Australia

**australianauthors.store/steve-eatts**

Eatts, Steve (author)
*StupIT People: Tales of Corporate Stupidity in a Business World Gone Mad*
ISBN 978-1-922452-52-8 (paperback)
978-1-922452-21-4 (ebook)
FICTION / Satire
HUMOUR / Business and Professional

Cover and book design by Green Hill Publishing

The characters and events in this book are fictitious and any resemblance to real persons, living or dead, is purely coincidental. Except for Amy. She's real and she is awesome.

*For Tracy*

# Acknowledgements

IMMENSE THANKS AND HEARTFELT GRATITUDE to Tracy, Ben and Sam for their unwavering support of me and all that I've sought to do in life. Also, to my extended family for their love and support through both good and challenging times. Lastly, a massive shout out to Michelle for her support, encouragement and editorial help.

# Preface

IT TOOK ME MANY YEARS in the industry to finally come to grips with the necessity of the sales function in an IT Services business, or any big business for that matter. Having started off as a low-level grunt on the delivery side of the house, I somehow thought that having new projects and interesting things to work on for clients was just an endless, never-ending cycle. It wasn't until I was eventually asked to assist with some pre-sales activities on a deal - because they wanted someone with at least a modicum of delivery substance to help present to a prospective client - that I really began to twig about the true importance of sales.

I still saw it as an evil empire, but I began to comprehend that it was a critical function required to operate effectively in order to continually feed the backlog of work to be done by the company. The best analogy to colour this, that I've heard, is around the real estate industry. You see, for real estate agents it's not really about selling property. Sure, it's important that they do a great job at marketing, and ultimately selling houses. But for the agents themselves it's really all about obtaining property listings so that they have something to sell.

Once that penny dropped for me, I started to see the sales function in a new and essential light. I also began to understand that I didn't have to sell my soul to the devil to succeed in sales. At least, that is what I hoped. Plus, it sure pays a damn sight better than your average delivery role in the services business, especially when the sales incentive bonuses kick in.

The sales function in the big technology business world has itself undergone a massive and quite radical transformation over the past twenty or so years. For example, cycle times for chasing business have reduced significantly. Where you may have once had five or six weeks (or even more) to put together a comprehensive proposal to a client, you are likely to now have two to three weeks, if you are lucky.

In addition, the idea of planning and mobilising for major opportunities months or even years in advance has also largely vanished. Now the cycle time within the business itself is increasingly driven by quarterly and in-quarter markers that define progress against short-term sales targets. The thirst of Wall Street - or in the case of the Australian Share Market, Bridge Street in Sydney - for updates against quarterly business targets is insatiable. And Senior Executives hell-bent on beating the short-term company targets set for them in order to achieve their own bonus-linked KPIs, drive the machine like a relentless, sales-hungry beast.

As we will see, this leads to some very stupid and short-sighted corporate behaviour. And this causes decisions to be made increasingly and primarily in the pursuit of near-term profits and shareholder value, rather than actually doing the right thing by clients and employees.

# Part I

## Chapter One

# The Telco Deal

THIS DEAL HAS BEEN A REAL GRIND. We've been at it for months now and at times it feels as if we are really no closer to getting it across the line than we were before Christmas. That was when it was seen as a 'must win, critical deal' for the quarter, and indeed the fiscal year.

I remember our arsehole of a Managing Director, Christiaan Joubert, bluntly telling the deal leadership team that we were all personally on the hook to deliver the signed contract by December 31st, or else there would be dire consequences. The real challenge to making that target was the client who, at that stage, had no bloody idea whatsoever of what they actually wanted included in the scope of services. So the idea of having a Statement of Work ready for signature before the year was out was a complete and utter farce.

But given that Christiaan had made commitments up the line to our global leadership that the deal was a sure thing for the year, the usual game of dodging and weaving around the truth was played until it finally became so obvious that Telco Pty Ltd had absolutely no intention of clearly defining their requirements, let alone engaging us in a sole-sourced contract negotiation process, until at least the end of March. So someone had to tell the MD.

That task fell by accident to Hamish, our Industry Leader for Govt and Telco, who was one of the very few people in the organisation who didn't fear Christiaan. Hamish has been around the traps for ever, is extremely well networked, and apparently also has a high personal net wealth. So not only has he seen it all before, he couldn't actually give a flying fuck if Christiaan threatened to sack him, which is Christiaan's usual modus operandi.

When it happened on the daily deal update call in mid-December, it was epic. Hamish joined the Skype call slightly late (it was something of a miracle that he joined at all, as he rarely bothered attending these), while Christiaan, who himself had decided to make a guest appearance on the call that day, was ripping into Dianne, our Sales Director. Dianne had just accidentally thrown some doubt onto the deal by suggesting that with the compulsory staff shutdown period over Christmas about to take effect, and knowing that it applied to both our company and Telco Pty Ltd, we may not have the right people on deck to get the deal done.

'What fucken resource constraints are you talking about? No one said that the deal team had to take the Christmas shutdown off.'

'But Christiaan, you said no exceptions at the Leadership meeting last week,' responded Dianne.

'I meant no exceptions apart from obviously critical deal resources, you fucken stupid bitch,' Christiaan matter-of-factly shot back.

It was at this point that Hamish chimed in, cheerily apologising that he'd missed the start of the call but that he had some new information from his connections at Telco Pty Ltd to share, that might help the discussion.

'I've been talking to the Head of Procurement and also the Program Director. Both of them have informed me that their committed decision timeline is to finish defining the requirements after the Christmas break, then to move forward through the pricing and contract negotiations with a view to signing a Statement of Work at the end of March,' he stated. 'So my suggestion is that we stop this nonsense and carry-on about signing anything this fiscal year, let the team have a proper Christmas break, and regroup in January after the shutdown period finishes.'

Silence. For at least a good 10 seconds, before Christiaan huffed: 'OK, send me that in an email, Hamish. Dianne, I want all Sales and Solutioning resources off over the shutdown, no fucken exceptions. Understand?' Then he dropped off the call before she could answer.

Awesome! This means that I do get to go home to Adelaide and have some sort of a Christmas break with Emily and the kids, rather than travelling back to Sydney to spend time in the deal 'war room' at our company office in an Industrial Tech park estate on the fringe of the city that will be even more deserted and soulless over Christmas than it usually is. And the war room would be populated with a bunch of equally grumpy colleagues who also didn't want to be there slaving towards a completely hopeless and unachievable outcome because the MD made a stupid commitment.

Thankfully, Hamish has ensured that sanity has prevailed, at least temporarily.

I used to despise the dreaded Christmas shutdown period when it first came into fashion, mostly from the point of view that it was my annual leave, and why should the company tell me when I have to take a large slab of it? Increasingly over the past few years, the time frame for the shutdown has expanded, as IT services companies like The Company worked out that many of their workers slacked off completely while most of their clients in turn were on leave. What started as a forced break of, say, 3 or 4 days between Christmas and New Year, evolved over a few years to become 8 or 9 days, or in extreme cases three weeks. Now I don't really care so much about having an enforced break imposed, as long as I get a half-decent break at some point - preferably without too many of the work interruptions which seem to be a hallmark of the modern, always on, always connected business.

Anyway, I'd better call Emily with the good news that it looked like I'd get some time off over Christmas. Oh shit, it was Dianne calling, guess she wanted to talk about the call....

'Hi, Dianne'.

'Hi, Mike. Listen, I think we need to rethink,' she says.

'Rethink what, Di?'

'That whole stand-the-team-down thing. Don't you think it would be beneficial if we kept the core team going over Christmas, so that we don't lose too much momentum? March isn't that far away and we've got an awful lot to do.'

'Dianne, didn't you just hear what Christiaan said?' I asked.

'Yes of course I did, but I want to go back to him with a proactive proposal that shows how committed the Sales Team is to getting this deal done.'

Shit, just when I thought I might catch a break! Now my pleasant thoughts of some relaxing down time with the family were evaporating right before me. Just because Dianne is a workaholic who is always on (mostly out of fear of losing her job), doesn't mean the rest of us have to be.

'But Di,' I say, mustering the most caring and compassionate voice I can find, 'don't you think we'll actually be better off letting the team have a little breather and coming back to the deal refreshed and more energetic than ever in the new year? I think allowing them to spend some quality time with their families and loved ones over Christmas would be a really great gesture on your behalf, and it will also allow you to comply completely with Christiaan's shutdown request too. So I think that standing the team down for the break is a win-win scenario for you, for the team – most of which haven't had a weekend off with their family for three months, and it will also be better for The Company.'

'You know what, I think you might be right, Michael.'

Phew!

She continued thinking out loud: 'I can sell this to Christiaan as the right approach. It's in line with his stupid shutdown policy, and I can let him know that we now have a plan to accelerate the deal early in the new year.'

'And I think the Sales and Solution Teams will be very grateful, Di, that you've been able to orchestrate a Christmas break for them this year. It hasn't happened for a few years now for most of them,' I said.

'Absolutely. Thanks, Michael. Leave it with me.'

Holy shit, that was a bullet dodged. I'd better call Emily, I thought. But before I could, I received a message from Tony, my trusty lead Solutioner on the deal. He's the hard-working, ever reliable guy who essentially pulls it all together, including the scope of services and the pricing. People like Tony are the backbone of any complex sales pursuit.

Thursday 4:11pm

> Hey Mike, heard about the call this morning, can you call me ASAP? Thx, Tony

Good timing that he's reached out. I can tell him the good news.

'Hey Tony, how's it going?'

'Thanks for calling, Mike. I heard that the call was pretty fiery this morning.'

'Yeah, it sure was. Thank god Hamish injected some reality and sense into the discussion. And the great news is that we now get to take some time out over Christmas,' I said.

Tony continued: 'Yeah, that's what I wanted to talk about, Mike. I'm really worried that we are going to lose too much time.'

What the fuck? Not Tony as well as Dianne... 'Why is that, Tony?'

'Well, we haven't been able to finalise the first draft solution yet. I don't have any initial pricing from our offshore support team in India, and there's a lot of content still to deal with…'

'Stop, Tony,' I interrupt. 'There's no draft solution because the client hasn't defined their requirements yet. There can't be any initial pricing until we have at least those draft requirements, and there is no point putting together any response content until we know what the fuck we are responding to.'

'I know, Mike. But I think I need to carry on through, to at least make a start.'

'Make a start on what though, Tony? We'd just be making up a mock solution without any client requirements. What's really going on here mate? Why don't you want to take the time off?' I asked bluntly, having known and worked closely with Tony for quite a while.

'Well, to be honest, Mikey, me and Renee and the kids have a big trip planned for June next year to the States, and I want to save my leave until then. Besides, I'd really prefer not to have to spend too much time with Renee's psycho family over Christmas, mate.'

'Why didn't you just tell me that, Tony, instead of talking BS about the solution, mate? I'm happy to try and get you an exception to work over the shutdown. We just need a plausible explanation of what work is essential for you to continue doing over the break, so that I can sell that to Dianne and she can convince the big South African prick to approve an exception.'

'OK. Thanks, Mikey. Sorry for beating around the bush, mate. I'll drop you a note listing some key tasks that I can complete, that will give us a head start for next year. Is that OK?'

'Sweet, mate. Send me an email and I'll brief Di as well. Cheers.'

Now, I'd better call Emily and let her know that I'm getting a break before I get any more crisis calls... 'Hi Emily, guess what? I get to take some time off over Christmas this year.'

'I'll believe that when I see it,' she says, ever the cynic when it comes to the demands of my job. 'How come?'

'They've finally realised that this opportunity with Telco Pty Ltd is still an early-stage deal with no chance of closing this year, so they are standing the team down over the shut-down period,' I explained.

'Like I said, I'll believe it when I see it,' she added, because let's face it, she's heard it all before.

## Chapter Two

# The Alternate Proposal

So HERE WE ARE. IT's now three weeks into March and most of the Telco Pty Ltd deal has been locked down and agreed with the client. That is, except for the support services component, which is the part that I am responsible for. Having worked in Managed IT support services sales for some time now, it's never a surprise that this is the component that always gets left to the very last minute. It's partly by necessity, as we need to know what the rest of the services solution looks like in order to be able to scope out and price the ongoing support services. But it's also partly because it's the less glamorous and interesting part of the whole deal, so it gets continually pushed to the back-burner while everyone fluffs around fine-tuning the design, development and implementation parts of the overall solution.

It's critically important to get it done, though. The Head of Procurement for Telco Pty Ltd has made it very clear that the overall deal will not be signed without the full scope of support services being included. Which is a good thing, as we often get our colleagues from the consulting part of our business, who do the up-front design work, pushing the client to just sign the Statement of Work for that component, leaving the rest of the development, implementation and support services to be contracted later. This is often the agenda pursued by Rudy Beaumont, the Director of Strategic Consulting and one of the biggest wankers in our company.

For Rudy it means that he gets his signing now, and his team can merrily start their often ill-fated design piece. For the rest of the business it usually means turning a multi-year, multi-million-dollar deal into a six-month scoping study worth just a few hundred k. It also often results in Rudy's army of consulting geniuses completely fucking up the initial work when they over-promise and under-deliver on expectations, destroying the client relationship in the process before we get the chance to conclude the rest of the deal.

So it's a good thing that that won't be the case here with Telco Pty Ltd. Rudy and his team have thankfully had very little to do with this deal so there's been no real interference there; and with us as the clear preferred supplier, most of the deal fully defined, and a signing ceremony booked for Friday 29th March, what could possibly go wrong? Oh, that's right, we haven't finalised my part (the ongoing support services component) yet; and with now just a week to go until the formal signing, I'm starting to really feel the pressure.

It actually turned out to be a good thing that Tony worked through most of the Christmas shutdown period. It was, though, a pain in the arse that I also had to work through most of it, because as it turned out when I sought exception approval for Tony it was agreed to by Dianne and Christiaan on the basis that I had to return to work straight after Boxing

Day to ensure that Tony had the 'right executive support to keep things moving forward' with our Global and Offshore Solution Teams. That was a fun conversation with Emily at the time. But Tony was delighted to work through, and he worked with gusto to marshal the offshore team in India and to develop a hypothetical draft support solution based on where they thought the design might land. I'm not sure if it was a fluke or the result of some very shrewd analysis and thinking, but they actually got it pretty close to the mark of the initial design solution, which wasn't actually provided to us until the end of February.

Since then, though, the design solution has changed on a daily basis, sometimes substantially. It seems that every morning in the daily team status call we are informed of some 'minor tweaks' to the design solution, which are of course never minor. We've struggled to keep our support component relevant and we must have gone through about a dozen approval cycles by now. Given the size of the deal, this includes reviewers from our offshore operations and Global HQ, meaning almost daily late-night conference calls. Tony is a master at setting these up and keeping them on track. He even lets me know which calls I absolutely need to attend, and gives me cues to say certain things that he knows will help progress our cause. I just follow his lead, as usually I am too tired after starting the day with the daily 8 am deal team status call, and often I am three or more glasses of wine deep in my hotel room by the time these calls start at 10:30 or 11 pm. So staying awake, not sounding like I've been drinking, and ultimately getting the tick of approval from people who will almost certainly never actually have anything to do with the Telco deal once it's been sold, is the mark of success on these calls.

There are also the multiple stakeholders to keep updated on progress. Especially Dianne, who seems to require updates at a frequency which of course narrows in line with how close the deal is to getting signed. I don't envy her, having to deal with Christiaan and a host of other interested bystanders demanding ad hoc updates on exactly where we are up to. But it's bloody distracting when you are trying to lock down the solution, get the Statement of Work finalised, and ensure that there are no last-minute glitches that impact the price.

There was Dianne messaging me again now.

Tuesday 8:45am

Mike, what's the status of the support soln? Need urgent update for ELM this morning. Thx, Di

Hi Di, same as my update when we spoke earlier this morning. Final solution changes approved last night. Team making last updates to SOW. We will be ready for legal review with client tomorrow. cheers, Mike

ELM, by the way, stands for Executive Leadership Meeting. It's the weekly coming together of Christiaan's leadership team. Thank God I'm not at those lofty heights in The Company; Dianne is welcome to that and all the crap that goes with it. The less I have to deal with some of the clowns and arseholes on the EL Team, the better - especially the MD himself, who is quite the piece of work. The fewer conversations I have with him, the better my quality of life is, I reckon.

Time to check in with Tony on the final changes, so I grab a coffee and one for Tony and head down to the deal war room. 'Hey, Tony. Here you go, mate. How are you going with the final SOW updates?'

'I've just finished updating the approval artefacts from the call last night, Mike. Getting onto the SOW changes now. Should only take me half an hour. Then I just need to check with Lu Lu that this last round of changes has no pricing impacts, and we will be locked and loaded.'

'That's awesome, Tony. Thanks. I'll give Lu Lu a heads up on what we need.'

Lu Lu is our Lead Pricer on the deal and she is an amazing mathematical and spreadsheeting genius. Especially when it comes to calculating her share of the Sales Team's commission from the deal! I don't know how she does it, but she manages to juggle multiple deals, her husband and several kids, all without ever appearing to sleep. Legend has it that she once made a mistake in a pricing formula, but it's never been proven, and quite frankly, I think that's just a bullshit rumour.

It goes to voice message. 'Hi, Lu Lu. It's Mike. Just wanted to give you the heads up that the final changes to the support solution flowing from Tuesday's design update were approved last night. Tony will give you the details once he's finished updating the SOW in the next half hour, but we expect zero impact to pricing from these minor changes. Would appreciate you confirming. Thanks.'

Tuesday 9:13am

Mike, CJ wants an end of day status update. Can you drop me an email by 4pm please. Thx, Di

No worries Di, will do. Just with team now and all on track. Mike

I added the bit about being with the team now because Di loves those small details. She can drop them into the ELM conversation to show how on top of her team and deals she is. It's her way of adding value so I help her wherever I can, as it keeps the heat off me too.

Tony wandered over and seemed a little agitated. 'What's up, mate? You seem a bit twitchy. How many coffees have you had this morning?'

'Just three, Mikey. Oh, and the one you brought me. I was just speaking with Dexter from the Consulting practice to let him know we had their final adjustments approved, and he mentioned that there might be some changes to the underlying technology solution. I told him that we were locked down now, but he kept babbling on about the need to introduce a different set of analysis tools that Gartner just rated as the leader in their latest Magic Quadrant. I told him you'd call him, Mike.'

Shit. Those pricks in Consulting have had hardly anything to do with this deal and now they think they can come in and mess with the solution this late. Any changes now would cause huge amounts of rework – solution updates, pricing changes, schedule changes, re-approvals, etc. Typical. And Dexter Bartholomew is one of the worst offenders. The so-called Chief Architect of the Consulting practice is an intellectual wanker who adds no value and constantly waffles on about meaningless technology stuff such as the latest Analyst rankings or some emerging piece of unproven tech created by an obscure start up-that has no place in a Tier-1, mission-critical technology system.

'Hi, Dexter. It's Michael Mansfield.' I'm going to have to cut to the chase with this guy before he gets his waffle on. 'I just heard from Tony that you are thinking about changing the analysis tooling in the solution, which I assume he misunderstood as I know that you know the solution is now fully locked down and we go into final legal reviews of the SOW from tomorrow.'

'Hello, Michael. It's nice to speak with you. Yes, I was just telling Tony that we are going to switch over to the newest Cone Systems software as the analytical engine. It's just been rated by Gartner as the Visionary Leader in their latest Magic Quadrant.'

'But, Dexter, surely you understand that this means we'll have to rework that part of the support solution to ensure we have skills in place around this technology - and we don't have the time to do this,' I say, appealing to his logic, if indeed he had any.

'I don't see why that's an issue, Michael. The solution won't be in place until mid-next year.'

'Yes, but the signing ceremony for the deal is this Friday and we have to have the solution, pricing and Statement of Work finalised today for legal review tomorrow and Thursday. Dexter, there simply isn't enough time left to change the solution now.'

'But it's essential for Telco that we use this latest technology in our solution,' said Dexter somewhat patronisingly.

'Why is that, Dexter?'

'Well, it's been rated by Gartner as...'

'You've already told me that, Dexter. Why else?'

'Because it will provide Telco Pty Ltd with a future-proof analytics platform that will enable them to use modern data mining techniques to detect outliers and...'

I had to interrupt again as he was getting on a roll now and my ears and brain were starting to hurt. 'How exactly does this fit with the technology guidelines that Telco Pty Ltd gave us to shape our solution?' I enquired.

'Well, Michael, Telco actually specified that we were to use their existing analytics platform, as they've already purchased enterprise licences.'

'So you are saying that this goes against the directions they've given us?'

'Yes, but...' stammered Dexter.

'And it will cost them significantly more, as they've already funded the existing platform.' Stay calm, don't overreact, I think, even though this complete tosser is giving me the irrits. 'So why exactly would we suggest something different now?'

Dexter responded firmly, mustering as much of his sense of superiority as he could. 'As I said, Michael, I believe that we need to embrace Cone Systems in our solution because it's now rated as the clear market-leading software.' He continued: 'I mean, even though it's not been fully deployed by anyone in our region yet, Gartner said it was a game-changing leader in this class of analytics solution...'

'Dexter,' I interrupted again, 'let me be very clear here. We are not making a last-minute change to adopt an unproven technology that our client doesn't want, at a significantly higher price than what we've already included. We have a signing ceremony booked for this Friday, and there are only two days before that to get through the final legal negotiations. So there will be no further changes to the approved solution. Goodbye.'

I turned to Tony. who'd been listening intently to my side of the conversation. 'For fuck's sake, Tony! These tossers live in an alternate reality. Here we are trying to get this deal over the line, and they come up with ridiculous and unnecessary changes that don't actually add any tangible value, introduce additional risk, and sure as hell will fuck up the financial business case!'

'Thanks, Mike. I'll keep going on the final SOW drafting,' said a relieved Tony.

Now I'd better let Dianne know we've avoided a potential land mine here.

| From: | Michael Mansfield – 26/03/2019 9:31am |
|---|---|
| To: | Dianne Johnson |
| Subject: | FYI – Late change thwarted |

Hi Dianne,
Just a quick FYI that I've just shut down a late attempt by Consulting to change the Analytics technology in the solution to ensure that we stay on track with our signing time frame this week. Dexter won't be happy but his proposal to change would have added significant cost to the solution for no tangible benefit and in fact would have been counter to the direction given by Telco Pty Ltd.

Anyway, just FYI in case you hear any noise.
regards,
Mike

Precisely 30 seconds after I hit send, my phone rang with a call from Dianne. 'Mike,' she said in hushed tones, 'what the hell is going on with these critical final changes, and what exactly did you say to upset Dexter?'

'What? I was very careful in pushing back to Dexter and didn't say anything that should have upset him. And what do you mean by "critical final changes"?'

'Rudy just got a message from Dexter and he went ballistic at the ELM. Apparently you are refusing to accept this minor change in the analytics solution that will, in Rudy's words, "differentiate us and clinch the deal" with Telco Pty Ltd. Luckily Christiaan had stepped out of the room, but Rudy will definitely escalate; so I need to understand the facts asap.'

'Righto, Dianne. Here's the facts. Firstly, since the use of their existing analytics technology is a mandatory requirement, by introducing a different technology, this change will violate the specific technology guidelines given to us by Telco Ltd. Secondly, it will significantly increase our cost base, and will definitely put us well and truly above the deal price that Telco have indicated is acceptable against their budget. Thirdly, this Cone Systems analytics technology hasn't actually been implemented anywhere in this region yet, as Dexter himself has confirmed. So the risk profile of the solution goes up, and getting hold of any skills in this new technology will be a nightmare. And lastly, Dianne, Dexter is a useless, theoretical wanker who just wants this change because he read about it in a Gartner report last night!'

"OK, Mike, I get it. Especially the bit about Dexter. But let's keep that between us. You didn't call him that, did you?'

'No, Dianne. As I said, I was composed, and pushed back politely but firmly; and I fought off the urge to call him a fuckwit. What do you want me to do now?'

'Keep finalising the existing solution and I'll try and calm Rudy down with these clarifications.'

I look over at Tony who has heard the whole exchange and is shaking his head in disbelief, having joined the dots on the other side of the conversation.

'Good news, Mikey,' he says. 'I've finished the SOW draft, and Lu Lu has confirmed that last night's adjustments did not require pricing updates. So, mate, we are good to go.'

'Awesome, buddy. Well done. I'll let Kim from Legal know that she'll have the final docs by lunchtime, ready for a big couple of days of final review.'

Later that morning the phone buzzes with a message from Dianne.

Tuesday 10:56am

M, Just forwarded you an email. Plse respond with facts ASAP! D

| From: | Dianne Johnson – 26/03/2019 10:55am |
|---|---|
| To: | Michael Mansfield |
| Fwd: | Urgent Escalation re Telco deal winning solution changes |

Mike,

Please give me a few dot points to assist with response below.

Thx,

Di

Sales Director

| From: | Rudy Beaumont – 26/03/2019 10:13am |
|---|---|
| To: | Christiaan Joubert |
| Cc: | Dianne Johnson; Dexter Bartholomew |
| Subject: | Urgent Escalation re Telco deal winning solution changes |

Christiaan,

As discussed just now I require your urgent intervention to ensure that we produce a ground-breaking and award-winning solution for the Telco deal. I am deeply alarmed that the expert advice from my Chief Architect is not being heeded by some ignorant individuals on the broader deal pursuit team, and that not including this small but critical final adjustment will severely jeopardise my team's chances of winning this vitally important business.

May I please request your personal intervention to ensure that the obviously sensible outcome is achieved here.

best regards,

*Rudy Beaumont*

Executive Director, Strategic Consulting

Oh, for fuck's sake! I need another coffee before I can respond to this crap. 'Hey, Tony, want another coffee? I'm heading downstairs to grab one and to take a few deep breaths.'

Tuesday 11:25am

> Di, Just sent you an email with 'the facts' in line with what we discussed earlier. I'm rather annoyed at being described as ignorant but I've let that go thru to the keeper for now. Let me know if you need anything else. Mike

> Also I let Kim know that we'll be ready with the docs later today to start the final legal review tomorrow. Assuming that we shut down this late change crap. Mike

Just after lunch, Di called. 'Good news, Mike. We've shut down the issue on that late change that Rudy and his team wanted.'

'That awesome, thanks, Di. I'll send Kim the final draft pack now.'

'Not so fast, Mike. There was a slight compromise that may require a few minor adjustments.'

'What do you mean by "slight compromise", Di?'

'Well, Rudy was very insistent on including this new technology, and whilst Christiaan was clever enough to push it out of the core solution lest we price ourselves out of the deal, he demanded that we include it in our alternative solution.'

'What alternative solution, Dianne?' I asked with trepidation.

'That would be the one that you and the team now need to craft to be submitted alongside our primary solution. You know, as an additional value-add to show how we can think outside of the box too.'

'Shit, Di. There's not enough time to prepare for the legal sessions tomorrow as it is, let alone if I have to get Tony, Lu Lu and the team to create this alternative solution.'

'I understand, Mike, and I made sure that Consulting are going to throw some resources in to assist you get this done. So Dexter is heading up to the North office to join you and the guys in the war room shortly.'

'Gee thanks, Di. That's great,' I mumble, thinking that will be far more hindrance than help.

'Come on, Mike. I know you've got this and will do whatever it takes to be ready in the morning. If you need anything urgent from me, just message anytime tonight as I'll be at the Industry Awards event with Christiaan and Rudy.'

'OK, Di,' was all I could muster as the dark clouds began to close in around me.

## Chapter Three

# Wankers from Consulting

IT'S WEDNESDAY MORNING NOW AND I'm heading into the office for a quick preparation session before the legal review. Through some hard work by the team last night, along with some tactical nous, some judicious interpretation of company policy and possibly a bit of luck, we've managed to cobble together a 'Supplementary Offer' document as an alternative solution that includes this piece of crap and largely unproven analytics software from Cone Systems. We managed to do it without impacting at all on the main solution Statement of Work and given that we were able to label it as a non-binding concept paper without pricing, we didn't need to take it through an approval process with our offshore delivery colleagues. Although we did set up what was meant to be a quick briefing call for them, just to ensure that they felt engaged; and it ended up running until 1:30 am, as they repeatedly asked the same questions about how we were going to ensure that it was indeed a non-binding concept paper that Telco Pty Ltd could in no way actually sign off on. Tony was his usual persuasive and patient self with our colleagues on the call. He'd skipped off home at about 10 pm so that he could take the call from there, so I headed back to my hotel room to grab something from the late-night room service menu. Another bloody club sandwich was probably the last thing I needed to eat, but there wasn't much choice. I must ensure that I have some fruit today, for fear of getting scurvy based on my recent deadline-driven diet.

When I left the office last night, I was rather pleased that I'd managed to get through the evening without completely losing my shit at Dexter or the decidedly useless Intern that he brought along with him. Dexter messed around drawing indecipherable diagrams on the whiteboard for the first couple of hours that they were in the war room, explaining them to Davie the Intern in a way that indicated that Dexter genuinely believed that not only was he the smartest person in the room, but he was also the only one that understood his own sheer genius. Oh, and in doing so he managed to rub off most of the '**DO NOT ERASE – BID MASTER TIMETABLE**' section from the whiteboard, which will send Mario our Bid Manager into a fit of apoplexy when he finds out!

In the end I suggested to Dexter that Tony and I had enough 'insights' from him to construct a strawman of the alternative solution, and that we would head off to document that and take delivery over it, but that we needed him and Davie to put together the graphic that would form the centrepiece of our paper. If he could please have that done by 11 pm, that would be great. He complained about the time frame and wanted to do it by Wednesday close of business, but I was having nothing of it. After all, he's the fuckwit that created this mess and prevented the team and me from properly preparing for the legal review sessions, so he can bloody well bunker down and help. As it turned out I got an email from Davie the Intern at 11:25 pm, cc'd to Dexter with a half-arsed diagram that one of Emily's 4-year-old kindy kids could have drawn, so clearly Dexter had buggered off leaving Davie with the work. Typical. But my care factor was next to zero, so long as I could include something with the Consulting team's fingerprints on it, in the Supplementary Offer document that Tony and I had essentially cobbled together using boilerplate from the main SOW along with some quick Google-based research on the Cone Systems technology part.

On my way in through the office foyer, I grabbed a flat white for myself and a long black for Tony, as I knew he'd already be in. I walked into the war room just behind Mario the Bid Manager, who was easily distinguished because the smell that always followed him around was that of an ashtray. It took about two seconds before he was screaming something like: 'Who the fuck rubbed off my schedule? I'll fucken kill the bastard...'

'Ciao, Mario. I think you'll find that Dexter from Consulting is the bastard you are referring to,' I stated, smirking widely. 'We were in here late last night and he was working on the additional document.'

'Why, that pompous fucken oxygen thief! How dare he come in here and destroy my master schedule. Just wait till I get...'

'Relax, Mario. I took a photo on my phone before he did any damage, I'm messaging you the pic now so you can recreate it.' As Mario mumbled away, I took the coffee over to Tony who indeed was already in the office; and despite the noticeable bags under his eyes, he was wearing a massive shit-eater type grin, as he clearly enjoyed this little panto-mime and me dropping Dexter straight in it.

As I set up my laptop I realised with surprise that I hadn't heard from Dianne yet this morning, asking for the latest update. Still, she was due in at 8:30 for the legal review prepa-ration session with Kim, the boss of our Legal Department and our head lawyer. 'Hey, Tony, any blow-back overnight from our offshore friends?' I asked.

'Nothing significant, Mike. Just a couple of separate requests to confirm in writing that the Supplementary Offer is non-binding,' he said, still grinning.

'Good thing that they aren't risk-averse, mate,' I responded sarcastically.

'Yep. Also, I just forwarded you a pricing summary pack that Lu Lu prepared last night for the sessions today and tomorrow. As usual it's a great summary of the pricing elements that make up the solution and what the key factors are that could cause the price to change as you negotiate.'

'Thanks, mate. She's awesome.'

The war room door slid open and in sidled Dianne, with a much meeker entrance than you'd usually see from her and with her sunnies firmly covering her eyes. She muttered something that sounded like 'morning' and started to unpack her stuff, so I responded with a chirpy: 'Morning, Dianne, how are you this fine morning?'

She slowly turned around to face me and said, 'I'm fine, thank you, Michael.'

'Big night, Dianne?' I speculated.

'Yes, Michael. As it turns out, last night was rather a big one. As you know, CJ, myself and a few of the EL Team attended the Industry Awards; and we won the award for Technical Design for that industrial maintenance system we developed over in Western Australia.'

Tony, Mario and I all offered our congratulations. But Dianne clearly wanted to share more and launched into a little story.

'The problem was, it was the second to last award of the night and Christiaan - being the self-centred sod that he is - had got bored, thought that the whole evening was beneath his standing because we hadn't yet won anything, and had left. So when we were announced as winners, with CJ having left the building, Clyde, as Industry leader for Mining and Industry, got up to accept the award. But before the poor bugger could take two steps, he saw that bloody Rudy was already on stage clutching the award and making his way to the microphone. So Clyde and I did the only sensible thing and headed out to the bar straight away.'

'Jesus, Di, that prick Rudy is a piece of work. I hope someone said something to him,' I offered.

'Certainly did,' responded Dianne. 'When he came swanning into the bar an hour or so later, he came straight over to us. I was on at least the third martini by then, so I just asked him straight up what the hell gave him the right to do that when it was clearly Clyde's award to accept.'

'What'd he say?' I enquired.

'He gave me that stupid does-not-compute look of his and then said that someone had to take responsibility on behalf of The Company, and as the clear 2IC to Christiaan, and given his standing as an eminent public speaker, who better than him to represent us.'

'Shit, bet that went down well?'

'Indeed. After he said that, Clyde leant forward and I thought he was going to take a swing at him. But he sat back, looked Rudy in the eye, and said something to the effect of: "Rudy, fuck off, you arrogant trumped-up prick! And you can stick that award where the sun doesn't shine while you are at it." It was gold!'

'Ha! Wish I'd been there to see it, Di. Sounds like a fun night.'

'It was fun from there onward, for sure. Now, I heard you guys had a less than fun and very late night, but you got that alternative proposal turned around in record time?'

'Sure did, Di. Big thanks to Tony for doing the hard yards to get most of it done, because our mates in Consulting were their usual useless selves.'

Mario piped up at that point. 'Well, you won't fucken believe how they see things, then. Check out the email I just forwarded. I'm heading out for a smoke to calm down.'

| **From:** | Mario Ricci – 27/03/2019 8:25am |
|---|---|
| **To:** | Dianne Johnson; Michael Mansfield; Tony Davidson; |
| **Fwd:** | Effort above and beyond - Thank you |

FYI

---

| **From:** | Rudy Beaumont – 27/03/2019 8:12am |
|---|---|
| **To:** | Dexter Bartholomew; |
| **Cc:** | Christiaan Joubert; |
| **Subject:** | Effort above and beyond - Thank you |

Dexter,

I understand that you rallied the team and worked through the night to get an amazing Alternative Solution proposal for the Telco deal ready for the client to review this morning. I know that in doing so that you overcame numerous obstacles including several non-believers on the deal team, so thank you for your persistence, dedication and for going above and beyond.

This outstanding work, on top of your thought leadership throughout the course of this long pursuit, continues to show the value that you and the outstanding Consulting team bring to the Company.

best regards,

*Rudy Beaumont*

Executive Director, Strategic Consulting

I was about to let out a torrent of loud abuse but caught myself just as Kimberly McDonald, our Head Lawyer and Lead Negotiator, walked into the room. Kim (as she prefers to be known) is an upright, highly respected member of The Company who is talked of in hushed and somewhat feared tones. One would not dare swear in front of Kim. She is a ruthless, rather commanding woman who can control a room full of suits with just a look and a few choice words. How she puts up with Christiaan has got me beat, but she is clearly one of his absolute favourites and he trusts her completely above everyone else on the EL team; and she is often engaged to assist with the independent review of non-legal issues within The Company as well.

'Good morning, everyone,' said Kim.

'Morning, Kim,' we responded almost in chorus. She sat at the head of the table, and just slid the absent Mario's laptop to one side to make room for her papers.

'Now, we need to be at Telco's city central office at 9:30 for the first session this morning, so we need to make this quick. As you know, we've only got today and tomorrow, with Friday set for the signing ceremony with Christiaan and Telco's MD. So we need to stick closely to the schedule.'

Kim then outlined the scheduled sessions for the two days, along with who would be there on the client side as well as ours. Interestingly, the client has retained as a Technical Advisor - a gentleman (and I use the term very loosely here) who used to work for The Company. I hadn't had a lot to do with him as he left not long after I started, but I knew him by reputation, which is to say that he is widely regarded as an opinionated prick.

Kim also set out the usual standard protocols for the sessions, including calling timeouts and confirming that only she had the authority on behalf of Christiaan to concede on any point of contention. 'Now, Michael, where did we get to with the Alternative Proposal that Christiaan told me we were tabling?'

'It's been drafted overnight, Kim. It has no impact on our final base proposal that they were sent yesterday, and it's essentially a non-binding description of some alternative technology options,' I offered.

'Interesting,' said Kim, 'Christiaan and Rudy described it to me as far more fundamental to our success with this deal, so I suggest that we table it at the very beginning to get agreement on how much time we need to allocate to discuss it.' We all nodded in agreement, before Kim turned to address me again. 'The other potential issue I'm told that may arise is around SLAs,' she said. 'Can you tell me, in summary, what we proposed there, Michael?'

I was very surprised to hear this. 'Kim, Telco set out quite detailed Service Level Agreement expectations in their requirements document, and our response was to fully and completely comply with their requirements. So given that we agreed with absolutely everything that they asked for around SLAs, I'm not sure why that would be an issue for them?'

'Interesting,' said Kim. 'We'll find out soon enough, then. OK, team, let's get going, I want to make sure we are there at least five minutes early.'

## Chapter Four

# The Negotiations Begin

THE TEAM FOR THE FINAL negotiation sessions on the Support Services contract - Kim, Dianne, Tony and myself - arrived at Telco's city offices right on time and we signed in with security and waited to be taken up to the meeting. While we waited, I contemplated how important the next 48 hours would be for getting this damn deal done and dusted. Not just because of the Signing Ceremony set for Friday morning between our MDs, but also because I had to be down in Canberra on Friday for a full-day strategy session on what was meant to be my next big deal assignment. So from my perspective, we just had to get these final negotiations concluded as quickly as possible, which really shouldn't be too difficult given the work we'd already put in and the fact that in our proposal we'd pretty much agreed with everything Telco asked for.

We were greeted by Telco's Legal Team Leader, Rachael, who escorted us up to the conference room. On the way up in the lift Rachael, an immaculately dressed woman of indeterminant age, reminded us gently that we had only two days to get the final support agreement locked down so she was expecting us to engage in a productive and cooperative manner. Kim responded quickly and softly that we too anticipated a highly collaborative approach with the mutual goal of getting through this without too much fuss by late Thursday.

As we continued up to the 44th floor, Rachael told us who would be in the room representing Telco Pty Ltd. As well as herself there would be Charles, their newly appointed Technical Advisor, and Kelly, a Para-Legal Assistant who was to control the master documents. Unfortunately, their CIO wasn't able to make these sessions so had asked Charles to represent his views. Bugger, I thought. That could only mean trouble, as we'd previously worked on the requirements with their CIO and we understood his point of view well and, quite apart from his reputation, Charles was a relatively unknown commodity.

We were ushered into the massive and immaculate conference room which had panoramic views across Darling Harbour and western Sydney. Clearly the Telco business was going pretty well. I was immediately approached very warmly by Charles, which put me off-guard as I think I'd only met him once before and even then only very briefly. 'Hello. Michael. So good to see you,' he said, gripping my right hand with both of his hands. 'It's been quite a while. I hope you are keeping well.'

'Thanks, Charles. Good to see you again too,' I said. 'You look well, mate. Haven't aged a bit, I see'. This last part was a blatant lie on my behalf, as Charles did look like a much more grizzled and older version of how I had remembered him. His beard was longer and much greyer than I remembered, he now wore spectacles, and he was sporting a tweed jacket which made him look more like a librarian. But the biggest surprise was how polite and friendly he was, given his reputation as a gruff, opinionated bastard.

After the introductions we assumed our seats at the huge conference room table. The three Telco representatives were on one side and the four of us from The Company on the other side, with Kim sitting at the end of the table directly opposite Rachael. In front of Kelly was a laptop hooked up to a ceiling-based projector, ready to show the documents up on the big screen which was now being automatically lowered into place.

Rachael kicked off proceedings and explained that in the interest of time, Kelly would mark up any agreed changes in the documents as we went. We all agreed that that was a great idea and proceeded to discuss the agenda for the day. Kim asked if we could please set aside some time right up front to discuss the Alternative Solution, and she asked me to pass over the hard copies we'd brought with us. As I handed them across the table Charles interjected: 'What's this alternative solution? I haven't been briefed on any alternative solution.'

As I began to answer, Rachael quickly and rather assertively cut me off, addressing Charles as much as the rest of us. 'We won't be considering any alternative proposal as part of these sessions, and we have no interest in anything other than gaining agreement on your core proposal. We thank you for your effort in putting this alternative view together, but we will defer consideration on it at this time,' she said quietly and firmly, as she gathered the three copies we'd handed over and put them behind her on the sideboard.

Kim looked at me and I shrugged, suggesting that there seemed little point in arguing the case, especially since I believed that the entire alternative proposal idea was a crock of shit. It was annoying given the effort we'd had to put in the night before to prepare it, but ultimately it was no great loss, in my opinion.

"OK, Rachael. I understand. I would request, however, that you ensure that this alternative viewpoint does receive appropriate consideration by the CIO, as Christiaan, our MD, personally sponsored its development,' said Kim.

'Of course, Kim. Now let's move on to the first discussion item, shall we?' replied Rachael, smiling broadly across at us.

The rest of the morning proceeded rather mundanely as we discussed and confirmed the scope of services. Charles offered a couple of suggested changes that showed a lack of understanding about how many rounds of debate the specific services had received over the past few months. They were already well articulated and fully in line with Telco's requirements, so his attempts to add value were quickly shut down by Rachael, who knew that the CIO had previously agreed in principle with the scope of support services and Charles was just distracting us all with topics that didn't progress the cause.

We broke for a quick lunch and huddled over coffee and sandwiches in a café a couple of doors down the road. Dianne was quick to apologise for the wasted effort on the alternative proposal and said she'd already sent a message to Christiaan to let him know that it was an unwanted distraction. He hadn't responded, but Tony and I were most amused by the prospect of Christiaan sending a rocket to Rudy for wasting our time. One could only hope that would happen.

After our brief adjournment for lunch we re-grouped and began to discuss the Service Level Agreement. Given Kim's comments this morning, I was somewhat nervous as I waited for this topic on the agenda. I still didn't quite understand what the issue would be, given that we'd provided exactly what Telco wanted here. Well, it didn't take long for me to find out...

Charles, who up until now had been relatively quiet and well-mannered, began to grandstand immediately. He said that he'd reviewed this area in particular detail given his extensive background and expertise on the topic of SLAs, and quite frankly wasn't sure why he'd bothered. They were, in his less than humble opinion, the 'worst set of non-committal SLAs he'd ever had the misfortune to waste time reviewing'. He began to bellow across the table at us that we'd been 'highly unprofessional' in proposing such a weak set of measures and that he couldn't believe that we'd try such a thing on.

This really sat us back in our seats. After all, the SLAs were in fact Telco's own requirements and had previously been reviewed and essentially agreed with their CIO and Head of Support. Kim and Dianne were both glaring at me with that 'WTF' look on their faces. Tony was sitting next to me, his head slightly bowed in disbelief. He had put so much effort into this agreement, especially the rather complex penalty and rebate system that was included in it. He lifted his head and leant forward. I thought he was going to lose it with Charles, so I put a gentle hand on his arm and then I interjected. I tried to calmly explain to Charles that this was a bit of a surprise since we'd followed the lead from Telco on these. He quickly got personal and said that he would expect better from someone with my experience and that I had a duty of care to ensure that we put up SLAs in line with modern industry standards.

Fuck me, this guy was a piece of work! So much for the friendly greeting this morning. Composing myself (when I really wanted to tell him that he was an idiot and should go fuck himself), I tried the tactic of asking him politely to be more specific on what the issues were in the SLA. 'Charles, could you perhaps give us one or two specific examples of where there are issues?' I enquired.

Charles responded with: 'There is no point in getting into specifics as the whole document is a joke.'

At this point Kim stepped in and said that it was a real concern to her that we had such significant issues around the SLAs. Could she please have a brief one-on-one conversation with Rachael to agree how best to progress the discussion. As Kim and Rachael got up to leave the room, Charles stood up too and said that there was no point in him wasting any more time on this until we came back with a completely different approach, so he was going back to his desk to 'do some real work'.

After Kim, Rachael and Charles had left the room, Kelly the Para-Legal excused herself too - I think more from embarrassment than anything, as she didn't want to be left in the room with the three of us after Charles' outburst.

'Shit,' said Dianne once Kelly had vacated the room. 'Where the hell did that come from?' she asked rhetorically.

'I thought that he might give us a hard time on a few issues to try and to prove his worth, but that was next level,' she added.

'What an arsehole,' was Tony's contribution as he rocked back and forth in his chair, no doubt thinking about how much work there would be for him if we did have to completely revamp the SLA.

'Di, apart from him trying to show how much of an expert he is meant to be in this field, I don't understand it at all. We've offered them exactly what they asked for originally, and we've worked closely with them to fine-tune some of the measures. And he wants to throw the whole thing out. There's no way that Christiaan can sign this thing on Friday if they want major changes. We won't get it approved on our side, for starters.'

'Let's not even contemplate that,' responded Di. 'I'm sure Kim will be pushing back pretty hard so let's see what she brings back.'

A few minutes passed and Kim came back in to the room. She said nothing immediately and we were all trying to read her face, which was giving nothing away. Remind me to never play poker with her as she's impossible to read.

'Well,' said Dianne, 'what's the deal?'

'Rachael is having a quiet word with Charles,' Kim responded, and with just those few words we all knew what that meant.

Rachael and Kelly came back in about 10 minutes later, and Charles was nowhere to be seen. Rachael said, 'We've had to ask Charles to engage on an urgent issue we have out at our data centre. He'll re-join us tomorrow. Now, I think we should move on to the next item, and we'll finalise the SLA schedule first thing tomorrow.'

Throughout the rest of the afternoon we methodically worked through the other schedules we had on the agenda for review. There was nothing major or too controversial to debate, but there were quite a lot of minor changes that Kelly marked up in the master document. We made pretty good progress, and if anything, we were a little ahead of where we needed to be. At 4:30 we decided to wrap up for the day. Tony and I grabbed a cab back to the office while Kim stayed on to discuss some other business with Rachael, and Dianne headed off to meet another client in the city.

At 4:42 pm I got a call from Kim. 'Michael, I need you both to come back to Telco, please.'

'Why, Kim? What's up?' I asked.

'We've lost the mark-ups from today's discussions,' she replied, and I knew that she wasn't kidding as that simply wasn't her style.

'What, how…?' I mumbled.

'Just get back here asap, Michael,' was the response.

We got the cabbie to turn around and got back in there just before 5 pm. When we got to the conference room on the 44th floor, Kelly was in quite a state. She had clearly been crying, as there were mascara marks running down her cheeks. Kim, Rachael and a bearded, hipster-looking young dude were hunched over Kelly's laptop. It turned out that he was their Desktop Support Technical Leader, and he was struggling to find a way to recover the marked-up version of the master document that somehow had vanished from Kelly's laptop. They'd been looking through various servers that were supposed to hold automatic document backups without success; and there were no temp files that seemed to contain the latest. The only version that could be recovered was from 9:47 this morning, before we'd really made any material changes.

Sonofabitch! That meant we had to re-review everything we'd been over through the day. I tried my best to feel sorry for Kelly, but I couldn't. The dumbass clearly hadn't saved the document properly and so now we were in for a very long night re-creating all of the changes that we'd agreed.

## Chapter Five

# Not Quite Done and Dusted

WE FINALLY FINISHED RE-CREATING THE changes for the day at around 11:30 pm. Most of it was pretty straightforward but there were a few issues where the negotiation and discussion had to be had all over again. I'm pretty sure that we got away with a few things that we'd conceded earlier in the day that Rachael just let go by, I think because it was essentially their fault that we'd lost the collective work of the day. Thankfully they couldn't blame us, as The Company doesn't provide their desktop support services!

We reassembled at Telco's offices again at 8 am on Thursday. We had all agreed the night before that we needed to push on quickly to accomplish what was needed. Kelly looked like she had hardly slept and she wasn't impressed when we gave her a USB stick and suggested she also back up on that throughout the day. Rachael was again immaculately presented, her perfectly combed dark hair cascading down her shoulders across her smartly tailored and (no doubt) designer label crimson suit. Rachael stated that Charles would be joining us at 9 am to 'finalise the SLA schedule'. On a side note, Dianne had messaged me last night from her client dinner, where an acquaintance who knew Charles said that he'd been out sailing earlier that evening. So much for the data centre emergency!

We launched into a recap of the agenda for the day, and agreed that all going well we would target to finish by 4 pm, to provide a little bit of contingency time if needed. Surprisingly - given the prior late night - there was good energy and a positive mood in the room, and we moved forward at pace for the first hour.

At 9 am on the dot in walked Charles, smiling and with quite a red glow about the face. On closer inspection it looked like he had a mild dose of sunburn, so clearly the story about him going sailing had some truth in it. He greeted us quite warmly and said that he'd spent some time going over the SLA schedule again last night and this morning. Great, I thought, here we go again. I couldn't have been more mistaken, though. Charles asked Kelly to bring up on the screen the version of the schedule he'd just emailed her and it seemed to have just a handful of relatively minor mark-ups in it. It seems that once Rachael had read him the riot act and explained that Telco were already OK with the SLA, in a face-saving attempt he too was now largely OK with it, aside from a few very minor suggestions. I guess at the end of the day he was being paid as a consultant by Telco Pty Ltd whether he got his opinion listened to or not.

There were a few tense moments later in the session when we got bogged down with some semantics on legal terminology. Neither Kim nor Rachael seemed to want to budge and it was quite amusing when Kelly offered an opinion that sided with Kim's view. Rachael was clearly not amused and it may well have been the final straw in terms of Kelly's future prospects as a Para-Legal with Telco Pty Ltd! We did, however, manage to get through all that we needed to, and just after 4 pm Rachael declared that we were done from their perspective and now had a support services agreement that could be executed with the rest of the contract between our two organisations. Success! There was relief and joy in the room as we said our thanks and goodbyes.

Yet again Kim stayed on to deal with some other matters. Dianne, Tony and I headed back to the local watering hole near our office for a quiet celebratory drink. I called Lu Lu and a few of the other key contributors on the deal to join us as we headed to the pub. When we got there, rather than being really celebratory, the mood was actually quite subdued - mainly, I think, because we were all so tired from the long hours over many weeks, especially with the added twists and turns of the past couple of days. After just a couple of beers I excused myself and headed back to my hotel room, since I knew that I had to be up early in the morning to fly down to Canberra, and I was very fatigued as well.

I ordered some room service and gave Emily a call while I waited for it to be delivered. I apologised to her for not calling last night due to the document stuff-up and she reminded me that in fact we hadn't actually spoken since Monday night. Oops, bad husband letting work take over again, I thought. Anyway, I'd be back home in Adelaide on Friday night and would get to spend the next couple of weeks recovering and working remotely from there while we started on this Canberra deal. That would be a nice chance to spend some time with Emily and the kids, since I'd been flying in and out of Sydney every week since Christmas

- after spending more than forty-five weeks on the road away from home the previous year.

I had a nice glass of red wine with my dinner and was just about to climb into bed for an early night when my phone rang. It was Kim. I assumed she was calling to say thanks, well done, etc; but no, that wasn't the case at all.

'Michael,' she said, her tone immediately notable for its seriousness. 'I'm here with Rachel, Charles and Kelly, and I've got you on speakerphone. We've got some issues with the Service Level schedule, specifically the penalty calculations.'

Shit, I thought we were done and dusted on this deal. 'What's changed, Kim?' I enquired.

'Nothing has changed, Michael; but it appears that there are some errors in the SLA penalty calculation mechanism. I assume that you'll need to get Tony on the line too, so can you please call him and patch him in?'

'Sure, Kim. Stay on the line and I'll get hold of him.' My head was spinning. We simply had to get this sorted because of the signing planned for tomorrow. And there goes my chance of an early night, I thought.

'Mikey, how's it going, mate?' was how Tony answered my call.

I cut straight to the chase. 'Mate, apparently there are some issues with the penalty calcs for the SLAs. Kim is still in at the Telco office with Rachael and Charles, and they've found some errors. I need to patch you into the discussion.'

'Yeah, nice one, Mikey,' he responded, thinking I was pranking him.

'Tony, unfortunately I'm being deadly serious.'

'Shit, mate. I've just got home from dinner with Renee and we knocked off a couple of bottles of wine.'

'I can tell that, Tony. You sound half-cut. Just leave the talking to me and I'll throw to you when I need you, OK?'

"OK, Mike.' And with that, I patched us both back through to the conference room with Kim and the representatives from Telco.

It turned out that they had indeed discovered an error in the calculations. It was quite a minor error, but nonetheless it had to be fixed. Unfortunately, in finding this error, it also undermined Rachael's confidence in the rest of the penalty and rebate calculations, so once we'd agreed the fix on the first error we had to work through all of those individually. Tony managed to sound sober enough to contribute where needed, and we worked our way methodically through all of the calculations. It was a little difficult following the conversation without being able to see exactly what they were looking at in the room, but I had a hard copy and was making notes on that as we progressed. At just after 2 am we were done, and it was agreed that Kelly would send me the marked-up version within the next hour, and I would provide Kim with the final stamp of approval from our perspective before I got on my flight in the morning. So I set the alarm on my phone for 5 am and fell into bed for a quick nap.

I awoke to the sound of the duck alarm on my iPhone at 5 am, logged on to my email, and found the document that Kelly had sent. Through blurry eyes I went over it, quickly comparing the changes to the notes that I had taken on my copy. It all checked out perfectly so I sent a confirmation note to Kim, quickly showered and dashed to the airport for my 6:30 am flight to Canberra.

## Chapter Six

# The Signing Ceremony

WHEN I LANDED IN CANBERRA, I messaged Dianne to let her know about the debacle last night and to assure her that it was sorted. She had already had an update from Kim and they had agreed that Christiaan didn't need to know the gory details, only that all was concluded successfully ready for the signing ceremony and photo opportunity at 11 am.

I arrived at our Canberra office and headed up to the room that was booked for the strategy session on this new opportunity. On the way in I bumped into Hamish, our ever-so-smooth Industry Leader for Govt and Telco.

'Gee, Michael, you look knackered,' he greeted me.

'Thanks, Hamish. That would be because of the nightmare of getting your Telco deal done in the last few days,' I retorted.

'Ha. Yeah, thanks for that, Michael. I have heard that it's been a huge challenge, what with the interference from Christiaan and Rudy. And I also heard that old mate Charles has been as charming as ever on their side. Anyway, thanks for your efforts and I'll see you in the planning session in a bit,' he said as he headed off down the corridor.

There were quite a few people in the room as we gathered for the internal deal strategy session. I knew many of them but there were a few unfamiliar faces as well. The opportunity we were discussing was to be released by the Federal Government as an open tender in four weeks' time, so this session was set up essentially to finalise our strategy for the response and to ensure that we had all the right resources lined up. Actually, it made for a nice change that we were this well organised in advance. As well as gaining a better understanding of what this deal was all about, my other key challenge for the day was to stay awake.

I remembered that I was in Canberra when the meeting commenced with a quite extensive 'Welcome to country' speech recognising that we were indeed meeting on Aboriginal land, followed by a safety briefing that was longer than the ones most airlines do. We then did the usual rigmarole of going around the table and having everyone introduce themselves, which took about half an hour, especially with all the various representatives from the Consulting team.

The most senior rep from Consulting was Chloe Lovett, an Associate Director who is essentially Rudy's second-in-charge. She's another immaculately dressed youngish woman, circa early 30s, who is rumoured to spend more on her wardrobe than some small nations' GDP. Chloe is always professional and polite, but she does seem to appear at the beginning of deals like this and then is never sighted by the deal team again.

Another familiar face at the table was Clem, a wizened old Infrastructure Solution specialist, who calls a spade a fucken shovel and then hits you in the head with it if you're not careful. He's the type of guy who thinks all this cloud hoo-ha is bullshit and is just the next iteration of the old-school bureau services he used to sell back 'in the good old days'.

The morning dragged on. I proceeded to check my messages roughly every two minutes, nervously awaiting any final twists or turns on the Telco deal before it got signed at 11 am. There was no news of note, and indeed 11 am came and went without any updates, so by 11:30 I was in desperate need of confirmation that all had gone well. You simply can't dedicate so much time and effort to a deal like that one and not get all wound up in it. So I messaged Dianne.

Friday 11:35am

> Hi Di, any news on the signing? I assume all has gone well? Mike

Unusually for Dianne, I didn't get an immediate response, which only added to my anxiety. Hamish would be aware of whether it had been signed or not, but he wasn't in the room to ask. So I just had to sit tight and wait for news.

As we broke for lunch just after 12, Chloe came over and asked 'if I was across the good news on the Telco deal?'

'I'm extremely familiar with the deal, Chloe. What news have you heard?' I responded.

She turned her iPad around for me to see, and said: 'I just got this on my Linked-In feed and thought you might be interested.'

It was an announcement trumpeting the signing of the Telco deal, complete with a photo of Christiaan with Telco's

Managing Director and CIO. Making up the foursome in the picture was Rudy, standing there front and centre next to Christiaan and beaming straight at the camera.

'Thanks, Chloe. It's great news, isn't it,' I said, while my internal voice was saying: *For fuck's sake, what is that wanker doing in the picture?* He had fuck-all to do with the deal apart from stuffing us around with that bloody ridiculous alternate proposal that could have completely derailed the deal. And where the fuck is Dianne, as she was meant to be there?

I finally connected with Dianne when I was at the airport later that afternoon. I was sitting in the Qantas lounge about to fly home to Adelaide, when she called and apologised for not getting to me earlier. She understood that the ceremony went well, not that she was there, as Christiaan told her that morning that she needed to urgently meet with another client across town rather than attend the signing as planned.

'Michael,' she said, changing tack as she clearly did not want to talk about the signing ceremony any more. 'Thanks so much for all of your efforts on the deal. We would not have got there without you, especially with all the twists and turns towards the end. I know you must be completely and utterly exhausted, so please take some time off next week and recharge your batteries.'

'Thanks, Di. I do really need to spend some time home with Emily and the kids, so I appreciate that.'

'Safe travels, Mike. Talk to you late next week.'

I wandered over to the bar to get a glass of wine, feeling completely and absolutely exhausted, but somewhat satisfied and very happy that I was heading home for a break. As I headed to the bar, I glanced up at the departures board and saw that my flight home was now delayed. Oh well, what else could I expect to finish off the week from hell…?

## Chapter Seven

# It Was Nice While It Lasted

WEEKENDS RACE BY, GENERALLY, BUT even more so when you fly back in on a Friday night and then have to re-pack to leave again either on Sunday night or first thing Monday morning. Even though I didn't get home until after 9 pm on Friday as the flight from Canberra was delayed, at least I didn't have to head out again this next week. So that made for a much more relaxing weekend back home with Emily and the kids.

Late March/early April is usually the best weather in Adelaide. The stifling heat of summer has usually gone and you tend to get beautiful, clear blue skies with temps around the mid-20s, which is great for heading outdoors. Emily and I had a very pleasant day on Sunday, cruising around to a couple of wineries in McLaren Vale followed by a late lunch at the Star of Greece, overlooking the clear blue waters of Port Willunga. Fresh King George Whiting washed down with a nice glass of Clare Valley Riesling. It sure was a good way to de-stress from the pressure of the past few months and all the corporate crap that goes with getting a major deal across the line.

It was also a good chance to properly catch up with Emily on her working world and general family stuff, since we'd hardly even spoken over the past few weeks. I'm very lucky that she is so understanding of the demands of my job and just gets on with her own life until I get the chance to re-engage properly. Most of the other people that I work with don't seem to have such understanding partners, and they always seem to be trying to make up for some debt supposedly owed for working long hours or being away on business. Emily isn't like that. She understands the demands and gets it. Mind you, when it does come to family time and holidays, she is far less tolerant of work interruptions - which I find is a good thing, as it keeps me grounded and stops me from being completely and utterly locked in as a corporate slave.

For once on a Monday morning, I woke up feeling somewhat refreshed and calm, looking forward, of all things, to catching up on some administrivia like my expenses and some other compulsory online Company training that I simply had to keep putting off in the heat of the Telco deal. As a reasonably senior executive in The Company, I did struggle a bit with the concept of doing my expenses, travel bookings and other basic admin. Seems that the days of having even a tiny bit of Executive Assistance support were now well and truly behind us. I always thought it was really the ultimate false economy, getting a specialised professional on a salary of a couple of hundred k to spend hours and hours doing basic admin tasks that could be more efficiently done by a proficient EA on about fifty k, or even much less if they offshored those support functions in the Philippines, like they had with some of the EL team EAs. The reality was, however, that you ended up doing tasks like your expenses essentially in your own time, either late at night, on the weekends, or between conference calls while at the airport. So, somewhat perversely, I was looking forward to a leisurely day or two of getting through my rather extensive backlog of expenses.

Just after 9 am local time I was logging in to my laptop, when my phone rang. It was Dianne. 'Morning, Dianne. How are you?' I answered.

'Hi, Mike. Good. Hey, time's up. I need your help on something,' she said.

'Very funny, Di. You must have had a good weekend too,' I retorted.

'No, seriously, Mike. I need you to get over to Perth asap to jump onto an urgent deal we have there.'

'You're fucking kidding, Di, aren't you?' I spluttered, realising already that she probably wasn't.

'Sorry, Mike. I really need someone with your experience to be part of a major deal pursuit we are kicking off this week. It's a critical, multi-year opportunity with one of the largest mining companies in the region, and our Global Industry Leader for that sector flew in from the States over the weekend. So I need you to get your butt over there and work with him and the local deal team we've assembled, to get this thing moving in the right direction from the start. We've got four weeks to get this one submitted and Christiaan is clear that it's a must-win, so you'll you have to take a break after this deal is done. Sorry, Mike, but I need you on this one.' Click. End of conversation.

Because I've experienced this type of on-the-fly corporate re-prioritisation so many times before, the shock was only mild. Indeed, once I'd fully absorbed what had just happened, I was more worried about telling Emily that my plans had been changed again. So I thought it best to buy some time on that and get my travel plans in place first.

I spent the next 45 minutes trying to get through to The Company's designated Travel Booking Agency to book my flight to Perth. I knew that there wouldn't be much choice to get from Adelaide to Perth today, but there was no way I was accepting the travel agent's first recommendation of flying to Perth via Brisbane with a two-hour layover. 'But Mr Mansfield, it's coming up as the lowest logical airfare, in line with The Company policy,' she said.

I managed to shut that down and assure her that I had written approval from our Sales Leader for a direct flight that had to be today. Which was BS, but it worked on this occasion and I got a direct flight that afternoon. Now to tell Emily the news that I was off again, and then do some background digging on this deal. Looking on the bright side, I reasoned that at least I could do some of my expenses on the plane on the way to Perth.

## Chapter Eight

# Divide and Conquer

Before flying out of Adelaide I had a good chat to Clyde, our Regional Industry Leader for Industrial and Mining, who held overall responsibility for the deal and was already on the ground in Western Australia. He was a good man, Clyde. He was Scottish by birth, and whilst you always sensed he could really fire up when needed, he exuded a cool and calm demeanour. He struck me as a 'don't get mad, get even', long game kind of guy. Very straightforward and not into the backstabbing bullshit behaviour of many of his Executive Leadership Team colleagues.

Clyde gave me the lowdown on the opportunity and his honest opinion was that, whilst we were a chance to win it, we were coming from a fair way back compared to a couple of our competitors. He laughed when I told him that Dianne was saying it was a 'must-win' deal as far as Christiaan was concerned. 'Every farkin' deal is a must win according to Christiaan,' was Clyde's dry response.

I found out from him, too, that although there had been plenty of people swarming around the deal over the past few weeks, very little actual progress appeared to have been made, so I needed to be prepared to roll the sleeves up. Clyde had also already batted away a couple of Rudy's Consultants because he was still pissed off at Rudy for his awards night credit-stealing stunt, and he sure as hell wasn't about to let him get too deeply involved in this deal to steal the credit on that too.

Clyde also mentioned that the Global Industry lead who'd arrived from the USA was an interesting character - a brash, outspoken American who seemed to think that all Aussies were as dumb as dog shit and that we weren't thinking big enough. Awesome, I thought. Whilst not quite in the hospital hand-pass category, it did sound like it would be a tough opportunity with plenty of challenges.

I actually arrived in Perth in pretty good shape on Monday night, mainly because I relaxed and watched a movie instead of working on my expenses. I didn't really have much choice about getting my laptop out to do work, since the dick-head sitting in front of me reclined his seat fully before the plane had even levelled out and the seatbelt sign was off. I could even tell he was going to do that before he did, as the moment the fat turd sat down, he started rocking back in his seat. That's always a sure sign that the seat is coming back at you and you've got no room to get your laptop out in economy - or 'povo' class, as I like to refer to it - which is the only way we fly these days. So the expenses would just have to wait for another day.

I headed into our Perth office bright and early on Tuesday morning, since with the two-and-a-half-hour time zone difference in daylight savings time, it was already past 10 am for me in Adelaide terms. I found the bid room and the only other person there was a Bid Manager, Grantley, who

I'd worked with previously a few times. A good guy. Really dour and experienced, and has seen it all before. He's fairly calm and methodical and has a wickedly cynical sense of humour. He told me that we were in a bit of mess and had been spinning our wheels for days now, and that there had been plenty of people injecting themselves into the deal, including our colleague from the US as well as some of the usual suspects from Consulting, but that no one was actually doing any useful and productive work on it yet. I asked him to elaborate.

'Well, Mike, we've got a very clear set of requirements from the client to respond to,' he said. Then he gestured with his arms towards the north wall of the bid room, where the whiteboards were covered with all manner of complicated flow diagrams, bullet points and general verbiage. 'The only problem is that all these fuckheads want to spend all day strategising on the whiteboard rather than actually reading the client's requirements, agreeing what our value proposition is, and starting to develop the response document!'

'Typical. I hear you, Grant. Seems to happen on most deals these days, unfortunately. Let's get hold of Clyde and we can agree a plan between ourselves to help you fix this and get us back on track,' I said.

So Grant and I hatched a plan with Clyde that morning, to essentially divide the deal team into two camps. One for the strategists who would have until Friday to flesh out the deal strategy and our company's value proposition. The other team would be made up of those who could actually make sense of the client's requirements and crack in and start developing the solution and responses to the client's questions.

We put the Global Industry Leader in charge of the strategists and sent them all down the other end of the bid room with fresh packets of whiteboard markers. Then we snuck off into another room and began the arduous process of dividing and conquering the real work that urgently needed to start. Of course, we told the strategists that we'd work on the non-core parts of the response, as we needed their strategic thinking to formulate the essence of the solution by the end of the week. That would just leave us enough time for Clyde to test some of their ideas (off the record, of course) with the client and then to include a couple of their 'gems' and put them back to work on the Executive Summary.

By the end of that Tuesday the core deal team had assessed the key requirements, done the client stakeholder analysis, distilled our thinking down into a series of key win themes, and divided up the response documents. The fundamental challenge that remained was that there appeared to be about four to five weeks of solid work required to get the solution, pricing and response into shape, not including all of the internal approval machinations. And we only had three and half weeks until the deal submission date. Of course, this challenge would no doubt be further impacted by interruptions and wild ideas from our colleagues in the strategy brains trust.

According to the response assessment criteria helpfully provided by the client, one of the key areas we had to address was under the heading of 'Corporate Social Responsibility'. In this part of the response, we had to provide comprehensive and detailed information on The Company's green credentials and policies - everything from our position on recycling, through to where we stood as an organisation from a carbon footprint perspective, and what our plan to be fully carbon neutral was. I wasn't the only member of the deal team to highlight this as being just a teensy bit hypocritical, coming as it did from a mining company that a quick online search showed was one of the biggest carbon polluters in the country!

By late that week, it was clear that there was still a mountain of work to go, so I made the call to stay over and work through the weekend to try and help break the back of it. It wasn't all just hard grind, however. Grant and I were kept amused through the rest of the week by those on the strategy side. Our Global Industry Lead came in every morning with some new thought bubble of an idea that he'd either researched or been fed overnight, obviously to show us dumbass Aussies how knowledgeable and superior he was, and to justify his trip Down Under, no doubt.

Not to be outdone, the local Perth head of our Consulting arm clearly had to show how smart and well connected she was, as she kept feeding in the latest 'ideas from our competitors that I've heard on the street', which we all knew were either made up bullshit or furphies, fed in on purpose by a smart-arse competitor to throw us off the track.

But the best part was late Friday morning, when a previously quiet young Graduate or Intern (not sure which), who had clearly had enough and was somewhat exasperated, stood up and gave a speech for the ages. In essence she said that the time for ideas was well and truly over and that they now needed to distil their ideas into the core value proposition for the deal. 'For fuck's sake,' she said, 'there's only three weeks left and those guys' - pointing across the room towards us - 'need our inputs now, not more bloody ideas.'

Grant, being the sarcastic bastard that he can be, stood up and applauded her. I found her at the Friday night drinks function in the office later that day and thanked her for speaking her mind and calling them out. My advice to her was never to let strategy for strategy's sake get in the way of driving towards the outcome, which clearly she had worked out as well. Besides, I contemplated, strategy developed in isolation from what a client or business actually needs in order to solve their problems isn't actually worth the white-board it's written on.

## Chapter Nine

# Back Under Control

FAST FORWARD A COUPLE OF weeks and I've just arrived back at Adelaide Airport after another week in Perth. It's late Friday afternoon and Emily is coming to pick me up from the airport. We've made some great progress on the Mining deal over the past three weeks, and we are now in reasonable shape to get a potentially winning proposition in the box by the deadline at the end of next week. I've come home for a quick weekend refresh before I head back over on the Monday morning red-eye flight, for the final push.

We managed to get the Global Industry Lead on a plane back to the US at the beginning of this past week, once he had finally run out of his own ideas and worked out that we were not all just hopeless ex-convicts who walked around scratching themselves and bumping into furniture. We also wrangled a couple of the better ideas from our strategy team into our response. Given that most of their brain-farts were completely unrelated to the core solution response that the client had requested, we included them under the auspices of an 'Innovation Scheme', which would see our organisation - should we win the deal - investing in some areas of the client's business on a value-added basis. It remained to be seen if these ideas held any real value for the client, because no one from our strategy team had had any direct access to the client so far during the response period, due to probity restrictions; but also because Clyde and myself didn't want any of them anywhere near the client. In the usual manner, once the strategy folk had passed on the gift of their exalted thinking and in their minds had saved the day, they all vanished off on other urgent business matters, lest we actually put them to work doing something tangible towards our response.

We also found out during the week why exactly Christiaan was so fixated on us winning this particular deal. It turns out that the company that he previously worked for before he became our MD (lucky us!) is the front runner for the deal. He's enough of a psycho usually, but he has an even deeper pathological hatred of losing to this other mob. Via Dianne he's indicated that he will approve single-digit margins to win this one; so again, no pressure on the deal team, because he's all over us like a cheap suit!

After I got off the flight home, Emily arrived to pick me up from our secret pick-up point at the airport (I'm not telling you where because then everybody would use it). I like it when she picks me up, as it provides an extra chance for us to catch up and chat on the way home. Also, it sure beats waiting in a queue to climb into yet another stinky taxi or watching your rideshare screen go from 'arriving in 3 minutes' back to 'arriving in 6 minutes' for 15 minutes before the car finally arrives. We were chatting away about our plans for the weekend (we had none, which suited me just fine) when the phone rang. It was Dianne, and I assumed she was after the normal end-of-week deal update, in preparation for her ELM grilling on Monday.

'Hi, Mike. I hear you made some great progress again this week,' she said before I got a word in.

'Yep, pretty solid. Lots to still do, but we are back on track,' was my response.

'So what exactly is left to do on the deal, then?' she asked - rather strangely, since she was never one for detail.

'Well, we've not got a fully approved solution yet, the legal review of their Ts and Cs is still underway, we've still got pricing to lock down, and the response content is at about 80%,' I responded.

"OK. So who can pick that up from you, Mikey?' she asked.

'What do you mean 'pick that up from me', Di?' I said looking across at Emily, who by now was grinning her arse off at hearing this conversation and seeing my reactions to it.

'Well, Mikey. I need you to drop the mining deal and head to Canberra on Monday morning. We've got two important pursuits that I need you to look into, because I think they are off the rails and I've committed to Christiaan that they will be closed out in June. I've just sent you an email with some background on the deals. Now, who can take over from you in Perth?' she asked.

'Shit, Di, I don't know. And what do you mean you've committed these other deals to Christiaan when I haven't even taken a look yet?'

'Geez, Mike. You know how it is. He gets me all worked up and I just tell him that I'll put my best guy onto them and make them happen,' she said, giving me a none-too-subtle and rather sucky compliment. 'What about Kieron?' she said. 'Could he finish off the Mining deal?'

'Di, have you been at a long lunch today? That guy is a complete waste of space and you know it.' Thinking quickly about how not to completely drop Grant in it, I suggested: 'I think if we can re-assign Lu Lu to finalise the pricing and maybe get Tony to help Grant remotely in locking down and approving the solution, then the rest can be dealt with by reassigning stuff to the existing deal team. If we can't get Tony then Rahul would be good, as he's awesome at getting things through the process, too.'

"OK. Rudy offered to rescue us by having Chloe get engaged, but I didn't think that would be the best in the circumstances,' she replied.

Huffily, I spat back: 'What the fuck is Rudy rescuing us from exactly, Dianne? We've got this Mining deal back under control, no thanks to his team and their complete lack of value on the deal.'

'That's not what I meant, Michael. Anyway, check your emails when you get the chance. I've sent you some details on the Canberra deals. Also, have you seen the Telco deal win bell note yet? Oh, gotta go, Mike. Christiaan is calling me...' Click.

Emily was most amused. She thinks that for a large, complex, multi-national organisation, The Company lacks some fundamental organisation skills, and I can't argue with that. She is also endlessly entertained by the game playing and back-stabbing from within The Company, and genuinely says that the four-year-old children in the kindergarten where she works have better manners and ethics than the executives that I get to work with on a daily basis. Again, I cannot disagree.

'So where to next week now?' Emily wryly asked.

'Canberra,' I responded. 'They want me on another rescue mission for some deals over there.'

'No worries,' she said. 'Just make sure to pack your scarf and coat as it'll be getting cold down there now. And make sure that our overseas holiday at the end of June isn't at any risk,' she added in her firm draw-the-line way.

After dinner that night, I got back online and tried to change my flights for Monday morning, without success. I would have to call the Travel Booking Agency tomorrow. I did quickly check my email, too, to see what Dianne had sent; but the first thing that caught my eye was the 'From the Desk of the MD - Win Bell Announcement – Telco Pty Ltd' note.

It's nice to see your hard work result in winning a deal and to get some kudos within The Company when it all comes together. Hopefully Shayna and her marketing team have done a good job on this one, as I know that they put these announcements together; and I gave her some inputs for this one last week. So far, so good; until I got to the section titled 'Deal Team', which said:

'Special thanks to the core pursuit team that worked tirelessly over many months on this important opportunity. Particularly to our Head of Legal, Kimberly McDonald, and to the exceptional contributions from Rudy Beaumont's Consulting team:-

- Dexter Bartholomew – Overall Deal Architect
- David Jacobsen – Deal Strategy Coordinator

- Chloe Lovett – Senior Strategy Adviser.

Also thanks to those from Dianne Johnson's Sales team that participated in the deal, including:

- Mario Ricci – Bid Manager
- Tony Davidson – Solutioner
- Lu Lu – Pricing
- Michael Mansfield – Support Services.'

I stopped reading as my blood boiled. Just then Emily walked in with a nightcap for me and sensed immediately that something was wrong.

'What's up, Mike? You look a bit worked up about something?'

As calmly as I could, I responded, 'It's OK. I just saw the win announcement from my last deal, and it's not exactly accurate in the way it portrays the contributions to the deal. I'll just send a quick message to Dianne and deal with this tomorrow.'

Friday 9:07pm

Dianne, I just read the Telco deal win bell. To say that it is highly inaccurate and that I am completely and utterly pissed off would be a gross understatement. If you want me to be in Canberra on Monday I expect to have a call from you tomorrow. Mike

## Chapter Ten

# Canberra Bound

I DID GET A CALL FROM Dianne on Saturday afternoon. I think she'd waited until after lunch and had had a glass or two before she called me to reassure me that she had spoken with Christiaan and he understood that it was essentially my deal and that my contribution to it was critically valued, etc etc. Which I knew was bullshit, as Christiaan couldn't care less that I was pissed off; but I wanted her to feel some discomfort over this too, as I was getting sick and tired of other people getting credit for work done by my team and me.

Dianne said she had also spoken with Shayna, the Head of Marketing, who was responsible for sending out these Win Bell announcements. Shayna had apologised and told her that one of her juniors had just mucked up the wording. I knew this was bullshit too, as I'd already had my own chat with Shayna. She and I go way back and we catch up for a few drinks a couple of times a year, which is always a hoot as Shayna is great company and has a reputation as a bit of a party girl. She told me (in confidence of course) that Rudy himself had asked to review the final draft and then sent back what was published, with a note saying that Christiaan had agreed to this version and it should be distributed immediately. Prick. I had a strong hunch that this would have his grubby fingerprints all over it, and sure enough that self-promoting bastard had subverted the process. Incidentally, my already clogged email inbox has now received the same win bell four times, probably from different mailing lists. I'd also received three 'what the fuck' emails from Mario, Lu Lu and Tony respectively.

Lu Lu, of course, was more concerned that her deal bonus would also be reduced or given to someone else, which whilst cynical, was a very valid question given the credit stealing behaviour we've been seeing of late. So I made sure that I got written agreement from Dianne that myself and the core deal team would be fully recognised for the Telco deal, in line with The Company's incentive plan and processes. While I was at it, I also got her to confirm that I would receive the appropriate deal incentive bonuses for both Canberra deals as well as a proportion of the Mining deal, should we win that one too. I used to be far more trusting of the system and thought that if I worked hard and drove the right outcomes, I'd be looked after. But having been shafted several times in recent years on projects and deals that I had done in good faith, I make sure now that I get upfront confirmation before I fully commit to the job at hand.

My personal philosophy has also always been 'don't applaud, just throw money'. Meaning that, whilst I get pissed off with stunts like Rudy pulled on the win bell, at the end of the day as long as they pay me what they rightfully owe me for the deal, I'm not going to die in a ditch because some other wanker got some kudos that they didn't deserve. Emily thinks I should stand up and fight every time I see an injustice like that, but I'd prefer to pick my battles a little more carefully, since these days it seems that there are just so many to fight.

Once I had Dianne's response on the win bell fiasco along with her confirmation around incentives, and her approval for my Canberra travel was in the system, I got around to booking my trip for the next week. That took about an hour on the phone on Saturday evening with The Company Travel Booking Agency, where the agent chastised me for leaving it so late to book a trip to Canberra, given that Parliament was sitting (for a change) over the next few weeks. So that required extra approvals, as the flights were in a fare category outside of policy, and getting accommodation was a bit of a nightmare. I took a mental note to arrange the rest of the travel I needed as soon as I got a good handle on these deals and what was needed to get them done.

## Chapter Eleven

# What's the Status, Kenneth? – Part 1

WHEN I ARRIVED IN CANBERRA on Monday, fresh off a packed early morning flight, I also made a mental note to book a hire car next time. I'd forgotten how bad the Monday morning taxi queue in Canberra could be. As I exited the terminal dragging my roller bag, that first hit of the bracing cold Canberra morning reminded me, too, just how bloody cold the next few weeks would be.

I'd spent some time on Sunday reviewing the information on the deals that Dianne had sent through. Not that it took me too long, as she didn't actually send much. Still, I wasn't willing to risk leaving it until I was on the plane over before I took a look at her email and any background documents. Too many times I've seen people on aircraft working on presentations or reviewing documents that anyone within a row or two could read, when they should have been highly confidential. I've walked off planes a couple of times far better informed on who our competitors are on a specific deal, simply because they were stupid enough to open their presentation, complete with the client's logo and their own, for all to see.

Anyway, it wouldn't have mattered here, as all I got from Di was a couple of paragraphs in an email summarising two deals. They were both for the same National Security Agency, which hopefully would make life and stakeholder engagement easier. One looked like a pretty straightforward extension of some existing services that we provide for them, and the other was for the implementation of a new system, somewhat related to the work we already do there. They were committed deals for the quarter for The Company and had to be signed by Friday June 28th, the last working day before June 30th. This in essence meant that Christiaan had included them in his forecast of what deals we would sign that he had to communicate to The Company Global HQ; hence they were on the radar as contracts that were 'must wins' and had to get signed. The other side note for me was that given that both deals were in the National Security space, all of the team that I might need to engage to assist needed to be at least Government baseline security cleared, which narrowed the choice considerably as far as deal talent went.

As soon as I got settled in at a Hot Desk in the Canberra office, having been told off by the Receptionist for not booking one in advance and then given a 15-minute rundown on the process to book one in future, I went looking for Hamish. He'd be right across these deals, given the importance of them to his Industry portfolio.

I found Hamish hiding out in a meeting room in between conference calls, and had a chat with him. He knew that I'd been asked to come down to help but couldn't really understand what all the fuss was about. The extension deal had to happen by the end of June anyway, and the other one, whilst unlikely to get done in this quarter, he believed was in good shape - at least, according to what Kenneth, his Account Manager for the National Security Agency account, had told him.

'Anyway,' Hamish suggested, 'get hold of Kenneth first up, to get the details from him and see where you might be able to help.'

So Hamish seemed to think the extension was a sure thing, and didn't seem too fussed that the implementation deal might not happen this quarter. His complacency on the implementation deal was probably due to the fact that Hamish was less worried himself about what closed that quarter. Whilst he is accountable to Christiaan for in-quarter signings, he (a) doesn't give a fuck what Christiaan thinks of him, and (b) is on an incentive plan that only counts his full-year results. So as long as he gets the deals done within this calendar/financial year, he doesn't actually care about a bit of slippage from quarter to quarter. Conversely, Christiaan, Dianne and also Kenneth are all on incentive plans which are very focused on quarterly results, hence the different views and focus. From my perspective the timing doesn't really impact my deal bonus, it's more about me being on the hook to Dianne, and therefore Christiaan, to get it done. But it's easy to see how this inconsistency of incentive plans drives some misaligned and often ridiculous behaviour within The Company. And it increasingly drives a very narrow, short-term quarter-by-quarter business perspective.

Kenneth McMahon is our Account Manager for the National Security Agency. I've met him once or twice before but never really worked closely with him. According to my background digging, apparently he was in the military at some point in his career, but the details of his stint there are scant. No one even seems to know which branch of the forces he was in, only that he has a military background. I've been told that he is hardly ever around the office, supposedly spending all of his time out at the clients' offices. He seems to get away with not doing much at all, but no one calls him out because of his self-proclaimed extensive book of contacts in the military and National Security space.

Tracking Kenneth down turned out to be a frustrating experience. I was told that he knew I was in town to assist with these deals and was eager to meet with me, but I spent a few days trying to lock down a meeting with him. At least it gave me some unplanned downtime to finally get my expenses somewhat up-to-date! I finally pinned Kenneth down with a commitment for a one-hour meeting late Thursday morning, but he was a no-show. Apparently, he had conflicting client priorities, and instead sent along a Graduate he had helping on the deals so far.

The Graduate, who only joined The Company at the start of the year, was a nice young man named Luke. I usually enjoy spending time with Grads, as they are often keen to learn and are yet to be fully poisoned with cynicism and corporate crap. Luke was a bright and enthusiastic chap who expressed a little frustration that he'd been largely left to his own devices without much direction, and no one was really feeding him with meaningful work to do. In his view this was hampering his ability to learn on the job, as it's pretty hard to learn on the job when no one gives you a job to do!

It turns out that Luke had got himself Government baseline security clearance and had had a crack at writing the Statement of Work for the extension deal - on the back of a forwarded email and not much real guidance from Kenneth. So I took him under my wing and spent some time reviewing that and providing some perspective on the deal lifecycle and what we needed to do to get that through The Company review cycle. Luke wasn't across anything on the implementation deal, and indeed didn't think that work had actually started on that deal yet.

After a frustrating week of trying to get clarity on the two deals and chasing down Kenneth, I hatched a plan to get to him. I tracked down Hamish and expressed my frustration, and I got him to call Kenneth from his number. As expected, Kenneth answered straight away, given that his boss was calling him. You could immediately sense just how pissed off he was when Hamish told him that he was with me and that we had him on speakerphone. Ha, finally got him! He was unavailable for the rest of the day, of course, what with all the client meetings he had arranged; but he absolutely committed to a one-hour workshop, which had to be first thing Monday morning to fit in with his schedule. There he would share the deal details with me and see how I could help.

Luke helped me with the logistics for the Monday morning workshop, ensuring we had a room booked, a data projector and a whiteboard, and that there was a meeting invite in

Kenneth's calendar. I needed to make absolutely sure there would be no excuses for him not attending.

On the way to the airport to fly home I gave Dianne a call, to give a quick download on the week's progress or lack thereof. She wasn't at all surprised that Kenneth had been avoiding me; in fact, she let me know that it was his lack of substance and waffling updates about client meetings in his deal review calls with her and Christiaan that led her to ask me to become engaged. I was becoming increasingly worried that I'd been sold a pup - at least on the implementation deal - and that it might require a lot more than some simple focus to get it through the process and signed by the client.

Once I got to the airport, I called the Travel Booking Agency to change my flight to Canberra the following week to Sunday night, as I couldn't afford the risk of being stuck because of fog, and missing the Monday meeting with Kenneth. It was a pain in the arse as I lost my Sunday afternoon/evening at home, but I convinced myself that it was a small price to pay as a contingency to ensure I would get there on time.

## Chapter Twelve

# What's the Status, Kenneth? – Part 2

I WAS ALREADY SITTING IN THE meeting for the workshop on Monday morning with Luke when Kenneth walked in.

'Hello, Michael' he said, extending his hand to shake mine with quite a startled look on his face. He went on: 'I'm really surprised to see you here already. I thought your flight in this morning would have been delayed as I hear the airport is completely fogged in.' Ha! Got him again, I thought, detecting just a hint of disappointment in him that I was actually there.

'Nice to see you, Kenneth. No, I came in last night as I figured there might be some fog around Canberra at this time of year and didn't want to take the risk of missing you again.'

After some relatively friendly chit-chat about The Company and Kenneth telling me more than once that he was sorry he couldn't fit me into his busy schedule last week, what with virtually 'back-to-back-to-back client meetings', he proceeded to say that he didn't actually see why it was necessary for me to get engaged on the deal at all, as he 'had it all under control'.

'You see, Michael,' he continued, 'I have some outstanding personal relationships at the Agency, and my contacts there have assured me that we will get both of these contracts signed by the end of the month. I've been telling Christiaan and Dianne this for months now, so I really don't see, with all due respect, why I need you to come in at the eleventh hour to take these deals away from me.'

Ah ha! So that explained his reluctance. He thought I was going to cut his lunch.

'Kenneth, I understand your concerns here,' I replied. 'I really do. And I don't actually enjoy being injected into these deals at short notice either. Rest assured that I am not here to take over. I'm simply here to help you get these contracts done.' I paused for a second, ready for the money shot. 'Besides, I'm on a deal bonus incentive plan which has no impact whatsoever on your compensation for the deals. You will still get full credit for them as the Account Manager, plus you'll not only have the benefit of my assistance in getting the deals done, but also the additional air cover I'll provide with Dianne and the leadership team.'

Kenneth nodded in understanding as the penny dropped, so I continued. 'So perhaps we can start with you giving me a clearer understanding of the state of play on the two deals, Kenneth?'

'Absolutely, Michael,' he said with a much-changed demeanour, before launching into spilling the beans on the status of the deals.

As I already knew, the extension deal was in OK shape, with the client expecting to receive a draft Statement of Work from us this week for that one. The implementation deal, however, was a different story. After a bit of probing I established that the client had selected the software system they wished to implement, and had asked us to give them a proposal to implement and integrate it with the other system that we already looked after. They had told Kenneth that they were keen to sign this initiative off under this year's budget, meaning by the end of June. The issue was that we had not yet actually started work on the proposal to the agency. Shit, with only four weeks left to get this done, and with an Agency noted for the glacial speed at which things usually happened, this deal would need a minor miracle to get done this quarter. And I was fucked if I knew how this fitted even remotely within Kenneth's description of it 'being under control'. But I would worry about messaging and recriminations later; just then we needed to scramble and get an action plan together.

So, I made Kenneth postpone the rest of his meetings that morning so that we could start to work through a plan. He was slowly starting to realise the gravity of where these things were at and the work required, and now knew that he needed to work with me in order to recover the situation, lest I completely drop him in it. Even so, he was very reluctant to introduce me to the client. I think he was just feeling threatened and was trying to protect the value of his relationships there, as I've seen that type of patch protection behaviour plenty of times before. But it turned out his issue was that they don't like 'sales' people, and sales is a dirty word to them.

'Well, call me a bloody Consultant or something,' was my blunt response. 'Whatever works for you, I'll play along with. And please get us in front of their project lead for this asap, as we don't have time to lose.'

Luke and I spent the rest of the day working up a detailed action plan. I also started to call in the cavalry in the form of getting some resources assigned to help with the solution, pricing, commercials and proposal content. I couldn't allocate the people I'd normally like in circumstances such as this, as they would have to be security cleared Australian citizens, and it is clear that these are fairly rare folk these days in our Company. Kenneth called to confirm that we had secured a meeting the next morning with the Executive Project Sponsor and the Project Coordinator at the Agency. Excellent. That would give me a much better perspective on their engagement and exactly where they were at with their thinking.

The next morning, I made sure I gave myself plenty of time to drive to the Agency's office for the meeting. Since my hire car didn't have satnav, I managed to get off one of Canberra's seemingly thousands of roundabouts early, and had to loop back around. Good thing there wasn't much traffic to speak of. I met Kenneth in the coffee shop in the foyer and we started to plan the meeting. It was in this conversation that he let slip that he hadn't ever actually met the two individuals that we were about to meet with.

What the fuck! He supposedly spends all his time out here, has these extensive relationships in the Agency, and yet he hasn't met these important individuals before. Apparently, he was dealing with some other Agency officials around this initiative, and they had recently moved over to other projects. In my mind the odds of getting this done were going down again.

After clearing security and having our phones locked away in secure boxes, we were ushered into the meeting room. Mr David Smythe-Jones appeared and introduced himself very formally as the First Assistant Secretary and Executive Sponsor for this initiative. He was a confident, well dressed type, quite possibly the most stereotypical white Anglo-Saxon male senior public servant I had ever met. Then bizarrely, given that I've not really worked with this Agency previously, I recognised the other person in the room. It was a woman named Lara Barnesworth, whom I knew from Adelaide. I worked with her a couple of years ago on a project in another organisation. Back then she was a Junior Analyst on the project team. Apparently, she was now an Acting Deputy Assistant Director, whatever the hell that meant. Lara greeted me very warmly, which was great; and it was somewhat ironic that I was already better connected to the deal stakeholders at the Agency than Kenneth.

We had quite a positive meeting where it was made clear that Mr Smythe-Jones (as Lara referred to him) would have ultimate sign-off on these initiatives and that Lara would be our primary liaison point to ensure that the Agency's requirements were being fully addressed. When I asked about their time frame, David Smythe-Jones responded by saying, 'Of course, it was most important that we not cut corners and that we go through a proper process of analysis to ensure that together we scope this work correctly; but there was also a strong desire by the Agency to see these initiatives committed in the current funding cycle.'

I took this to be code for: 'Be seen to do the right the right thing, don't stuff this up and embarrass me, but bloody well get it done by the end of June'. At the end of the meeting, David summarised and gave a little speech thanking us and The Company for our continued support and for helping the Agency ensure that Australia is kept safe.

Kenneth and I debriefed after the meeting, and agreed that they needed this to happen too. There was a bit of risk for us in that Lara seemed relatively new to the Agency; and indeed, she was only acting in her role which, according to Kenneth, was reasonably junior in the scheme of things. Still, we'd have to rely on her as our conduit to the Agency to get things done.

Once I got back to the office, I set up a conference call with Dianne and Hamish to let them know what I'd uncovered. I also needed their support for the resources we required and to ensure that we had as much clear air as possible, free from internal distractions if we were to get these deals done in June. I let Dianne know pretty firmly that I'd send her a single daily progress and status update at the end of each working day and that there would be no other random updates provided. I also asked Hamish to keep Kenneth somewhat out of the way, as he didn't have a lot of value to add beyond ensuring that we got access to Lara and the Agency stakeholders when needed. It was going to be a tight race to get this implementation deal done, and on the side we still had to work the extension deal through our approvals and get the Agency to agree and sign it.

Luke and I spent the rest of the week mobilising the implementation proposal team and fleshing out the Action Plan to include the Agency inputs we needed. I also had to argue my way off a 'compulsory' training course that I was assigned to for the last week of June. Seriously, what friggin planet were these Sales Administration people on, arranging sales training in the last week of a quarter?

I got to the airport Friday night feeling like we finally had a clear view of the challenge at hand, and that we were gaining momentum to make it happen. As I boarded the plane to Adelaide, I was surprised to spot Lara sitting in seat 1C, and we exchanged smiles and pleasantries. Apparently even public servants at her modest level of seniority are entitled to Business Class travel, while we in the corporate world slum it back in Economy. Great use of my tax dollars, I thought, as I trundled down the plane towards row 21.

## Chapter Thirteen

# Closing Out in Canberra

Three weeks on and it was getting colder every day in Canberra. Not that there had been much time spent outdoors, as apart from trips to and from the Agency's offices, the deal team had been locked away in a windowless bid room in the secure section of The Company office. We'd been pulling 12- to 15-hour days plus plenty of weekend work to get this implementation deal scoped in line with the Agency requirements, which we also had to extract from them. Then we had to document the proposal and price it all up, and of course get through the internal approval processes.

Apart from ensuring the Agency moved at the pace that we needed, the other major challenge on the deal was with our colleagues from the Security practice. We gave them pretty clear requirements as to the security inputs that were needed, including the cost envelope for their components. Unfortunately, they came back a little over-costed, which was a big problem given that we knew the exact budget the Agency had for the initiative and had pretty much locked in all the other requirements price-wise. We asked the Security guys to do a cost scrub and they then came back with a cost base that almost doubled! The fuckwits in Security clearly didn't understand that the concept of a cost scrub is to reduce our scope and cost so that we can get to a price that the client can accept. They also couldn't explain why the cost estimate had gone up versus the one they had quoted previously, so I was eventually able to stitch them up and get them to agree to provide exactly what the Agency needed for the exact price to meet the budget. It was all a great learning for young Luke, who seemed to understand the concept of price scrubbing better than the seasoned professionals in our Security practice.

The other annoyance for me was having to change accommodation almost every day for the last week of the deal. Since Parliament was still sitting before their mid-winter break, all the regular accommodation options were pretty much fully booked. The Travel Agency booked me Monday night in one hotel, Tuesday in another on the other side of town, and then Wednesday and Thursday in a shitty little apartment booked through Air BnB. It was only for two nights, but I really didn't enjoy dodging the needles each morning on the footpath to get to my iced-up car, which was parked in the street. Anyway, it was nearly over and I could go home again to Emily and the kids, ready to pack and leave on our holiday next week.

So with the incentive of my looming holiday as a positive motivation, and the threats of abuse from Christiaan as a negative motivator, I got on with the deals and managed to get them under control. With the luxury of nearly a whole day to spare, we now had them all approved and agreed from our side, and we had final agreement from the Agency.

We had also agreed the signing process with them, as they needed three signatures as part of their process.

I must admit I was starting to get a bit sick and tired of saving stupid people (and organisations) from themselves. I mean, here we were roughly four weeks after Kenneth assured me that it was all under control for signing this month, when we'd had to inject a team of some half a dozen people working at least 12-hour days, to get these deals even remotely under control. Honestly, how did he think it was under control? And how exactly was he going to get it through the process at all, let alone in the space of four weeks?

There was a time when I used to get personal satisfaction from saving stupid people from themselves, but the more I do it, the less I seem to enjoy it. Perhaps because I've been shafted so many times once the rescue mission is complete, that it's lost the gloss of satisfaction it once had. Don't get me wrong, it still pleases me from a personal contribution perspective when it comes off, but now I want them to damn well recognise and reward me for it as well.

Come Thursday evening, we had two of the three signatures needed from the Agency on both deals. The final signature required was from Mr David Smythe-Jones himself, and we had that lined up for late Friday morning with plans to have Kenneth out at the Agency to ensure it happened. Kenneth was especially keen to secure the final signature, so that he could recover some of his lost reputation with our senior team once they figured out that this whole mess was pretty much his doing - or lack of doing, as it turned out. I had also heard him on a recent call with Christiaan, grandstanding that the deals were all under control (see a pattern there?) and giving his own personal business commitment that they would be signed this week. No doubt Kenneth also wanted to ensure that he got his Q2 bonus.

With nothing left to be done on our side and nothing left to chance, I ventured out that evening for a few drinks with those of the deal team that were still in Canberra, including young Luke. Dianne was in town too so she came along, which was good as it meant we could leverage her corporate credit card. I did warn Luke at the beginning of the night not to try and keep pace with Dianne, but by 9 o'clock he was well and truly pissed so I made sure he got safely into a cab home. I also took the opportunity to remind Dianne that I was on annual leave from Friday night and that I'd be out of the country with the family. Her face told me that she'd forgotten, so it was good for all concerned that I reminded her. She did go on to say that when I got back she wanted to have a chat with me about my next assignment, so she was clearly lining me up in her mind for my next deal.

At noon on Friday I called Kenneth to check if we had the final sign-off, since Dianne had already messaged me twice in the last hour to find out. He said that he didn't have the signatures yet but wasn't concerned as Smythe-Jones was certainly there in the office and he had acknowledged to Kenneth that he had to provide some signatures for us.

I headed off to the airport since I'd booked an earlier flight home today, to ensure that I would get there ahead of my holiday. I'd messaged Dianne to tell her the news and let her know that I'd left it in Kenneth's hands out at the Agency.

The plane home didn't have WiFi, so my phone lit up like a Christmas tree when I turned it back on upon arrival in Adelaide. There were multiple voicemails and messages from Kenneth, Dianne and even Hamish. It turned out that David Smythe-Jones had signed the contract for the implementation deal but he hadn't signed off on the far more straightforward extension deal. Instead, he left that contract with his Executive Assistant to look at again on Monday, and headed off at 3 pm in order to beat the crowds as he drove down to his lake house at Jindabyne for the weekend. He had told his EA to let Kenneth and me know that he'd sign the extension deal next Monday when he got back, and that he trusted we'd ensure the continuity of services in the meantime.

I was gobsmacked. The bastard. He knew that we wouldn't switch off the support services and leave them in the lurch, so he'd just buggered off having only signed the new implementation agreement. God only knows why he didn't just sign both, but I guess he was just playing a power game and showing us who was boss.

According to Dianne, when Christiaan found out he demanded that we stand down our support services team to 'teach that mother-fucker a lesson'. Hamish talked him down from this, reminding him that in Q3 and Q4 we had a further $20m+ worth of deals to commit with the Agency. Dianne herself was also livid and was venting, because of course Christiaan had given her absolute grief over this, even though he would have known there was nothing that she could do. He never missed the opportunity to be a prick.

Kenneth had apparently taken full responsibility for the deal missing the quarter, as in his words 'I was the one there on the ground with the relationships'. He offered to resign but Hamish wasn't having that.

I was also feeling very let down because after all that effort and hard work we'd only got 50% of the outcome that we'd set out to achieve. And it was the bloody easy extension deal that missed.

I hung up from my call with Dianne just as Emily pulled in to pick me up. I was about to call Hamish to get his perspective when Emily politely but firmly asked me to put the phone away, because I was now on holidays and if it rang again, she was going to answer it for me…

# Part II

## Chapter Fourteen

# The Offer

I'D HAD A GREAT HOLIDAY break with Emily and the kids, all things considered. We travelled through Vietnam and Cambodia so the heat was a bit of a shock to the system, especially for me after weeks in freezing cold Canberra, but getting some winter sun and warmth was all part of the plan.

As usual our travel plans, organised with Emily's inevitable precision and attention to detail, went smoothly. I'd had relatively few work interruptions too, possibly in part due to being without phone coverage for a few days whilst in the more remote regions we visited. There were just a handful of calls, a couple of urgent messages and a few sly emails done on the phone when I snuck away for a few minutes - mainly to keep an eye on things and prevent a potential disaster or two, I told myself in justification. I also received a rather rambling voice message from a chap named Neville, who works for a business partner that The Company works with quite a bit across the globe, but I thought that could wait until I got back.

Dianne's EA had set up a one-on-one conference call with Dianne early on my first day back, so I figured that would be the discussion about my next assignment that Di had mentioned before I left. There were no clues in my emails about pressing deals so I was a little curious as to what she wanted me to take on. Just as I dialled in to the Skype call, I received a message from Di.

Monday 7:59am

> Sorry Mike, stuck on call with CJ. Will call you direct when I can. D

Guess I would have to wait a little longer to find out what was next.

Dianne finally rang me late that morning. 'Welcome back, Mike. We've missed you,' was her chirpy greeting. 'How was the trip?'

'It was great, thanks, Di. We had a good time and it was great to get just a little bit off the grid too, especially after that Canberra debacle,' I responded.

'Yeah, I struggle being off the grid, as you know, Mikey. But we sorted out that Canberra extension deal pretty quickly, so we've all moved on from that. Even Christiaan moved on once Hamish and I talked him down from starting a major conflict with the Agency.'

'It's good that some sanity prevailed, Di, since that would have definitely been a no-win outcome for us,' I said.

'Now, Michael,' Di said, changing to a slightly more formal tone, 'I need to talk to you about a tremendous opportunity that I've lined up for you.' Oh-oh, I thought, as the somewhat cynical voice inside immediately thought that it sounded like I was being set up for something here. 'I've been working with Christiaan and the Executive Leadership team and we are going to be making some changes in the structure of the extended Sales team. And we would like you to take on a critical Senior Sales Management role as part of the revamped structure.'

'Gee, Dianne, that's very flattering,' I spluttered, trying to buy some time. 'What exactly would it entail?'

As she started to respond, inside my brain was flashing 'warning, warning'. In my experience - having been in sales leadership and management roles several times before - it really means a whole lot of extra pain, administrative hassle, and downright frustration when compared to the relatively more straightforward role of being an individual contributor. It brought with it a truckload of HR crap and people management challenges to deal with, hiring and firing, and an endless cycle of reporting upwards on the status of deals, etc, etc. Shit! How would I get out of this one?

Without really giving any specific detail on the expectations of the role apart (of course) from what a great opportunity it was for me, Dianne went on to explain that everyone on the EL team agreed that I was clearly the best person for the role.

When she finished, I gathered myself up and said, 'Dianne, I really am flattered that you've thought of me for this role, I really am. But I honestly think my value to The Company is better used as an individual contributor on your key deals. That's where I think I can truly add the most value. So thanks, but I'd rather keep on doing what I've been doing.'

'Wrong answer, Michael,' was her rather stern comeback. Shit, I'd upset her now. 'We know what you are capable of and this is a great opportunity for you to take your career here to the next level.' Normally Dianne doesn't sprout corporate crap, but she was certainly in full flight now, and she seemed rather determined for me to say yes. After she finished her little sermon, she said, 'I'd like you to think about it overnight, Michael.'

I did ponder it overnight, without really knowing exactly what I'd be in for, and because of the many scars on my back from previous leadership roles, I arrived at the same decision time and again. To say thanks, but no thanks. I just needed to figure out how to have that discussion with Dianne.

The next morning Dianne rang me at 7:15 am. She sounded a bit flustered and blurted straight out that Christiaan had approved my appointment, and when I got the chance I should check my email since, along with a raft of other new appointments, it had been announced overnight. So, to try and prevent any further protestation from me, she suggested that I 'should just bloody well get on with this terrific opportunity'.

Fuck, fuck, fuck! It sounded to me as if Dianne and I had been completely backed into a corner on this, so I needed to salvage something.

'Shit, Dianne,' I said once I composed myself a little, 'you know I didn't really want this. What's in it for me if I take this on?'

'You mean now that you *are* taking this on, Mike, will I get you a compensation increase?'

'Yes, Dianne. That's exactly what I mean.'

She replied that in addition to still being able to get deal bonuses, it had been agreed that this year I'd be eligible for the general staff bonus as well - something that is never available to members of the Sales Team. OK, I thought, that's something. However, I was a little sceptical about the real value of the general staff bonus as that seemed to be at The Company's discretion really, and seldom seemed to amount to much for anyone. What I was more concerned about was the comment around 'still being able to get deal bonuses', so I queried that to ensure that the past deals I'd done, for which they still owed me, were at absolutely no risk.

'Of course your past deals will be honoured from a bonus perspective,' Dianne said, 'but given that I'll also need you to continue to run and execute some key deals for us, which I know you are keen to do, I've made sure that you remain eligible to get paid for those as well.'

She made it sound like she'd done me an enormous favour. What she was actually saying was that I'd be expected to help with running some deals on top of whatever this damn leadership role was. Shit, now I thought I knew what it felt like to be shanghaied.

'Gotta go, Mike. I'll call you later today to fill you in on the role in more detail,' were Dianne's parting words.

I was working from home that day so after I'd thought through exactly what had just occurred, I explained what had happened to Emily over breakfast.

'So did you get an actual pay rise for this?' she asked.

'Well no, Emily, but I am now eligible for a further bonus pool on top of my usual deal bonuses,' I explained.

'Congratulations,' she said wryly. 'It looks like you just took on a whole bunch of extra work and stress for no extra money!'

## Chapter Fifteen

# A New Role

SURPRISINGLY, I DID GET A follow-up call from Dianne later that morning and she filled me in a little more on the role that I'd now been 'gifted'. It was great that she called, as I couldn't tell from the email announcement anything material about the role, apart from the fact that I was one of three new 'Senior Sales Managers' in the Sales Team 'charged with focusing and re-energising the sales function for the rest of the fiscal year', whatever the fuck that meant. I was also inundated with a series of calls and messages from people who were either:

a.    Congratulating me on my new role

b.    looking for a job or new home within The Company, or

c.    were senior colleagues also appointed to new roles, who were seeking my view on the various roles announced as they desperately tried to piece together what it all meant.

So it appeared that I wasn't the only one stitched up at short notice on these new roles, which somehow made me feel just a tiny little bit better.

I also had a follow-up message from Neville, the business partner from T9One Solutions, congratulating me on my promotion and letting me know how excited he was to be working with me.

Dianne outlined that I'd be forming a team of about half a dozen sales specialists to help push sales in a particular facet of the business that I was quite familiar with. So far so good. She told me it was all because the results of the first two quarters were not great, and we needed to double-down in the back end of the year if we were to achieve the goals that we'd set for the business. This, trust me, was code for the Executive Leadership Team having an epiphany that they were not going to get their executive pool bonuses at the end of the year if we continued to deliver the same shit results for the last two quarters as we clearly had for the first half of the year.

I also loved the corporate speak around 'the goals that *we'd* set for the business'. As if Dianne or any of the Senior Leadership Team, including Christiaan, actually had any real say in the sales, revenue and profit targets that they were given each year, let alone mere minions like myself, as we all knew that the targets were rolled downwards to us. Yet they were always referred to as 'our' targets or 'your personal commitments to the business'.

Now, I've never been afraid of commitment and I love embracing a challenge. But I do prefer it when I've had at least some sort of say in deciding on the commitments before they become mine. Being given pre-ordained, often unachievable commitments and expected to just swallow them has unfortunately become a very common thread in modern business. And the dysfunction that this creates has to be seen to be believed sometimes.

Anyway, the long and short of it was that I had a couple of weeks to fully mobilise my team, get a clear line of sight on the deals for the rest of the year, and prepare an action plan setting out what I would achieve for a review with Christiaan and some of the EL Team. That last part didn't thrill me at all; but whatever, I'd do the best I could to get moving, to get the facts and play them back.

In terms of my team, it looked like I'd inherited a mixed bag of three or four existing sales specialists, depending on which ones accepted my offer, which I found strange in that it was implied that they had a choice in the matter when I hadn't. Plus, a recent Graduate recruit and I also needed to recruit two more experienced sales people to round out the team. Of the existing resources, a couple actually had great reputations which was positive; but the other two were unknowns to me, so I needed to do some digging. It also turned out that the Graduate I'd been assigned had arrived two weeks ago as part of a mid-year intake. Apparently, the poor bugger turned up and no one knew he was coming or what to do with him, since the person that originally recruited him for their team had been immediately walked from The Company two months ago after resigning and announcing he was leaving to go to a competitor. I felt quite sorry for the Graduate, as he probably would have felt a bit unwanted for that first couple of weeks and must have wondered what sort of tin-pot organisation he'd joined. I needed to get hold of him as a priority, to reassure him and find something meaningful for him to get engaged on. Once I'd done that, I'd do the rounds with the others and introduce or re-acquaint myself, so I could see exactly what sort of talent pool I now had in my keeping.

Just before Dianne and I wrapped up the call I asked her whether she had any insights into what this Neville chap from T9One Solutions might be chasing me on.

'Oh, sorry, Mikey. I forgot to mention it. That's the other part of your new role. You are now our regional representative on the world-wide team that sponsors T9One as one of The Company's most important global business partners. So I've passed on your details to Neville and I'll get you looped in to our Global Practice Lead for T9One later today.'

Great, I thought. When I hear words about being a regional representative in a global team, that really means only one thing: late night or early morning conference calls, since Australia unfortunately always draws the short straw with regards to time zone considerations. Later that night, my fears were confirmed when I saw a welcome email from the Global Practice Leader, which also asked his EA to forward me the weekly call invitations. Sure enough, the calls lobbed into my calendar with a regular start time of 10:30 pm, which meant that they'd kick off at 11 pm most weeks when I would be on the east coast. Awesome. Who needs sleep anyway!

I called Neville and arranged to catch up with him face-to-face the following week, when I'd be in Sydney. I thought I'd met him before and it turned out I had. We were both with different organisations then, but I remembered him as a bit of an old-school wine and dine relationship guy. It looked like he had very high expectations of how much time I'd be devoting to the partnership, so I would need to set that straight.

## Chapter Sixteen

# A New Team

I SPENT THE REST OF THE week working out of the Adelaide office, catching up with the local team whom I hardly ever had the chance to see these days, what with all the travel and the deals interstate. I had been especially looking forward to seeing Amy, one of the Account Managers in South Australia. Amy is simply awesome. She is one of the most positive people I've ever met, is super-fun to be around and also works hard to get stuff done. She's my go to person on the Sales Record system and is always willing to help me out by updating the tricky parts that I've really got no idea on. I had been most recently indebted to her for helping me fix the Agency deal records just before I jumped on the plane to go on holidays a few weeks back.

Most of my time in the office that week was spent on the phone, devoting the effort to get to know my new team, and to gain an understanding of what they were working on. It was mostly positive, although I had to do a bit of a 'Dianne' to one of them and explain that her assignment on my team wasn't really up for debate, but whilst it was really a foregone conclusion, I was sure that I could help her career with The Company flourish. Her name was Amber and she had been with The Company for about five years now. My first impression was that she might be a little high-maintenance. So after we'd spoken and I'd done my best to welcome her to the new team, I checked in with a connection of mine who'd worked with her before. Her feedback was that while Amber lacked nothing for confidence, she was indeed regarded as a high-maintenance employee, and she didn't actually have a great history of closing out deals in recent times. At least, not since she closed out a nice deal with a new logo client in her first year with The Company. My connection also told me to tread carefully, as Amber could be 'a bit sensitive to criticism' and was well regarded by some in the Executive Leadership Team. Excellent, I thought. With that combination of data points, what could possibly go wrong here?

It appeared, too, that I had been given one dead-set dud resource, by the name of Larry. A bit of quick discovery work informed me that he'd been moved around across a whole series of teams in the last couple of years, hadn't sold any deals, and didn't appear to have much to offer apart from everyone agreeing that he 'was a nice enough guy'. Indeed, Larry did seem like a nice guy, and he was enthusiastic towards me and his role on the team; so I was more than happy to give him a go, provide him with some coaching, and make up my own mind.

The final highlight for the week was an all-staff virtual Town Hall meeting. These were a regular occurrence where Christiaan and the Executive Leadership Team would update all employees on The Company's results, focus areas for the business, key initiatives, and the like. Some genius decided to schedule this one for a mid-afternoon start on a

Friday, which I, along with practically everyone else in The Company, didn't think was a great idea, given that many people are tired and busy just trying to wrap up for the week by then.

They run these things as virtual meetings these days, with employees joining in online to watch the live-streamed broadcast. It's meant to minimise disruption and travel back to the offices in each location, and it has the added benefit of allowing real-time employee questions through the broadcast's online chat portal. Real time online questions and feedback can, and sometimes do, backfire spectacularly. And yes, it did today!

The Town Hall opened up innocuously enough with Christiaan outlining the structural changes that had been implemented for the second half of this year and talking very positively about the business results so far this year. He spoke about us winning new business and dominating the market. Real rah-rah stuff. He then went on to show our financial results for the year to date, emphasising that profit for Q2 was up by nearly 6% to $35m, which had exceeded all expectations. At this stage the platitudes were flowing in the online chat portal. 'So proud to be part of this business'. 'Awesome result Team Australia'. 'Well done Christiaan. You are an inspiration'. These were just some of the comments, and you could see they were mostly from the usual sycophants since the portal shows the name of who posts each message.

Then I noticed, as I'm sure everyone paying attention did, a couple of questions sneaking in amongst the arse-kissing comments. Such as: 'Do these results mean that we get pay rises this year as we haven't had any for three years now?' 'Assume this great profit result means there will be a significant general staff bonus pool at the end of the year?' And so, in the blink of an eye, the whole vibe of the Town Hall call shifted, at least for those online.

That's because Christiaan, and most of the Executive Leadership Team that he makes sit in the broadcast room with him, can't see the comments yet. Selected comments and questions are fed in later by someone from the Marketing Team in the Q&A session at the end.

But it got worse, much worse. Christiaan invited Stephanie Martin, the Head of HR, to join him for the next topic, titled 'The Way Forward'. Stephanie proceeded to outline how tough the IT services market was at the moment, and said that we needed to make some changes and implement some measures to ensure that The Company stayed competitive. She went on to announce that there would be another round of involuntary redundancies starting the following week, and that there would also be a raft of further austerity measures put in place from now until the end of the year. These measures would include, amongst other 'initiatives', a pay freeze, and travel and training restrictions – all, of course, whilst Christiaan stood next to her with a confident, smug smile on his face.

The live chat feed exploded. I could hardly keep up with reading it as the messages scrolled off the screen. Even though their names were associated with the comments, many people didn't give a damn and loads of them unleashed here. 'What the hell?!?!? I thought he just said we had record profit'. 'This company is fucked because it doesn't give a crap about its most important resource – the people'. 'I bet the clowns running this show all get their executive pay rises'. This is just a sample set of the comments.

Unfortunately, I had to drop off to take a client call, so I missed the Q&A session at the end. I found out later that the Q&A part was very brief. Before Christiaan shut down the meeting, he had become extremely pissed off with the poor guy from Marketing who was reading him some of the questions from the chat feed.

So after an eventful first week back from leave, and with the Town Hall now done, it was time for me to head off down the pub with Amy. I owed her a few drinks for all the favours she'd been doing for me, and she would brighten my mood with her positivity; and, of course, we could have a good laugh about the Town Hall call too.

## Chapter Seventeen

# Performance Management

SHORTLY AFTER ARRIVING IN SYDNEY on Monday morning, I received the first curveball for the week. I had a call from one of the HR Managers who was assigned to 'assist' the Senior Sales Managers such as myself with people management issues. At first I thought it was a nice courtesy call to check and see if I'd connected with my team yet or to see what help I needed. But that was wishful thinking, really. He'd actually called me to see where I was up to with the 'PMP for Larry'. PMP stands for Performance Management Process and is code for the process of managing a poorly performing employee out of the organisation.

I was a little gobsmacked to say the least, given that I'd just inherited the guy onto my team less than a week ago. I pushed back and told him that so far I'd only just spoken to Larry once on the phone as my team had only come together in the past week. He was well aware of that but still wanted a commitment from me on when I'd progress the process of managing him out.

For fuck's sake! Give a guy a chance. I was giving no such commitment until I'd at least spoken to Dianne, so I told him I'd get back to him once I'd clarified the situation. While

I was at it, I asked him to send me the salary and compensation plan details for my team, since no one had provided them yet and it's pretty hard steering a Sales Team when you don't have this crucial information.

Monday 10:47am

> Di, Can you please call me as soon as poss re Larry. HR are suggesting he needs to be on PMP?! Thx Mike

About 10 minutes later my phone rang and it was Stephanie Martin, the Head of HR. Her nickname was 'the Cleaner' since all she ever seemed to do (apart from step on land mines in Town Hall broadcasts) was to go around dealing with the mess created by Christiaan or some of the other geniuses on the Executive Leadership Team as they overstepped the mark. Like the time last year, that had since become folklore in The Company, when Christiaan had allegedly called one of the Queensland Account Managers a 'fucking useless dumb c**t' in front of the entire State Leadership Team - apparently because at the client meeting they'd just attended, Christiaan had had to deal with some criticism of The Company's hiring freeze policy, which had left the client exposed to some IT issues, which naturally occurred right at their busiest time of year. Of course, it was the Account Manager's fault, because even though they'd briefed him beforehand that this issue would be raised, Christiaan doesn't take kindly to any form of criticism. Still, Stephanie had managed to quickly hose that whole story down and placate the

Account Manager involved with a quiet promotion and pay rise, or so the story goes.

I'd had a few dealings with Stephanie, but didn't know her that well. She'd always seemed to be pretty level-headed and pragmatic, which I guess you'd have to be in her role. After some chit-chat about the fallout she'd been dealing with since the Town Hall call last Friday, she hit me between the eyes with the issue she was calling about. She'd just been told that I was refusing to progress Larry's PMP. She put it nicely enough, so I didn't crack the shits; but I simply explained that since I only just took responsibility for Larry as his Manager last week, I needed to gather some more background and understand all of the relevant facts about his performance or lack thereof. I explained that I was all for effectively managing our poor performers and that I wouldn't shy away from the hard discussions, but it was just that I needed to talk to Dianne, gather the facts, then engage with Larry.

'I understand completely, Michael. Sorry to put you in this position as a new Sales Manager. It's just that Christiaan is demanding immediate action and you know what he's like,' she said.

'I sure do, Stephanie. Let me get right onto this and I'll confirm with you once we have things moving forward,' I closed with.

This was a great first-up example of why I wanted to stay as an individual contributor.

I was already forming a theory on just what was happening here, but I needed to test that with Dianne who, as happenstance would have it, was calling me now.

'Morning, Dianne. How are you doing?' I answered.

'Good morning. Mike. I'm doing great. thanks,' she responded, then launched into: 'Now, it's good that you've reached out about Larry as we need to get that moving fast.'

'Get what moving fast, Di? His PMP, I assume?'

'Exactly. Christiaan made it very clear when we were planning the restructure that Larry is a waste of space and has done nothing of value for years now, so he wants him gone asap!'

'So Di, if I can be a bit frank here, I've just been handed a dud resource that no one else has bothered dealing with previously, despite what sounds like a history of continual under-performance, and now it's my problem? And it's urgent?'

'That would appear to be the case, unfortunately, Michael. I know you can deal with it. That's why we put him on your team,' she said.

'What the fuck, Di,' I let slip. 'You did this on purpose and didn't bother to tell me up front that I'd have to deal with it? I've already welcomed the guy to my team and told him that I'm here to provide whatever coaching I can to help him succeed. Now I have to manage the poor bastard out straight away!'

There was quite a pause before Dianne responded to this, so I thought I might have gone a bit hard on her given how paranoid she can be, especially when it comes to anything that Christiaan has an opinion on.

'Mike, I'm sorry,' she said, in a tone that seemed genuinely apologetic that she'd dropped me in this. 'I really meant to tell you when we spoke last week, but it just slipped my mind, what with all the other staff and restructuring issues at the moment. I'm sorry, Mike, but I need your help to make this happen.'

I'll give Dianne one thing, at least she is always willing to admit a mistake and say sorry. Unlike most of her peers on the Executive Leadership Team, who wouldn't ever admit even the slightest fault and would usually try to throw someone else under the bus instead.

'I understand, Dianne. Leave it with me.'

As soon as I finished speaking with Dianne, I rang the HR Manager I'd spoken to this morning, and gave him some grief for escalating me straight to Stephanie before I had the facts. I also asked him to send me the current Company Performance Management Process details including the guidelines and forms. These things can get tricky and the Australian laws for performance-based dismissal are a bit of a minefield, so I needed to be armed with all the current information to do this correctly and to also do the right thing by Larry. I also asked him to send me a couple of sample forms showing how other Managers had recently done PMPs within The Company, and he committed to get back to me by close of business.

I was sitting in my hotel room that night when his email came through. He provided a template form designed to help track progress on the PMP, and a one-page guideline on the process, which described in very simple terms a three-month long process I'd need to follow. He apologised that he couldn't locate any sample forms for me, as in his words 'it appears that your PMP with Larry will be the first one undertaken here for several years'.

Awesome! That tells me that all the other duds I'd heard were 'managed out' of The Company over the past couple of years were probably given a nice little pay-out to leave quietly, with no one bothering to follow a proper process that either deals directly with real poor-performers or gives the employee a chance to turn things around. What a cop-out. His note also asked me for my feedback on the one-page guideline he'd sent, as he indicated: 'I've drafted it this afternoon based on what I could find in some online HR and workplace forums.'

So now I was trailblazing on a process that it seems our HR Department itself doesn't understand or have experience with. Fabulous! It's a good thing that I've done a couple of these before in other companies I've worked for previously, because I understand how critical it is to get these right and I have some understanding of what's required.

He had also attached the salary and remuneration information for my team that I'd requested, which was good. I opened up the password-protected spreadsheet and took a glance at the details. The first thing I thought was *Geez, no wonder they want to move Larry on - he's on a pretty good wicket*. Then I spied the figures next to Amber's name. Holy shit, that couldn't be right! She'd only been in The Company and the workforce for less than five years and she was on a base salary package that was almost 50% higher than even Larry was getting. And her base salary was quite a bit more than mine, too. Perhaps that was because she wasn't on a compensation plan that allowed her to get other bonuses? Nope. The Comp tab in the spreadsheet showed that she was on the same deal bonus plan as myself and the rest of the team. So according to this information she was on a very, very good wicket.

Hmm, I pondered. Maybe the figures aren't right. Or perhaps there is some other history or background there that I'm not aware of yet. I'd better have a quiet chat to Di on this one; and perhaps I should revisit the discussion on my salary at the same time, too.

## Chapter Eighteen

# Qualifying Stupidity

AFTER SPENDING ALL OF THE previous week in Sydney, I had a much more hectic travel schedule that week, with visits to Melbourne, Canberra and Sydney planned. I needed some face-to-face time with Larry to kick off his Performance Management process formally, and I wanted to spend some time with the other team members in Canberra and Sydney to get some more insights on their deals as input for the deal review session with Dianne and Christiaan. Plus I had dinner with Neville from our partner T9One Solutions, and a belated celebration dinner with the Telco deal team on Thursday night. This might sound rather glamorous to the non-regular traveller, but believe me it's really just a hard grind with the odd moment of fun or excitement thrown in very occasionally.

I also had several deal qualification sessions to get through, along with a deal review briefing session with Dianne in preparation for the big review with Christiaan and some of the Executive Leadership Team the next week.

The first deal qualification session on Monday afternoon didn't go so well. To provide a bit of context for the unini-tiated, deal qualification is the formal process of deciding which particular deals or opportunities The Company is going to pursue. Since we don't have infinite resources to chase every single opportunity or Request for Proposal (RFP), the idea is to go after the ones that we have a very good chance of winning, and those deals that are truly of strategic importance to The Company - meaning that they will position us for further future business, expand our capabilities substantially or will enhance our market reputation in some positive way.

There are processes and criteria by which deals are qualified, and often these calls get very opinionated and heated, because every Sales person naturally wants to pursue the deals that they have been nurturing or for which they see a good (sometimes misguided) chance of success. There's also the unwritten MD rule that gazumps everything else in the process, meaning that if Christiaan wants to go after a deal we will. And if he doesn't? Well, you get the drift.

The deal we started with on the qualification call on Monday afternoon was one that we'd known about for a while. It was for a banking client with which we had a solid relationship dating back several years, and we'd previously done some work for them, although nothing in the past twelve or so months. The services they were seeking were a good fit too, right in our sweet spot; and we would actually be very well placed to deliver a good outcome for them, which made a pleasant change. We'd been talking directly to them about this opportunity for several months, and we were pretty confident that we'd been positively influencing what they had actually decided to come to market with.

The problem began on the qualification conference call when Rudy started questioning our ability to deliver what the client was seeking. Myself and the Account Manager responded confidently that we certainly could deliver what the client was looking for, backed up with some examples of some very similar projects we'd done recently with other clients. I assumed that because this deal wasn't in his area of our business, Rudy seemed determined to shoot it down.

Unfortunately, we see this behaviour quite frequently - where the self-serving ulterior motive of one area of the business tries to stifle another area of the business from succeeding. That way they have more chance of getting scarce Company resources such as Bid Managers for their deals. It's perverse, but internal competition and politics often results in completely dumb-arsed business decisions when the bigger picture is thrown to one side.

That's exactly what happened on the call. Once he got on a roll, that prick Rudy started to question everything, even picky details such as the fact that the client was in the process of appointing a new CEO and that we'd missed out on attending the briefing for the opportunity last month when the Account Manager was away ill. That didn't really matter as they never say anything useful in those briefing sessions that's not on the slides we already had, anyway. But as Rudy was getting busy grandstanding, saying things like 'we don't have deep insights' and 'this is risky as the new CEO may not support the initiative', Christiaan joined the call.

Hearing these somewhat biased snippets of opinion were all that he needed to completely shoot down any chance of chasing this business. Instead he went on to berate the

Account Manager for 'wasting our time with bullshit opportunities like this'. Go figure. A perfectly good piece of potential business and we were not going to invest in going after it. I bet that the client would have been highly pissed off that we were not going to respond, and that our competitors would in turn have been delighted when they got word that we were not in the game.

Christiaan then proceeded to issue instructions that we needed to go full steam after another opportunity with a Financial Services client. This was news to all of us on the call, including the industry leader for Financial Services, Helen Holmes, who was also on the call and always pretended to know everything about all the opportunities in the market in her patch.

It seemed that Christiaan had been introduced to the executive who was leading the RFP process for this client at an Industry event the previous night. Even though the RFP had been released more than a week ago to a select group of organisations that did not include us, the gentleman from the Financial Services firm had kindly offered to extend the RFP invitation to The Company as well. Which of course he would do, as he has nothing to lose by getting a response from us as well. He might actually get some 'free consulting' from us in the form of some good ideas that he could lob at the suppliers that presumably he'd been working with for some time and that he was really considering.

Helen protested a little as even she, as industry leader, had to admit that we'd done no business with this particular organisation and had no relationships in there. She also didn't think that we had the specific capabilities in this region to provide exactly what it seemed they were seeking. Christiaan, however, remained adamant that we needed to put in a 'disruptive response'; and of course, Rudy supported him by saying that 'this could open up a strategically important new relationship' for The Company, whatever the hell that meant.

So a call that was set up to qualify us in on a good opportunity with a known client, finished with us being committed to chase a different deal that up until last night we had no idea existed, where we had no client relationships or track record, limited if any relevant capabilities, and where we were already at least a week behind the competition who got the RFP a week ago. It sounded to me like a complete and utter waste of Company resources. But I didn't get a vote - I just had to ensure that we got a team behind it to get it done. At least the team we'd tentatively lined up for the banking deal that was earlier qualified out from under us could be allocated, so I was thankful for that small mercy.

I was also glad that I wasn't in Helen's shoes. She'd lost the chance to chase a good deal and had to now chase a bad one that she would lose. In doing so she would have also expended effort and scarce resources that wouldn't help her hit her industry targets for the year. None of which would be factored in when her Annual Performance Review occurred early the next year.

## Chapter Nineteen

# Deal Reviews and Dinner

B Y THURSDAY MORNING IT HAD already been a very full-on week. I'd met face-to-face with Larry and used the opportunity to let him know that we'd be putting him on a Performance Management Program. I explained to him that as a Sales professional, he needed to have a consistent track record of delivering signings to the business, and when I'd looked at his history of signings for the last few years, there was no evidence of him doing this. Because of this lack of success, the Executive Leadership Team had lost confidence in his ability to deliver successfully for The Company, but I was there to give him a fair go and to ensure we went through a proper process that gave him every chance of success. He agreed and after some further discussion almost seemed relieved that someone had actually had an honest conversation with him about his future. Deep down he knew that he hadn't been performing, so now he had some help to either turn it around, which even he admitted was unlikely, or a way to quietly exit The Company. Those conversations are never fun and I find them particularly draining; but you need to be honest and show some integrity in these situations, otherwise you become part of the problem too.

I'd also caught up with Amber for a coffee chat. From the outset of that discussion she was clearly very keen to make sure that I was fully aware of her outstanding success in selling a new logo deal for The Company. She told me in great detail about the significance of that first deal she signed within a year of joining The Company, fresh out of University. I tried to find out what other deals she'd done since that one but she batted those questions away and proceeded to provide some high-level commentary around some of the other opportunities she was working on that Christiaan was 'very excited about'.

When I gently prodded her for a bit more basic information on these deals - such as which clients and what stage they were at - all I got back were some sound-bites and clichés about 'other prospective new logo clients', 'breakthrough industries', 'making the market' and 'changing the game'. Nothing at all about the specific clients or opportunities that I could put my finger on. At least Christiaan was excited! So I asked her very politely to email me a brief paragraph to summarise each of the key deals she was working on, along with the Sales Record system number for each, because as I told her: 'I'm really keen, Amber, to include these important deals that you are leading in my review with Christiaan and Dianne next week.'

On Wednesday night I had dinner with Neville from T9One at the Bentley in Sydney. It was a pleasant enough conversation over dinner. I took the opportunity to assure Neville that whilst I was fully committed to the partnership between our two organisations, I did need to focus most of my time over the coming six months on the critical deals that I had in the pipeline, including at least two that The Company and T9One were already working on together. He said that he completely understood this, as he ordered another round of drinks for us both without actually asking me if I wanted one. Oh well, he seemed to think we were going to work together splendidly and that he could sense 'the mojo' between us. It was an agreeable evening with Neville; however, I did have to politely decline his kind invitation to kick on at a 'gentleman's club' that evening, since I needed to attend the global call with my colleagues from headquarters and the other regions to learn about how they were working so well with T9One.

That global call droned on until almost 1 am Thursday morning for me, but I thought it important to attend to get the lie of the land. And to set some expectations about how often I might or might not attend such calls in the future.

Fortunately, my pre-review review session with Dianne wasn't scheduled to start until mid-morning, which gave me some time first thing to gather my information and thoughts. The session had been set up as the chance for me to take Dianne over what deals I had in my patch for the next six months and what new deals or information I'd uncovered from the team since I took them on. It was all in preparation for the full review with Christiaan late the following week. It also was a chance for Dianne and me to agree on the priority deals and which ones we really needed to put the best resources on.

We'd booked a few hours for this, which was good as we needed plenty of time to cover off the deals in my patch that were in the pipeline for the next six months. We started by confirming the reallocation of resources from the 'good' Banking deal to the 'bad' Financial Services deal that Christiaan had qualified in earlier this week. Dianne provided some commentary that Rudy had injected a number of his Consulting people into the account to assist with the pursuit.

Ordinarily this would be distracting and would piss me off, but given that we had a snowflake's chance in hell of winning the deal, we'd use that to our advantage and hopefully Rudy would cop some guilt by association once we lost the deal.

A few of the other deals we reviewed included the following three gems:

1. A deal with a client in the Commercial Building industry that there had been a critical escalation on at the beginning of this week. Our team on this deal needed an urgent injection of additional talent to assist with the final phase and a presentation to the client scheduled for Friday. Late on Wednesday, after mobilising the extra team members, getting them to drop everything else they were working on and flying them down to Sydney, we found out that the Bid Manager had actually misread the notification email. We were, in actual fact, *not* down-selected and as such would not be invited to present on Friday.

2. An opportunity with a Government client that we'd been pursuing for over six months. It was a full-on tender process that we thought we had a good chance to win, and we'd invested a lot of effort into chasing this business. We were actually down selected as the preferred

partner, and were about to enter into contract negotiations. However, the client in question had had a recent change of IT Manager, so in their wisdom they decided to not proceed any further with the tender process and shut it down.

3.   A very promising deal with a Retail group. The Company had done some good work with them in other regions of the world and we qualified it in to pursue, and mobilised a strong team to support the Account Manager on the opportunity. It became apparent in the first week of the pursuit that our Account Manager, despite actually being assigned as The Company lead for this particular client for around two years, and the fact that this was the only client in his portfolio, had never actually met anyone in the client apart from a single low-level procurement resource.

In amongst those train wrecks there were a few good opportunities as well. They didn't all always go belly up, but sometimes it was pretty amusing to my warped sense of humour when they did. Dianne had a great sense of humour too, but she often didn't see the funny side of these, since she was all too frequently the person who had to front Christiaan with some sort of story about what had happened to the deal and why we lost. That was never a problem with the winning deals. The old adage that 'success has many fathers, failure is an orphan child' is never more true than in the cut and thrust of IT deal making.

During our meeting I mentioned to Dianne that I was waiting on some information from Amber on her key deals, and I took the opportunity to raise the question of her salary and compensation package in comparison to others, especially mine.

Dianne said that she was well aware that Amber was paid a fortune, and explained that in part it was due to a role change shortly after she signed her first deal, that new logo one.

'So in effect,' I asked, 'she was promoted several levels within the first twelve months of being with The Company and signing a single deal?'

Without confirming, or denying this, Dianne told me to tread carefully as she was clearly a personal favourite of Christiaan, given that she made him look good with a new signing almost the moment after he too had arrived at The Company.

'She's a protected species, Mike. So do your best to manage her, but please be careful,' was how Dianne closed out the topic.

That night we had the rather belated celebration dinner for the Telco deal. It was postponed from last quarter because Dianne was told not to do anything last quarter due to spending restrictions. Which is interesting since, as announced at the recent Town Hall call, we now had even more onerous austerity measures in place for the rest of the year. I guess it all came down to timing and Di had the cost of the celebration approved in a small window between the two spending restraint regimes. My personal prediction was that by the end of Quarter 3, the austerity measures would be ramped up further to include a stop to all travel except that personally approved by Christiaan, a complete hiring freeze, the cancellation of any client Christmas functions and the removal of all cutlery, crockery and glassware from the kitchens.

The dinner at Café Sydney was a great chance to chill out and catch up with some of the team from the deal, including Tony, Lu Lu and Hamish. I hadn't caught up with Tony since his holiday so I asked him about it as soon as we met at the venue. 'How was the big family trip to the US, mate?'

'Mike, it was nice. But after six weeks away with Renee and the kids I'd had enough and was ready to come back to this crazy company,' he said. 'Besides,' he added, 'with Renee spending money like a drunken sailor for the entire trip and with the shitty Aussie dollar exchange rate, it cost me a friggin fortune. I'm gonna have to work for the next 40 bloody years to pay it off!'

'Geez mate, that's no good. Let me know if Renee plans another holiday and I'll happily find you an urgent deal so that you have an excuse to cancel,' I quipped in response.

Unfortunately, Rudy was there for the celebration dinner too, dressed up in his usual outfit of a flashy sports coat, equally vibrant shirt and contrasting trousers. At his age he really should tone it down a little, and he certainly should stop with the short trouser leg, no sock look that only really young graduates and people under 30 can carry off. Tony and I were debating whether this particular look was more 'pimp at the races' or 'pox doctor's clerk' when he came over to say hello. He greeted me pleasantly enough, but I checked my fingers after the handshake to make sure they were all still there. Rudy said that he wanted to talk to me later about what his team had discovered on that amazing Financial

Services opportunity. Which I think is fine, since I know that he will not bother chasing me on it and I sure as hell won't be chasing him.

During dinner I had the misfortune to end up sitting next to Dexter, one of Rudy's chief wankers and the dickhead that almost completely disrupted and derailed the Telco deal at the 11th hour. Tony and I had to listen to him prattle on and on and on about the latest analysis on analytics, or something about the latest evolution in agile human-centric design. Boring! Don't these people have any outside interests apart from technology? Every time Tony and I switched the conversation to sports or current affairs or entertainment or anything else, it always went straight back to boring technobabble.

After dinner wound up and people started to leave, Tony and I decided to kick on for a bit so I told Dianne, who loves a good after-party, that I'd message her when we found somewhere good to have a quiet drink, since she had to stay and settle the bill and see everyone else off.

Tony and I walked a couple of streets down to Hemmesphere, a really nice, upmarket bar that we'd visited once before while in the midst of some other long-forgotten deal. It was a pricey place but was very classy with leather lounges and good service, and you could at least hold a conversation against the music being played.

When we walked in we immediately spotted Taylor, a quite senior Commercial Manager from The Company, sitting on a couch with two rather attractive young women. Both Tony and I knew him well from a few previous deals that we'd all worked on, and Taylor did have a bit of a reputation as a ladies' man and was rumoured to enjoy a bit of a snort from time to time. But Tony and I hadn't really seen that side of him when we'd worked with him before. Sure, he was always pretty 'on' and seemed very energetic, but he also never seemed to actually do much actual heavy lifting on the deals. He was more the conduit guy, communicating up the line to members of the Executive Leadership Team, and helping make background stuff happen.

Taylor saw us and waved us over enthusiastically. We wandered over and he welcomed us warmly, introducing us to his 'business associates' Cynthia and Nadia, and offering us a drink since he had a tab running already. When I tried to politely decline his offer to buy us a drink, saying that we would get this next shout, he responded by saying, 'Don't worry, Mike, it's on The Company tab since I'm entertaining on official business, lads.' And he grinned and waved over the hostess to take our drink orders.

OK, we can have some fun here, I thought as I caught Tony's eyes. So I relented and let Taylor order us a couple of dry martinis. While we waited for our martinis to arrive I sent Di a message to say where we were and to tell her that Taylor was here with a tab running.

Dianne arrived fairly quickly and Taylor greeted her warmly with a big hug. He introduced Dianne to his young business associates and then proceeded to order Dianne some of that expensive French Champagne that she is particularly fond of. While he was doing that, Dianne started to chat with Cynthia and Nadia, and it was immediately clear that they were not in any way involved in the IT industry. Dianne by now had a glass of Champagne in hand and a manic grin on her face, so we got into the swing of having a few laughs and some more drinks.

About an hour in, Taylor and Cynthia and Nadia coincidentally headed off to the bathrooms at the same time. Perhaps their bladders were aligned or perhaps they just needed to powder their noses.

Dianne leaned over and said to Tony and me: 'I'm sure you've worked out that neither of those women are business associates, nor is one of them his wife.'

'Geez, Di, how could you possibly know that?' I sarcastically enquired.

'Because I spent a weekend away water skiing with Taylor and his very lovely wife earlier this year,' she said. 'And I'm sure,' she added, 'you've worked out the rest yourselves!'

After Taylor, Cynthia and Nadia returned, we kicked on for another couple of hours, absolutely smashing Taylor's bar tab before we called it a night and left him to it with his female friends. As we thanked him for his hospitality, I was wondering how the hell he was going to get his expense claim approved through The Company process. Dianne capped off the night by thanking Taylor too, and asking him to pass on her best wishes to his wife.

## Chapter Twenty

# The Morning After

I WAS WOKEN UP IN MY hotel room the next morning by the phone ringing. Shit, it was almost 8 o'clock and I'd clearly slept through the alarm I had set for 7. My head was pounding and my mouth was as dry as the Simpson Desert. It was those three consecutive rounds of 'roadies' at the end of last night that did the damage, I think.

It was Dianne. 'Morning, Michael,' she said, sounding as bright as a button. 'How are you feeling this morning? A little under the weather after all those martinis, maybe?'

'Yeah, thanks for helping me show restraint last night, Di,' I answered, wondering how the hell she'd managed to drink so much and be up and about so brightly the next morning. It comes down to practice, I guess.

Dianne went on to play back some of the late conversation with Taylor and his special friends from the night before. Not only does she appear immune from hangovers, but she also never forgets anything, even after downing a couple of bottles of Champagne. That's not what she wanted to really talk to me about, though; eventually she got stuck back into business after amusing herself at Taylor's expense. Clearly she would have some fun with him for a while moving forward.

She was really calling me because apparently all hell had broken loose as word got to Christiaan yesterday that we'd lost what was meant to be a very straightforward renewal deal for some services that we'd been providing to a client in Brisbane for many years. Evidently there had been lots of blamestorming going on, as those close to the account and the deal tried to distance themselves from the stigma and stench of losing the unlosable.

Given that I wasn't involved at all in this deal, Dianne wanted me to do a quick, independent review to find out exactly what went wrong. Naturally it was urgent. And my findings needed to be included in the overall Sales Review session with Christiaan and Dianne late next week, so now I had some schedule shuffling to do in order to get to Brisbane for a couple of days early next week. And I'd need to quickly line up some meetings with those involved in the pursuit, including the client.

After some coffee and a nice greasy bacon and egg roll, I headed into the office. I gave Emily a quick call on the way in since we hadn't spoken yesterday. She was most amused at my self-inflicted pain and comforted me with a nice 'serves you right'. I confirmed what flight home I was on that after-noon and she reminded me that we had dinner plans that night, which my still-foggy brain had completely forgotten.

Great, I thought. All I wanted to do was to get home and put the feet up in front of the TV and watch some Friday night footy, after a week on the road. I'd effectively already dined out four times this week, including two restaurants, the Qantas lounge at the airport and the hotel bar. But that was my issue, not Emily's. She had been busy working and running the household and cooking for the kids while I had been galivanting around the country, so the least I could do was spend some quality time with her over a nice dinner at a restaurant that she had chosen for us.

So, as often seemed to be the case, before dashing to the airport I spent the rest of my Friday re-arranging my schedule for the next week, setting up as many meetings as possible for the Brisbane review, getting my flights and hotels organised, and doing some overdue email follow-ups. One of these was to give a gentle prod to Amber to remind her that I still needed her deal updates.

---

**From:** Michael Mansfield – 09/08/2019 2:47 pm

**To:** Amber Barberson

**Subject:** Deal updates

---

Hi Amber,

It was great to catch up with you face to face earlier this week. I've really enjoyed getting to know you and the other members of our new team and I think we'll have a very good second half of this year.

Just a quick reminder that I need you to shoot me through that summary information on your top deals asap. I need just a short paragraph on the current status of each deal and a link to the deal Sales Record number from the system.

From our chat it sounded like you have some exciting prospective opportunities, so I am very keen that these are included in the Sales Review that I'm preparing for our Exec team. If I can have your response by midday Monday that would great.

Thanks and have a great weekend.

Regards,

Mike

## Chapter Twenty-One

# The Loss Review

AFTER A PLEASANT ENOUGH WINTER weekend with the family back in Adelaide, all too soon I was packed up again and off on a Sunday night flight to Brisbane, or Brisvegas, as the locals seem to hate it being called. Given the circumstances of the deal loss, I'd had a reasonable acceptance rate in securing meetings with the key people involved from The Company. Getting a meeting with the client, however, was proving to be far more difficult than I expected. So my plan was to start with interviewing the folks from our team to get their perspective, and to continue to chase the client for a representative meeting to validate what I'd found, before I had to head down to Sydney for the Sales Review session on Thursday. I'd also arranged to catch up with an old industry mate who lives in Brisbane and works for another IT Services mob there.

By Tuesday night I'd done the rounds and spoken to virtually all of the people from our Account Team and those involved directly with the deal. The picture I was forming was all a bit puzzling, really. This was a client with whom we'd had a long and successful track record. We had a very solid group of people from the Account Team providing the services and they had managed to avoid any real staff turn-over in recent times, even dodging the never-ending rounds of forced redundancies to maintain a set of consistent faces to the client. We'd shown tangible continuous improvement in our services over the past few years, we'd had virtually zero service outages, and we had introduced to the client some nice innovation based on productivity initiatives from a similar client of The Company based in the Netherlands.

Our Account Manager herself was devastated that we'd lost the account. She seemed to be a very good operator and had clearly put her heart and soul into her work with the client. She had also had an excellent relationship with the CIO, who had gone out of his way to call her after the decision and reassure her that it had nothing to do with her, without actually telling her why they'd made the decision.

I continued to try and get hold of the client CIO but he wasn't responding. His EA directed me to a bloke in their Procurement team; but he was very junior, and in any case he said that he wasn't authorised to provide any feedback at all 'at this stage in the process'.

When I asked him at what stage he thought we might actually be able to get some feedback, he dithered and said he'd have to check and would get back to me 'at some stage'.

Awesome! It's not like someone simply ordered the wrong type of staples for the stationery cupboard. There were several million dollars' worth of complex services involved here. (Note: Stationery cupboards existed before the days of endless cutbacks and the bean counters took full control. You used to actually be able to go and grab a pen or a notepad etc, if you needed one. I guess the demise of stationery cupboards doesn't really matter now, since no one ever takes notes in meetings anymore, anyway...).

So, with no real inkling from the Account Team, I turned my attention to the Deal Team. Perhaps we had been complacent in thinking that we'd just get our contract extended and had put in a half-arsed response?

After interviewing the Bid Manager, Deal Leader, Solution Lead and Pricer, I was even more confused. It seemed that we had put an 'A-Grade' team on this opportunity, and even given them enough time and runway to put together a really good response. That in itself was astonishing since organisations like The Company hardly ever seem to pay much attention to actually retaining the clients they already have. All too often they chase the glory of new logo clients or that next big game changing deal.

I knew Rahul, who was the Solution Lead on the deal, quite well; and he's a really solid, no BS guy who gets stuff done. A good all-round operator. He assured me that we'd not been at all complacent, that we'd put in a really compelling response which involved better service at lower prices, and had all the innovation from the Netherlands account built in.

I browsed through the written Bid Submission myself and what he was saying seemed to be spot on. It was a great response, especially for an incumbent client.

So without any open feedback from the client, it seemed that we were all at a complete loss as to why we had lost this business. Apart from trying to show that the collective Account and Deal Teams involved here seemed to do a good job, which I knew wouldn't go down well with

Christiaan, I really didn't have any other insights to offer for the review.

After just over two solid days of digging with no real answers and a client that refused to provide a proper loss debrief, there wasn't much more I could do apart from my scheduled catch up with my old mate to find out what the industry goss was in Brisbane these days.

Brian is a wily, experienced, very considered and well-connected chap, so I thought maybe he'd have a view from the street on why we lost. He works for a competitor who also made a bid for the work - albeit reluctantly since, as he told me when we sat down to lunch, he originally thought that we 'were a shoe-in' for the contract extension and in his view it was a complete waste of his company's resources to even put in a response.

After the waiter opened the nice bottle of South Australian shiraz that we'd selected, and we'd had an initial toast to celebrate catching up for the first time in a couple of years, it turned out that Brian did indeed have some very interesting and specific insights on why we had lost.

'Michael, it turns out that you were never going to win that business,' stated Brian.

'Really, Brian? What makes you say that?' I responded, prising him to elaborate.

'Well, you see, this apparently was an over-rule decision directly from the CIO himself to not award the work to your Company,' he said, pausing for a moment before continuing. 'It seems that you chaps rather foolishly and somewhat clumsily overlooked his wife for a job in March this year,' he added, somewhat matter-of-factly.

'Holy shit, Brian!' I blurted, almost spitting out my first sip of shiraz. 'How do you know that for certain?'

Without actually directly answering my question, Brian calmly continued: 'I'm reliably informed that your local team interviewed this lady for a senior Consulting role earlier in the new year and everything was proceeding quite nicely, with expectations that a formal offer was imminent. Then she was invited to attend what she believed was a final discussion with one of your Senior Executive Team. You know, Michael - as a final sanity check on what would be a quite senior appointment, and to explain a bit more about her role and the expectations that went with it.'

He paused to take another sip of shiraz himself at this point, and there was no way I was going to interrupt this flow of information.

'But apparently, Michael, that discussion did not go at all well. Your senior chap told her that she was just one of many candidates in the mix, that perhaps she lacked the experience needed and wasn't quite the calibre of candidate that they were looking for after all. From all accounts he treated her very poorly and with a distinct lack of respect. It certainly did nothing to enhance the standing of your Company in her mind whatsoever.'

Wow! This is all made perfect sense, given how blindsided we were by the decision, and how we'd encountered a wall of silence from the client and their CIO since then.

I paused to take it all in and then said, 'Brian, thank you so much for sharing these candid insights. This definitely sheds some light on an otherwise dark mystery for me.' I proceeded to top up his glass, before I went on: 'I have two questions that I'm not sure you'll be willing to answer, but any further information you feel you can share would really help me in providing some off-the-record context to our leadership around this.'

'I'll help you if I can, Michael, as long as you protect me as well, of course,' he responded.

'No doubt in that at all, Brian. You know me well enough to know that I would never compromise my sources, nor betray your trust here. What I really want to know is how you know this for certain; and secondly, whether you may know the identity of the senior Company executive involved in this rather poorly executed interview process?'

Brian paused for a moment, removed his glasses and looked directly at me before looking around the space near us to ensure that he couldn't be overheard.

'Mike, I know this for certain because she works for me now. And I also know that it was that prize buffoon Rudy who heads up your Consulting business that did the damage.'

Without reacting, I simply raised my glass of wine and said, 'Cheers. Thanks, Brian. By the way, how's the family going? The kids must be close to finishing high school now, eh?'

Once I got to the airport after my lunch with Brian, I found a quiet spot in the lounge where I couldn't be overhead and I called Dianne to give her the feedback on what I'd discovered. Without disclosing my sources, of course.

Surprisingly - or perhaps not - she was not shocked at all by what I told her. She asked me to prepare a short summary on what I'd learnt, minus the names, and to paraphrase the feedback 'from the street'. In the meantime, she'd have a chat with Christiaan to give him a heads up.

I added what she'd requested to my overall Sales Review report, before I left Brisbane. I also gave Amber a quick call but without success, since she still hadn't sent me through the information on her deals that I needed for the review.

At the gate for my flight to Sydney I got a pleasant surprise when my boarding pass flashed red and beeped at the scanner. 'Change of seat allocation today, Mr Mansfield,' I was informed as they handed me a new boarding pass for a Business Class seat. Nice.

As I settled in on the plane, a young girl of about five or six years of age who was boarding with her father spied the plush seats at the front of the plane and said, 'Daddy, how do we get to sit in these nice seats?' Quick as a flash, her father responded with, 'Honey, you need to go to school, study hard and do all of your homework.' My fellow travellers in the front section all laughed out loud at this snippet of uncommon wisdom.

## Chapter Twenty-Two

# The Sales Review

A S WE STARTED OUR DESCENT into Sydney after a far more pleasant flight than usual, my mind started to think a bit more about the Sales Review session with the Execs tomorrow. It filled me with a bit of dread as these things were never fun. They nearly always evolved quickly into a full-on grilling session. You had to prepare for the unexpected, with rocks being thrown from all angles; and even when you had solid answers to their questions they never seemed to finish on any sort of positive note. It was apparent that no one really wanted to talk about, let alone acknowledge, how some good things were actually happening; even on the deals that were being run well and in the teams that were kicking goals, we seemed to always find the dark side to critique.

After the plane touched down, I turned my phone back on from flight mode and a message from Dianne popped straight up.

Wednesday 8:12pm

Mike, don't bother adding the Brisbane deal loss info to the review report. I'll explain tomorrow. cheers, D

Interesting. Assuming that Di had spoken to Christiaan, this could mean many things ranging from Christiaan going ballistic and castigating Rudy (wishful thinking) through to him being in complete denial and not wanting to hear the truth so that he could shoot some other poor innocent bystanders. It was best not to speculate, I thought; I'd just take the Brisbane deal information out of the report when I got to the hotel room that night.

After a fairly quick taxi ride to the city I got another pleasant surprise when I checked into the hotel in Sydney. 'Welcome back, Mr Mansfield. Thank you for staying with us again. We've upgraded you to the Harbourview Suite this evening, which of course also provides you with full access to our Executive Lounge,' said the nice man at Reception. It must be upgrade day today, I thought, as I thanked him.

As a very frequent traveller it was always nice to receive an upgrade every now and again. There was another irony that wasn't lost on me as well: how come I only ever seemed to get upgraded to some massive, palatial suite when I was travelling on my own and only staying for one night? It never seemed to happen when I travelled somewhere with Emily and could actually make good use of the salubrious facilities. It seemed to me that the quality of the room provided was often in direct contradiction to the length and personal importance of the stay.

The same goes for Executive Lounge access. I love a good Executive Lounge with the offer of evening drinks and canapes, but more often than not - as was the case here - I was so late checking into the hotel that the Executive Lounge had closed for the evening and thus I couldn't enjoy this privilege. Oh well, first world problem, I thought. In any case, I still had some work to do and a late conference call with the Global Team to stay up for. Oh joy!

Emily was more miffed than I was when I rang her to chat and told her about the upgrade to a suite. She agreed with me that it never happened when she travelled with me. She changed her tune a little when I told her that I'd bring her home the complimentary chocolates that were left for me in the room. I didn't tell her that I had a nice complimentary bottle of wine too, since I figured that rather than take that home tomorrow as well, I might actually need some of it to keep motivated and working until after the Global call finished much later that night. A glass or two tonight would also help to calm my nerves a little ahead of the Review tomorrow, which I was increasingly dreading.

After another late night followed by a deep six hours of sleep, it turned out that I needn't have stressed about the Review call after all. As I was enjoying a quick breakfast in the Executive Lounge, Dianne rang me to say there had been a change of plans. The Review with Christiaan and the other Executives had been postponed indefinitely. She still wanted to meet with me later that morning, but we wouldn't need the full 90 minutes set aside for the review session.

When I quizzed her as to why it was postponed, she waffled something about the Executive Leadership Team just wanting us to focus on the key deals and getting on with them. OK, I thought, nothing like a week or two of hard effort in getting ready for this going straight down the toilet.

Still, it wasn't all wasted effort, as at least I now had a good perspective of what was going on in my patch. Apart from, of course, Amber's deals...

When I caught up with Dianne in person later that morning, I asked her straight up about Christiaan's response to the feedback on the Brisbane deal. She said that for once he didn't react at all. He just seemed to take it all in, and only asked about how confident we were in the source of the information. Dianne said she had replied that it came from very well credentialled sources who had no ulterior motives. She said he even thanked her for the information, told her not to share it with anyone else, and to effectively shut down this whole deal review process and get on with the remaining deals for the year.

Interesting, I thought. I wondered what repercussions, if any, we might see Rudy hit with on this one.

Dianne also hit me with another little surprise. She told me to expect a call from Stephanie Martin from HR. It seems that Amber had contacted HR and had raised a formal bullying case against me.

Before I could fully blurt out, 'What the fuck, Dianne...' she immediately put her hand up to stop me. She told me that she knew me well enough to know that I wasn't the bullying type, that she was confident that I wouldn't have done anything dumb, and that she had my back. But she couldn't and wouldn't discuss anything about it with me until HR had made their enquiries.

'I just wanted to give you the benefit of a heads up, Mikey, before they got to you,' she said.

I just sat there and shook my head in disbelief before thanking her for the heads up and telling her that I thought I may as well head off to try and catch an early flight home.

## Chapter Twenty-Three

# Global Curveballs

FOR THE PAST WEEK OR so I've been absolutely fuming inside about these allegations of bullying by Amber. I started by racking my brain over everything I'd said to her on the phone and when we met face-to-face. I honestly couldn't recall anything that could be construed as aggressive or bullying. That really isn't my style and I've always strived to be more of a collegial, consensus-style manager. Knowing the little I did about Amber's reputation for promoting her own early success with The Company, I'd completely put aside any concerns over her inflated salary and had been careful to be extra sensitive when getting to know her and also in following up for her deal updates, which never came through anyway.

As the investigative process continued and my mind continued to churn on the issue, I knew I was wrong to think this way, but I couldn't help feeling that she was being an overly sensitive self-entitled princess, using these types of accusations to actually divert attention away from the fact that she had no real current deals and hadn't had any for some time now. Anyway, I was extremely keen to clear my name and I was happy to go through a thorough and very transparent process so that the truth came out.

I must say that Stephanie and all the HR team involved were very professional in their handling of this case. Clearly, they'd been called upon to do this type of review process a few times recently, unlike the Performance Management Process where they remained clueless. They explained the investigation process to me, asked for copies of all communications I'd had with Amber since she joined my team, and arranged a formal interview with me, which was recorded. They also ensured that while this was happening I'd have no contact with Amber, as she had been temporarily shifted to report to another Sales Manager.

In amongst all this, my learned colleagues from the Global Team had been creating some angst as well. Don't get me wrong, there were some amazing people in our Global organisation that I really respected and who offered some real value for those of us working at the coal-face with clients and deals. But some of these people from Headquarters in the US are so far removed and disconnected from the reality on the ground here Down Under, that their harebrained schemes and thinking don't even surprise me anymore.

The most recent example occurred when it became known that there was a deal team from The Company's Global Team working in Sydney on an opportunity with a multi-national client. The usual protocol for this would be to connect with The Company Leadership Team locally, both to inform them of the opportunity and to seek local assistance and insights; however, we had no idea they were here until, during one of the late-night conference calls that were fast becoming the low point of my week, someone casually asked if I'd met them yet.

It seemed that there had been a team of around six people here for more than three weeks, working to gain inroads with this client in order to win their trust to compete for the local services component of an initiative we'd done some work with them on in the States. They just forgot to bother to tell us, or indeed to check and see if we had any existing relationships that might help. As it turned out, we did already have some excellent senior relationships in Sydney with this particular client, which would have really helped to fast-track our invitation to compete for the business. In conveniently overlooking the standard protocol of advising the Regional Leaders of our Company, these clowns got their junket Down Under, but didn't really do any good whatsoever for our overall chances of successfully competing for the business.

Suffice to say that when Dianne and Christiaan found out, they both went berserk. Christiaan demanded that they be expelled from the country immediately and naturally commenced a witch hunt to find out who, if anyone, in our region knew in advance. So in order to prevent myself being a scapegoat in all of this, I went pretty hard with the Global Practice Leader, who was actually a nice enough guy. He was apologetic but fairly sure that he'd raised the opportunity on one of the Global Team calls a few weeks ago, before they arrived down here.

Oh-oh. Perhaps I hadn't been paying enough attention on the late-night calls and had missed a trick? Nope, I don't think so. Even if I had been out for dinner and drinks beforehand, which was often the case given the timing of these calls, my ears would have quickly pricked up at the mention of any opportunities in Australia. Anyway, the Global lead agreed to pen an email to Christiaan to apologise for the oversight and he offered to assist in any way he could when he was down here in three weeks' time.

Wait. What?!

Before I could interject and ask exactly what he was on about, he asked me, 'If you could please check with Dianne on how the agenda for my visit is coming together?'

'Sure thing - no worries,' I said, immediately joining some dots together and thinking I might be able to have some fun with Dianne on this one.

Once I connected with her on this, Dianne went unusually silent for a moment then sheepishly admitted that she knew about the planned visit but that it had completely slipped her mind and she had pretty much done nothing to set up the agenda. The fun for me ended immediately when she delegated to me the task of setting up a whole series of Client and Account Team meetings for our Global colleague. Her EA could assist, of course, but I knew that this really meant that I now had the unenviable task of cajoling a number of my Account Management colleagues and some of their clients into meeting this guy from Global, which would completely distract me from focusing on the real business of helping my team close out deals.

Towards the end of the week I was invited to a one-on-one meeting with Stephanie from HR to discuss the finding of the bullying investigation. Stephanie was her usual professional, no-nonsense self and she cut to the chase quite quickly.

In summary, their investigation had found the allegations to be completely unfounded and that I had no case to answer. Phew, that was a big relief! Even though I had remained quietly very confident that I'd done nothing wrong, there was still this little voice of doubt that maybe I'd inadvertently said something inappropriate to upset Amber.

Stephanie went on to tell me that Amber herself was now being counselled over raising such 'frivolous' bullying allegations, as it was not the first time she'd voiced concerns that were investigated and found to have no basis.

I smiled widely upon hearing that, but Stephanie put me straight back in my box.

'Michael, whilst there was clearly nothing of substance in her allegations, you do need to be extremely careful with your choice of words to avoid them being mis-interpreted. You should especially avoid using aggressive or quite masculine terminology,' she stated.

'What do you mean, Stephanie? Do you have a specific example?' I asked.

'Well, apparently in your deal update request email, you asked Amber to "shoot through the deal summary asap", and her perspective was that this was an aggressive request and the reference to shooting had violent connotations.'

I carefully considered what Stephanie had just said, thought about a couple of response options, and responded with, 'Thanks. I understand, Stephanie. I'll work on that,' - while my inside voice was screaming, 'Oh for fuck's sake…'

Stephanie closed out the meeting by confirming that going forward Amber would continue to work for her current temporary Sales Manager. In other words, she was being transferred out from me to another team. And even Stephanie couldn't resist adding: 'She is now someone else's problem to deal with.'

I couldn't resist responding with: 'She is someone else's very expensive problem to deal with now.' Which made Stephanie smile wryly.

As we left the meeting room, I also made a mental note to keep an eye on the 'Sales Results by Seller' report for the rest of the year, so that I could see if Amber actually managed to achieve something of value for The Company in return for her very extravagant salary and her waste of expensive company resources to investigate bullshit, petty claims that might affront her all-too-sensitive and overinflated sense of self-worth.

## Chapter Twenty-Four

# The Simple Extension

I'D STARTED TO GET A bit jittery lately whenever Dianne reached out to me, mainly because it seemed that every single time she called me it resulted in some form of left-field request for me to drop everything, completely change what I was focused on and fix up someone else's mess. Instead, for once, she called me with what seemed like more of a free kick than a hospital handpass.

There was a contract The Company had with a client in the financial industry sector, that needed to be extended. It seemed that this one had been overlooked by Helen Holmes, who was our Industry Lead for this area, until the client themselves had come knocking on our door to remind us that the contract was due to expire soon and to ask if we could please consider extending it. On the surface it seemed that we just needed to do some simple paperwork to grant an extension - once it had gone through the usual internal Company approval process, of course.

This all fitted into the 'too good to be true' category, so I threw a bunch of questions at Dianne to verify that it was indeed as straightforward as it seemed. She knew exactly what I was thinking and reassured me.

'Listen, Mikey, I'm giving this one to you for two reasons. First of all, I know you can just get it done without fuss. Secondly, I owe you a bit of a freebie with some of the other crap I've thrown your way recently. And you will get full deal bonus credit for this, so think of it as an early Christmas present from me,' she said.

'OK. Thanks, Di. I appreciate it. I'll connect with Helen to get the details and I'll get it done as soon as I can,' I responded, thinking that in spite of Dianne's assurance I'd still do my own due diligence to check for any skeletons in the closet on this one. Besides, this would be a welcome distraction for me from the recent grind of organising the agenda for the Global Practice Leader's visit, which was one of the crappier jobs that Dianne had thrown my way.

I managed to get hold of Helen pretty quickly to get her perspective on the deal. Helen was another interesting member of our Executive Leadership Team. She was quite the charmer, and was extremely adept at creating and building relationships. Helen was a consummate schmoozer and networker, forever on the move opening doors and creating new connections for our business. She was, however, absolutely terrible at following up on actions or getting into any detail on specific pursuits. So it was really not surprising that she had overlooked a potentially major extension deal in her patch, since that was more in the detailed category of business-as-usual operations.

Helen was delighted that Dianne had asked me to take care of this for her. Since it was also a free kick for her Industry numbers for the quarter as well, and given that she'd been reluctantly qualified out of a good deal recently, she needed all the help she could get.

Helen's answers to my questions didn't unearth any real concerns for me on the deal and she confirmed that the client had requested a straight-forward three-year extension with no other changes to the services or contract. Her excuse for overlooking the extension previously was that we were between Account Managers on this particular client, the previous one having been made redundant a few months back. She reassured me that this hadn't impacted our service delivery to the client, and they remained very happy with the services The Company were providing. Quite a rarity these days, I thought.

While we were talking Helen, who as usual was multi-tasking, sent an introductory email to the client's lead, introducing me as The Company representative who would take care of the extension for them.

I wasted no time in sending an intro note of my own to the client, asking for a quick meeting to confirm the details so that we could get the ball rolling on the paperwork. Next I reached out to Lu Lu for help on the pricing, and legal on the SOW, since even with simple extensions we needed their engagement as part of the internal Company approval process.

Lu Lu's reaction was similar to mine. She could immediately sense a good bonus for not a lot of effort and like me was keen to make sure that there were no hidden pitfalls in the deal. Once I assured her that I couldn't see any, I also reached out to my mate Amy in Adelaide, to call in another favour and get her help in creating the Sales Record entry for this, since every time I tried to do this in the system on my own I seemed to stuff something up and incur the wrath of our Sales Administration Team.

With the wheels now in motion on the Simple Extension deal, I returned my attention to the preparations for the impending Global visit. Getting all the necessary client meetings lined up for our Global Practice Leader was taking loads of time. Naturally our Account Managers, who were the first point of call to line up any client meetings, were always reluctant and suspicious of such visits. Many of them had scars from previous Global visitor interactions with their clients. To the Account Managers it must have seemed that there was a never-ending procession of people from The Company, especially Global, wanting to meet with their clients. Often these meetings seemed to involve a high degree of over-promising and commitment by the fly-in visitor on behalf of The Company to make improvements, provide free innovation, or offer extensions to the scope of our services at no additional cost. The poor old Account Manager then had to live with and manage the client's expectations around these promises whilst being completely constrained by The Company's spending restrictions, meaning that they really had no chance to positively act on the commitments that had been made. So the reluctance of the Account Managers was completely understandable and their natural inclination was to 'protect' their clients from these visits.

I had to admit that I agreed in principle with the Account Managers' position. In my experience with these types of executive visits, regardless of whether they involved local or international executives or (even worse) Christiaan himself, they tended to create a cycle of perpetual client disappointment where The Company routinely over-promised and under-delivered. This always left a bad taste in the mouth of the client and eroded a bit more trust from the relationship every time this occurred.

Anyway, it wasn't my job to judge the value or otherwise of this, but merely to convince enough Account Managers and their clients to meet with our Global Practice Leader when he was down here in a couple of weeks' time. Fortunately, this particular chap had a pretty impressive Bio and a good Linked-In profile, which had so far made it much easier to secure a few good meetings with appropriately senior representatives from our clients. However, much more work was needed to fill the agenda and I needed to continue to work the phone and follow up a number of Account Managers to get enough sessions locked in, while also making the simple deal extension my number one priority.

On the deal extension, I managed to get Legal to send me the existing contract and Statement of Work (SOW). They checked out fine and the contract had clear provisions for unlimited extensions by mutual agreement of both parties. It took me quite literally less than ten minutes to update the changes in the SOW to reflect a three-year extension period, which I then sent back to legal for them to provide a quick once-over review on.

Meanwhile, Lu Lu had come back with the updated pricing for the extension, taking into account the price index provisions in the contract, allowing us to vary the pricing once every year in line with CPI. Lu Lu was also very excited by the prospect of getting this deal done and had already done her calculations on the deal bonuses that we would be in line for if we got this signed.

The bonuses are based on some formulas that take into account the total value of the deal, the type of services being provided, the length of the contract and the profit margin that it is sold at. Lu Lu knew these calculations inside out and wanted reassurance that we'd get credit for the deal. I let her know that Dianne had already sent me an email and cc'd our Head of Sales Administration to confirm that I was the allocated lead for the deal, and that myself and the team that I allocated to work on this were pre-approved for the deal bonuses as per the calculation guidelines.

'That's awesome, Michael,' Lu Lu gushed happily. 'Please let me know what else you need me to help you on'.

Just after I'd finished with Lu Lu, I had a call from Patrick, who was the client contact for this extension deal. He was very keen to get this done, and wanted to know how quickly I could assist. He was delighted when I told him I'd already redrafted the SOW and that it was going through our internal review process right now. We arranged to meet the following day so that I could walk him through the changes in the SOW and pricing, as by then I expected to have our internal review completed.

As I hung up from his call, I thought somewhat sceptically that this was all moving at a pace and with a smoothness that felt like it was far too good to be true. Best to keep it moving quickly, I thought, before my luck runs out or there is any chance of it being derailed.

The following day arrived and I was meeting Patrick at 1 pm, so overnight I'd kept up the pressure on our Legal Team to review the simple SOW changes and provide their approval, which they had done by 10 am that morning.

Lu Lu had also obtained the necessary 'price release approval' overnight, so we were good to go. The only slight distraction that morning was a call I received from our Security Practice, who had got wind of the extension deal and wanted to review the proposal for Security risk before I discussed it with the client.

I politely but firmly told them to fuck off. The scope and risk profile had not changed at all, and there were no services in there for them anyway, which was ultimately their angle, to selfishly see what they could get out of the deal for their Practice.

To ensure that I had the air cover I might need, I pinged off quick messages to Dianne and Helen to let them know, just in case the Security guys decided not to let it go and tried to get to either of them to escalate this on me. In doing so I also let Dianne know that in this case I had used my judgement to be 'appropriately aggressive' with my colleague from Security, to get my point across clearly, since he was probably quite used to being told to fuck off, anyway.

I headed out to the client's offices in North Sydney to meet with Patrick a bit early, stopping to grab some sushi from my favourite sushi joint on that side of the harbour along the way. I signed in at the client's office and Patrick came straight down to fetch me. He was a really nice fellow, probably about mid-40s, dressed in a nice navy blue suit and sans tie, which it seems is de rigueur even in the financial sector these days.

Patrick was very thankful that I'd been able to turn this around so quickly for them, as he'd been worried about this extension for a few months now and didn't want them to be left in the lurch without services. He said he'd struggled to get The Company's attention on the extension but was grateful now he had it.

Go figure. A client that wants to do more business with us and we obviously hadn't been responsive, at least until now. So on behalf of The Company I offered my sincere apologies that we hadn't been more responsive until now.

We went over the fairly basic changes in the documentation and I explained the minor uplift in pricing due to the CPI provisions in the contract, which he understood and accepted. Once we'd agreed that all that was in order, Patrick dropped his bombshell.

'Michael, thanks again for getting this three-year extension together so promptly. As I said earlier, we are very keen to ensure that we lock these services in and avoid any regulatory risks or issues, what with all the current Government murmurs about shaking up the Financial Industry even further following the Royal Commission. We were wondering if your Company might perhaps consider a longer contract extension? Say five years instead of three. That would certainly give us some longer-term surety, if you were open to it?'

Trying to contain my utter delight at hearing this, I responded positively and calmly, stating: 'I'm sure we'd be very open to considering that, Patrick. Could I perhaps confirm that to you tomorrow? And if all is good, I should be able to have the updated paperwork with you the same day.'

'That would be excellent. Thanks, Michael,' said Patrick, who was, as of this moment, my new best friend.

## Chapter Twenty-Five

# The Best Free Kick Ever

Plans for the Global Practice Leader's visit had been progressing slowly but surely over the past few days. As the week drew to a close I had almost a full agenda lined up for our esteemed visitor. I had secured a series of client meetings in Sydney, Melbourne and Canberra, including a session with one of our newest client CIOs, whose nickname in the industry was 'the Celebrity CIO'. It had been bestowed on this particular man as he was rather fond of self-promotion and loved every opportunity to big-note himself on social media. I'd filled in a couple of slots with meetings with Partners including Neville from T9One, who was delighted to have the opportunity to host a dinner with our guest from Global. I'd also set up a meet and greet session with our local Practice Team in Melbourne, to give them the chance to meet the Global Leader for their area of expertise. All up I was happy with progress on this, as was Dianne when I shared the draft agenda with her. In reality I just wanted to get it all lined up then get the visit out of the way, as it had been a real distraction and had prevented me from engaging and helping on some other deals.

Apart, of course, from the Simple Extension deal, which was still turning out very nicely indeed. After Patrick had requested that we consider offering a five-year extension, I was able to quickly confirm that we would commit to this, and to get the pricing updated and the SOW amended and approved. Everyone was delighted; including Dianne, Helen and the client. However, no one was more delighted than Lu Lu, who understood the very positive impact that the increase of total contract value would have on the deal bonus calculations for us.

I was being careful not to count my chickens until they hatched; but once they did, it stood to be the biggest payday for me for the least amount of effort on a deal ever. Even the share for Lu Lu as the pricer on the deal was set to earn her a bonus payment of more than $20k for what amounted to a couple of hours of direct work on the opportunity. My bonus as the deal lead would be around three times that, and I made sure that I got an email confirmation from Dianne that the revised five-year extension would all count in the calculations for the deal bonuses, to ensure that we wouldn't get shafted on the additional bonus dollars for the extra two years.

Experience and being handed the 'rough end of the pineapple' a few times before on bonuses had shown me that you've got to dot every 'i' when it comes to these things. Assume nothing and protect yourself! I'd also learnt not to tell Emily what might be coming into our household coffers until I was 100% certain of the value and the timing of the payment.

As I went about finalising the visit agenda, I must admit that I was a little nervous while waiting for confirmation of the signed contract from Patrick. He'd been super responsive previously and had now had it for more than 24 hours, so I was very keen to hear positive news before I jumped on the plane home that night. Lu Lu and Dianne were also both badgering me every half an hour or so for updates, so it was with some relief and outright joy that I took the call from Patrick to say he'd just emailed the signed contract to me.

Awesome! This indeed would be the biggest free kick of a deal I'd ever had, and it made for a very welcome change from often doing the hard yards for no real reward or recognition.

It would also make for a very pleasant weekend back home, too. For once I had a sense of some success and that I had closed out the week with some positivity. I had even managed to get the final draft visit agenda off to Global before I shut the laptop for the weekend. When Emily picked me up at the airport, she immediately sensed my good mood. After all, she was used to me arriving home mentally battered and bruised from another week of corporate battles, tired and usually in a pretty shitty mood.

I just told her that I'd had a really good week and had managed to close out a small but important opportunity, which was why I was so happy with myself. I'd planned to surprise her with my deal bonus amount once the payment was confirmed, which should be by the end of November in line with The Company policy. A very nice little kicker just before Christmas, I thought to myself.

## Chapter Twenty-Six

# Wheels Falling Off

IN THE NEXT WEEK, THINGS had continued to progress quite nicely early on. Our Global practice lead was very happy with the agenda I'd prepared for his visit, and his EA confirmed his travel plans for the following week. Naturally I had been asked to accompany him around on his visit, in effect to chaperone him and keep him out of trouble while here. I was fine with this as, whilst it was a distraction, at least it gave me the opportunity to make sure that everything went smoothly and he did seem like a very decent person, especially for a senior exec from Global! It also meant that I could arrange some other team member catch-ups while on the road, including a follow-up Performance Management session with Larry.

With the Simple Extension deal now in the bag, I also got to work and wrote up a deal win bell for the opportunity. I did this as a pre-emptive strike and to ensure that there was to be no rewriting the history on this one as had happened on the Telco deal.

I got it approved by Dianne and then sent it direct to Shayna in Marketing to prevent any such interference on this one. Shayna was pretty happy to receive my draft notice, as it saved her having to get her team to do it. Much to my surprise it was sent out to all staff the next day, almost exactly as I'd written it.

Lu Lu messaged me to thank me for recognising her straight away, and Helen even called me to offer her belated personal thanks for getting this deal done and at a much higher TCV than she had been banking on. I also got a few 'hey Mikey, well done, drinks on you mate' type messages from colleagues, who recognised from the announcement and deal value that I was in line for a nice pay day soon.

I didn't get any thanks from Christiaan despite providing him with what appeared to be the single biggest signing for the business in the quarter. Still, I didn't expect him to thank me as I wasn't one of the sycophants in our organisation that kissed his arse, and I was pretty sure that he regarded me as just some disposable, low-level deal guy. Besides, he'd never bothered to reach out to me directly on anything, and always had Dianne deliver his messages, which was completely fine with me.

It was late Wednesday before the wheels started to fall off my week. First of all, I got a message from Sales Administration asking to see a copy of the contract for the Simple Extension deal.

When I asked why they wanted it, I was told it was 'because we are checking this transaction in detail against the deal bonus policy'. This was a worry because, whilst I was confident that I had done everything properly on the deal, and that I'd confirmed Dianne's express approval for me and the team to do the deal and get the bonus, these people in Sales Administration had a reputation as the 'payment prevention police'. Almost no one in the broader Sales team trusted them, and it was widely believed that Christiaan instructed them to find whatever loopholes they could to enable The Company to withhold deal bonus payments wherever possible. So much for providing consistent incentives and motivating a high-performance sales team by actually paying sales people what they are entitled to under the written Company policy!

I let Dianne know about the request from Sales Admin and she said not to worry, this was just standard procedure to check the details for all deals of this size.

Hmmm, we'll see, I thought.

The second wheel to fall off happened on the Global call late on Wednesday night. The Global practice leader informed me that he'd been summoned to an urgent meeting in Company headquarters the next week, so he was now unfortunately unable to come down to Australia. Instead he was arranging to send his Chief Digital Technologist, Digby Barnes, in his place.

Shit, fuck and bugger! This was bad news. Digby had a terrible reputation and I'd heard him waffle on enough on conference calls and at a couple of Global seminars previously, to know that this was not going to be a good experience. Digby is a self-styled 'digital evangelist' and he genuinely believes that he is not only the smartest person in the room, but quite possibly the entire IT industry. He can always be found at conferences, often as a guest speaker representing The Company, and he inevitably rolls out the same indecipherable and meaningless drivel of a presentation every time. In my experience, ninety-five percent of people in the room think he's a wanker and for some reason the remaining five percent think he's a technology rock star.

When he is not attending conferences, Digby seems to spend more time updating his LinkedIn feed than anything else, usually just re-posting articles and ideas from other 'evangelists' and regurgitating them as his own.

Of course, Digby himself was delighted that he could adjust his own busy schedule at such short notice to lend us his expertise, and he was looking forward to his 'tour down under' next week.

I thanked Digby for stepping in, and thinking quickly about the repercussions of him meeting with some of our most valued clients, I went on to tell him that whilst I had sent over the final draft agenda, 'there were likely to be some final minor adjustments to the agenda as we locked it all down'.

That would give me the chance to consult with the Account Managers and quickly scramble to take out a couple of high value clients that I thought might not find Digby to be quite their cup of tea. So, having worked so hard to get all of the meetings organised, I knew that I now needed to do further work to undo some of them in order to prevent any 'Digby damage' to The Company's standing with these clients and our future opportunities with them.

## Chapter Twenty-Seven

# The Global Visit

I FLEW INTO SYDNEY ON THE Sunday night in order to be ready for Digby's arrival first thing on Monday morning. I chuckled to myself when I read my LinkedIn feed while in transit and saw that he'd tagged me in a post that wanked on about him 'evangelising the digital message down under…'.

In setting up the agenda for these types of visits we usually leave the Monday morning free of any client commitments, to give our Global visitors the chance to freshen up after a long-haul flight and to spend some time briefing them in detail on the plans for the week. Since the call last Wednesday night, I had also had the chance to remove a couple of sensitive client meetings from the agenda and to substitute them with internal meetings to keep Digby occupied, but as out of harm's way as possible. So I needed to take him over the final agenda and plans for the week.

I went to meet Digby at his inner-city hotel early Monday afternoon and I wasn't disappointed. He came out wearing dark jeans and a dusty pink sports coat with a black t-shirt underneath that simply had the word 'digital' written on it. All in lower case. This was, at least to me, the ultimate modern-day technical wanker's outfit.

True to form, Digby then spent the majority of the one-hour briefing session talking about himself, the journal paper he was working on, and how the global MD of The Company had asked him to represent The Company on some supposedly important US industry board. I couldn't get a word in edgeways! Not that I really cared, as I knew that this whole week was going to be a train smash, and I'd already decided to just try and minimise the carnage and amuse myself as much as possible at the same time.

So in that spirit, and since we had no client meetings organised for later that day, I asked how would Digby like to divert to the hotel bar and tell me some more about this paper he was working on?

With much the same approach, we eventually managed to get through the week. I said goodbye to Digby in Melbourne on Friday as he headed to the International Terminal to board his plane back to the US, and I headed to the Domestic Terminal for my flight home to Adelaide.

As it turned out, the damage had been relatively light. Between myself and the respective Account Managers, we managed to set the expectations for each meeting with the statement that 'Digby was there to share some insights into global trends and what he is seeing with our clients elsewhere'. Then for the next hour he would prattle on about himself and his theories of what was happening in the market. He'd mention the word 'digital' at least 50+ times per session and he never actually engaged in any dialogue on the client's challenges. Which was a good thing, as any specific discussions on client problems was sure to lead to Digby showing them how smart he was and telling them how to suck eggs.

A couple of clients were less than impressed that we wasted their time with this guy, so the respective Account Managers had some work to do to smooth that over with those particular clients. But, in what I thought was a pretty good hit rate, there was only one client who pulled me aside immediately after the usual Digby session and said very clearly, 'Michael, please make sure that I never lay eyes on that fuckwit again.'

'Absolutely understood and guaranteed,' was my quick response back.

In stark contrast, there were actually a couple of sessions that went OK. The first was with Neville from T9One over dinner on Tuesday night. I think this was mainly because I just zoned out, took a couple of calls, and had a couple of drinks while they talked about technology trends and god knows what. Neville was also delighted that Digby accepted his invitation to continue 'this riveting conversation' at his favourite 'Gentleman's club' after we'd finished dinner, which I again politely declined and left them to it.

For some reason, and much to my amusement, Digby appeared quite ginger and subdued the next morning when we met quite early at the airport for the flight to Canberra!

The other session that went OK was one of the sessions in Melbourne. It was with the so-called celebrity CIO, Blair Jaymes. Talk about two peas in a pod! Blair also has a well-earned reputation in the industry as a bit of a tosser who just spruiks buzz words about emerging technology trends and never actually delivers anything of value to whatever business has the current misfortune to employ him as their CIO or Chief Technologist. He certainly never seems to last long enough in any single organisation to actually implement anything.

The briefing document we'd prepared for Digby on Blair was testament to this. It showed that Blair had been with eight different organisations in just the past five years. He is also prolific on LinkedIn and Twitter, which impressed Digby when he looked at Blair's LinkedIn profile, so much so that he'd invited him to connect before they'd even met.

Given that Blair is always at conferences, appearing on panels or as a guest speaker at them, it was really a minor miracle that Digby and Blair had not crossed paths previously. Anyway, despite both talking across each other constantly for the entire duration of their meeting, they hit it off famously. They finished off by taking a selfie together that was immediately posted on their social media feeds as some sort of cathartic meeting of the great minds behind worldwide digital transformation.

Watching the whole thing unfold really made me want to puke, but instead I just smiled and nodded throughout the meeting knowing that the ordeal was nearly over. It also taught me that when two such idiots meet, the main and only enduring outcome is that they post clichéd and vomit-inducing quotes about each other on social media that they themselves think are inspirational - Whereas in my humble opinion #DigitalDisruptor = #Wanker!

Before we let Digby go, we had a final session which was the internal one that we had originally set up for the local Practice Team to meet the Global Practice Leader. Instead they had to make do with Digby again talking about his favourite subject - himself - sprinkled liberally with buzz words like digital, big data, omnichannel and blockchain.

I could tell from the reactions of those in the room that they thought Digby was a complete prat, except for Dexter, the Chief Architect from Consulting, who'd invited himself along to this session to meet Digby and clearly thought he too had found his digital soulmate. After the session had ended I had to prise the two of them apart in order to bundle Digby into a car and get him to the airport. After all, there was no way I was going to risk him missing his flight after the week that I'd just endured!

After a full week of seemingly endless and mind-numbing meetings, in the end there were only two and a half people who enjoyed Digby's visit and didn't think he was a complete and utter wanker. They were Blair the Celebrity CIO, Dexter from Consulting, and Neville from T9One. Neville only accounted for the half since he'd phoned me on Wednesday to say that Digby had become rather inebriated, untidy and 'handy' later on Tuesday evening at Neville's 'club' and had got himself ejected by the bouncers, which Neville described as 'highly embarrassing and inappropriate'.

Geez, I would have thought that taking business partners to strip clubs these days was in itself highly embarrassing and inappropriate, but whatever. That little nugget of information about Digby's inappropriate behaviour provided enough extra amusement for me to actually make the week worthwhile.

## Chapter Twenty-Eight

# The Long Weekend

WITH THE FUN OF THE global visit now in the rear-view mirror, the next week, which was the last full week of Quarter 3, virtually flew by. It was a veritable blur of seemingly endless reviews or so-called 'cadence' calls to check the latest status of the deals due to sign in the quarter, along with numerous 'fire drills' which were urgent requests for Quarter 4 pipeline updates. There's nothing quite like being asked for the same information three or four times in one day, all requested by different stakeholders and in slightly different formats. It quickly wears you down and sometimes I lapse into simply forwarding the previous update to the new requestor, just to make a point. It's also clear that those up the line on the Executive Leadership Team often really don't want to hear the truth when it comes to deal updates. For example, when I point out the difficulty of now suddenly overcoming some long-standing and quite complex sticking points in our commercial negotiations with a client - meaning that there is no realistic chance that deal is going to get signed this week - I get told that 'I'm not being helpful' or that I 'need to be more agile'.

I, however, would much rather tell the truth and be accused of being unhelpful (or in my view realistic) rather than playing the stupid smoke and mirrors cadence call games that many of my colleagues seem to delight in. Typically, it involves keeping alive the hope for a deal signing in the current quarter well after all realistic hope has been extinguished. They seem to think that putting up this false front until the deal finally slips into the next quarter due to some completely uncontrollable, usually client-dictated event, deflects any blame from the slippage away from them personally. Kind of like: 'I did my very best but, you know, unfortunately shit happens...'.

The other aspect of these calls that provides me with endless amusement is the sheer ability of some people to bullshit about their deals. As we rattle our way through the list of deals helpfully provided by Sales Admin, an Industry or Sales Leader will sometimes interject, trying to be helpful but really just to show how on top of their patch they are. So, more often than you might think possible, they'll quote the wrong deal leader, talk about a completely different deal or client, and even then get the status of the deal completely ballsed-up. Apart from those minor utterly incorrect details, I'm sure they think they've added immense value to the call.

During the final week of Q3 they also announced new, more onerous travel restrictions for Q4, which was usually standard practice for this time of year. On reading the announcement it did seem that this year the restrictions would be particularly harsh, which was fine by me if it meant the chance to work remotely more often and to spend some time at home rather than in and out of hotels and airports, especially since I'd spent over 30 weeks on the road working away from home this year already. But unfortunately in the fine print towards the end of the announcement, it clearly set out that the Sales function was exempt as it was 'critical to maintaining our sales momentum' for the year. Bugger!

With the working week out of the way and after a pretty full-on year so far, I was really looking forward to the October long weekend. It's the first public holiday since June, so it's always such a welcome relief to the regular grind when it comes around. I'd purposely asked Emily not to plan to do too much and certainly not to plan a trip away anywhere. I just wanted to sleep in my own bed and spend time with her and the kids, getting around to some favourite local haunts, hopefully with some nice spring weather to boot. I really just needed a little break to unwind ready for the final push through Q4 to Christmas.

The weekend started nicely enough with breakfast and shopping at the Adelaide Central Market on Saturday morning. We picked up some nice supplies for the weekend – some barbecue and deli meats, Adelaide Hills cheese, fresh vegetables and some lovely fresh local seafood. We'd invited some friends around for a barbecue that night so this fresh produce was put to good use, along with (of course) liberal servings of Coopers Pale Ale and some amazing Shiraz from the Barossa Valley that we thoroughly enjoyed.

Feeling just a little dull on Sunday morning, even after an unprecedented sleep-in until around 8:30, I was jolted back to earth by a call from Dianne. After some pleasantries and profuse apologies for disturbing me on a Sunday morning, she got straight down to it.

'Mike, I'm really sorry but I need you to get to Sydney as soon as possible to help us get out of a bind we've gotten into on a deal. It seems that we've completely missed part of the scope of services and simply can't move forward on it until we fill the gap. We've only got two weeks left until the submission is due, so it's super urgent.'

'OK, Di. I'm sure I can rearrange my schedule and get down there Tuesday morning or perhaps even late on Monday night if I have to,' I responded.

Di was quickly back with, 'Sorry, Mike. I need you there today.'

'What, Dianne? You do know it's a long weekend, don't you?' I shot back.

'Yes, of course,' she said, seeming just a little cranky that I was pushing back. 'Listen, Mike. The last thing I wanted to do today was to put this onto you, believe me; but the deal team in Sydney is working through the weekend, they've just found this glaring hole, and Christiaan has been screaming at me this morning saying that I need to fix it with someone on the ground there today.'

'Shit, Di. Doesn't that prick realise that people have a life outside of The Company?' I asked, rather rhetorically really.

'Mike, I know that you know the answer to that question already. Please, I just need you to get on the ground, understand the real extent of the issue, and get him off my back.'

'Hey, Emily, guess what,' I said as walked down to the kitchen where she was already busy baking something that smelled rather nice.

Taking one look at my face, and knowing that I'd just had a call from work, she smiled broadly and replied with false cheeriness, 'What time do you need me to drop you off at the airport, Michael?'

She'd been around me and seen the ridiculous things this industry and its clients demand for long enough now, so nothing really surprised her anymore either. She also knew that short of telling them to stick their job where the sun doesn't shine, this kind of disruption to one's personal life went with the territory of being a senior IT Services sales professional.

Even so, on the way to the airport early that afternoon she gave me some stern advice about me starting to put myself and my family first a bit more and letting other people sort out their own messes. Point taken. I really was getting sick and tired of digging other people out of their shit, including Dianne. I was also well over dickheads like Christiaan who seem to think that we are on perpetual standby for The Company, and that weekends are just working days in casual clothes.

## Chapter Twenty-Nine

# The Utility Co Deal

I ARRIVED IN SYDNEY AT 3 pm and headed straight into the office, where the deal team was supposedly gathered. Given that it was a long weekend and the start of school holidays, it had been one of those rather depressing flights for me. The plane was full of families and excited kids who were heading off on their holiday breaks when I was yet again heading to work, away from home and my family.

I was pleased when I got to The Company office out at North Ryde and my security swipe card actually worked to give me access to the building. I'd been caught out before, working interstate out of hours, when my card strangely stopped working. As it turned out later, in that instance it was because some butthead in security decided off his own bat to cancel out-of-hours access for all staff members who weren't permanently based in that particular office. Clearly, that individual in security was challenged by the notion that someone might actually need to visit another office out of 8-6 working hours - so I don't know what planet he or she lived on.

I dragged my well-worn trolley travel bag to the deal war room that Dianne had told me the team was working from.

When I arrived at the door, I could see that there were two people there. A Solutioner from the Cloud practice and a Graduate from Consulting. As I introduced myself, they seemed surprised to see me and said that the rest of the deal team members were pretty much working remotely from their homes for the long weekend. That also included the overall deal leader, Jonathon Davies, who apparently would be back here late on Monday.

Great, I thought. I'd been told categorically that I must be here on the ground to work with a team that is pretty much not here. I had a good mind to turn around and catch the next flight home, but I knew that whilst that might send a message, it would also be highly likely to backfire on me spectacularly. So it would be best, now that I was here, to knuckle down and find out as much as I could about the deal and its real state of play. As soon as I'd sent Dianne a quick update...

Sunday 4:27pm

> Dianne, Confirming that I've arrived in the deal war room. It's a good thing I got here as the 2 people here were getting bored with the limited companionship, what with the rest of the team including Jonathon the deal leader working remotely this weekend. Mike

Funnily enough, Dianne read my message but didn't respond.

So I spent the rest of the day trying to glean as much as I could about the deal from the two team members in the room. They gave me access to the requirements document from Utility Co and were also able to point me to the team portal for the deal, which contained the bid plan, templates and draft responses constructed to date. So at least I could do some homework and get myself up to speed on this before I got the lowdown from Jonathon.

After consuming this information on Sunday night, there wasn't a lot else I could do on the deal itself on Monday until I had some further insights from Jonathon. So instead, I spent most of my holiday Monday preparing some sales reports that Global had requested, updating the files with details of Larry's lack of progress on his PMP, and gathering some data for my forecast call with Dianne and Sales Admin. Really, I tried to convince myself without success, who needs a long weekend? I fought off the feelings of depression and anger at having been coerced yet again to forgo my personal life to satisfy someone else's misguided and downright dumb demands.

Jonathon finally rocked into the war room mid-Monday afternoon and, although I had left a couple of messages for him to call me on Sunday, he was surprised to see me there.

'I wasn't expecting you until tomorrow,' was his warm welcome to me.

Clearly much had been lost in translation with this escalation to get me on the ground in Sydney immediately, which presumably went from Jonathon to Christiaan to Dianne and back down to me.

Jonathon is one of our Complex Deal Leaders. He has a reputation for being a hard-arse, no-nonsense, get-it-done type of guy. Having worked with him before on a couple of pursuits, I knew that to be true. He was quite possibly the most time-poor person I'd ever worked with. He always seemed to have way too much on his plate and he ran his deal status sessions with absolute ruthlessness. He didn't want any details. All he wanted to know was: yes or no, are you on track for the deadline or not? Any attempt at explaining or adding further information would simply be cut off as he moved to the next person for their update, and any real issues that managed to be raised would be met with his instruction to 'take that up with me offline'.

Jonathon gave me a quick synopsis on the deal. It was with Utility Co but had been given the codename 'Project Gravity'. He had no idea why we called it that, and said, 'Some dick-head in Consulting who obviously thought that he was being clever and cool came up with the name,' and he just ran with it to shut him up. He felt that most aspects of the bid were in good shape, and that they were actually well advanced in a couple of areas. There were, though, some challenges with a few aspects of the overall solution, especially around the commercial model for support services; and that is where Jonathon had reached out requesting my help.

Essentially, I had to quickly mobilise a team to take the inputs from the other stakeholders on the team, and distil it all down into an ongoing support services model that would allow the client to pay as they go, or 'buy by the drink' as he termed it.

OK, I thought, should be quite doable, even with only two weeks to get it done. As long as the other contributors stuck to their commitments and assuming that I could get some good assistance from the offshore Solutioning and Commercial teams to help me pull it all together.

## Chapter Thirty

# Project Gravity

Jonathon liked to start every day at 8:30 am with a team status update session. Basically, it was a quick whip around to gauge the current status of each component of the deal. The first of these I attended was on Tuesday morning and the update session did not disappoint.

The full deal team was now back in the war room at North Ryde and the room was packed. There were quite a few familiar faces that I'd crossed paths with before. Dexter was there as the lead for the Consulting team, which I didn't really understand, since there was no real scope for them in the deal and I couldn't see his name as having any responsibilities or inputs on the detailed project plan task list.

Jonathon kicked off proceedings by introducing me to the team and throwing straight to me for my update. Knowing his style, I kept it extremely short and factual. I'd done some rapid ground work and had called in some favours, I was able to announce that I'd lined up an excellent onshore Solution lead in Tony Davidson, who'd be joining us today, and that he'd already put the offshore Solution team in India on notice to assist. I also had Lu Lu assigned to do the pricing for our component. My only gap was in getting someone assigned from the Commercial team, which I was actioning.

'Great progress, thanks, Mike,' said Jonathon before moving quickly on.

About 20 minutes later, and just after Tony joined me in the room, things got interesting. Jonathon had finished going around the room and asked for any final issues before we were all to get on with it. Dexter, whom Jonathon had skipped in going around the bases, said that he had an issue. He told the room that apparently the codename 'Project Gravity' had previously been used by another bid team in The Company, and therefore we needed to change it and come up with a new codename.

Jonathon immediately cut him off and said, 'You can't. We haven't got time to muck around with distractions like that.' And with that, Jonathon closed the meeting.

Dexter stood up and glared at Jonathon for a moment before barging his way out of the war room in quite an angry manner. Sheesh, he's a bit sensitive, I thought. Anyway, I found it quite funny as did Tony, so we had a quick chuckle as we headed off to grab a coffee.

'Now with this deal, Tony, the first thing I need you to do is to confirm who our lead from the offshore team in India will be, so that we can get them on a call when they come online later today,' I said.

'Already fired off a note last night, Mikey, so I'll check my emails in a minute to see what they've come back with,' he replied.

'Good. Now, can you also check for me that there are no holidays in India over the next couple of weeks that might impact? Like, will Diwali cause us any challenges in the next few weeks?'

'It shouldn't do, Mikey, as I think it's later in October, but I will double check that and see if there are any other scheduled holidays or holy days that might cause us an issue, mate. The good news,' he added with a cheeky smile, 'is that the most sacred and least productive day of all for India, the Indian Premier League final, has already been held this year.'

For the rest of the morning, I continued to chase down help from our Commercial team, with a less than desirable the end result. It seemed that the only option available at all was a chap named Kieron. I was hardly thrilled by this as I'd had prior experience working on deals with Kieron. In fact, 'working with' aren't quite the right words to use, as I've never actually seen him do any work. He is a complete and utter bludger, who is never around when work needs to be done. Yet he seems to be worshipped by some in the organisation, as some sort of enigmatic hero. That in itself remains a mystery to me, as the vast majority of people regard him as a lazy, manipulative bastard, but bizarrely there are a few who will quickly and feverishly spring to his defence. I just knew that I had my work cut out getting the Commercial elements I needed from him.

That afternoon, when I told Tony that we had been allocated Kieron he was dismayed as well. He quickly moved on, though, as it seemed he had been dealing with some challenges of his own in confirming who our Solution lead in India would be. He showed me a series of emails on his laptop that you simply had to see to believe. The emails went along these lines:

*The first note was from Tony to the head of the team there, Rajesh, asking for the urgent allocation of an experienced Support Services Solution leader for Project Gravity.*

*Rajesh forwarded the note to Meeraj asking him to 'take care of this'.*

*Meeraj then sent it Prakash 'FYI&A'.*

*Prakash routed it on to Anand, 'looping him in to do the needful'.*

*Anand responded back to Prakash saying 'that perhaps Sathya is best placed to take this on…'*

*Sathya injected himself into proceedings to let Anand and Prakash know that he was unavailable due to leave commitments.*

*So Prakash wrote back to Rajesh asking 'for clarification of the situation'.*

My head hurt trying to follow all this.

Tony just said, 'Fuck me, Mikey, all they've done is waste the whole bloody day going around in a big circle. I've asked Rajesh to call me as soon as he can to get this sorted, and I'd like to patch you in when he does'.

'Sure thing, Tony. I'll help put some pressure on to get them off this roundabout,' I said, my brain still trying to assess how many of our offshore colleagues had avoided this assignment, kind of like a deadly serious game of pass the parcel.

## Chapter Thirty-One

# The C Word

IT TOOK UNTIL LATE WEDNESDAY night for Tony and me to finally get someone from the India Solutioning team on the hook to run their end of the requirements. We had numerous conference calls with them on Tuesday night, continuing to go in ever-decreasing circles until I pulled the plug and told them to sort it out themselves and get me an answer by the next morning. That answer never came so the calls continued, from when the India-based team came online just after lunch Australian time, until we finally sorted it at 11 pm that night. Which, of course, was just in time for me to jump on to the weekly Global conference call.

That call was a cracker too. We all had to provide our firm and final estimates around what Q4 deals we would sign, which this early in a quarter is a very speculative game to play. So I did my usual thing and gave them my honest assessment of the likely outcome in signing values, which they didn't like because it was short of my budget. So now I had to prepare an urgent 'Gap Plan' to address the shortfall.

No worries, I thought. Since these deals don't just materialise out of nowhere, I'll just miraculously pull a couple of deals out of my butt! Deals that can get closed in the next

two months when the usual cycle for these complex trans-
actions is six to eighteen months. It was a good thing that I
didn't say that out loud because they definitely didn't get my
dry, sarcastic Aussie sense of humour.

I was also very amused on the call when the Global Practice
Leader thanked me for my contribution in arranging Digby's
recent visit. Apparently, and according to Digby, it was an
amazing success and he had uncovered a myriad of significant new business opportunities for The Company whilst he
was down here. He truly must have been in different meetings to the ones I was in. So to prevent me from being left
with the task, I asked Digby to send me a summary of his
notes on these deals so that I could ensure that we captured
them all in the Sales Record System. I was betting on the
likelihood that that summary would never arrive.

It was late Thursday afternoon before I finally tracked
down Kieron to talk about his assignment to the deal. He
still tried to dodge and weave his way completely out of
it but I was having nothing of that. I let him know that it
had been agreed all the way up to Christiaan that this was
now his number one priority. After I briefed him on what
I specifically needed, and told him that I would send him
the document template, he said that he'd get onto it first
thing Monday, since he was tied up on Friday entertaining
some clients at our marquee at the golf tournament that The
Company was a sponsor of.

Flabbergasted, I told him that I didn't think he really had
time for that now, but in any case I didn't actually care when
he actually started on his documents, as long as I had them
by close of business on Tuesday.

Bizarrely, when I voiced my concerns over Kieron's commitment to get this done in the 8:30 am status meeting with Jonathon on Friday, he immediately leapt to Kieron's defence, saying that he trusted him to get it done. I made a mental note that Jonathon was a Kieron apologist and as such not as smart as I'd pegged him as.

In the Friday status meeting I was also able to confirm that Tony and I had the India Solutioning team back on track and that they had already produced a nice first draft solution for us. As I finished my rapid-fire update for Jonathon, I let him know that I'd be working from Melbourne on Monday to take care of an HR issue before returning to the war room in Sydney on Tuesday for the rest of the week. I needed to keep progressing with Larry's Performance Management Process, but the Project Gravity deal team didn't need to know that detail.

As the update meeting came to a close, I observed that Dexter no longer seemed to be an active member of the Project Gravity deal team, because I hadn't seen him since he'd stormed out on Tuesday morning.

The weekend came and went in the usual haze of unpacking, logging on to a late night call with the India team on Friday night, trying to unwind on Saturday with some family time with Emily and the kids, occasional work interruptions throughout Sunday, repacking and then heading to the airport again for a red-eye flight to Melbourne on Monday morning.

When I arrived in the Melbourne office, I went to grab a hot desk but there were none available even though I was there quite early at about 8:15 am. This seemed to be a growing issue in most locations where we had offices, and I'd been caught out a few times having to work from the office kitchen, or in one instance simply heading back to my far more comfortable hotel room to dial in to conference calls.

Like most other similar organisations, The Company seemed to be swinging the pendulum from pushing people to work from home more often so that they could cut back on expensive office space, to calling for all staff to come back and work from the office when HR and other leaders figured out that some people were either becoming disconnected from The Company or simply bludging off. The net result seemed to be that when the cry came for all staff to return to working from the office most of the week, there were simply not enough hot desks to go around. Of course, that never directly impacted the Executive Leadership Team or the people in HR, since they were exempt from hot desking and all had their own permanently allocated desks.

I made my way to the office kitchen to find a perch from which to dial in to the 8:30 am status call. Shit! The kitchen was almost full too. In fact, it was half full of kids and looked more like a child care centre. It was school holidays and clearly the office - or in this case the office kitchen - was more like a creche for some frazzled Company employees who were also parents trying to 'balance' their work-life responsibilities.

When I came off mute to provide my update, such was the background noise that Jonathon immediately cut me off to ask if I was down at the local playground. Very fucken funny I thought… 'No, Jonathon, I'm in the Melbourne office, which apparently is having their annual bring your kids to work day today,' I fired back.

After the call I retreated to the meeting room that I had booked to meet with Larry and discuss his PMP. First of all, I had to somewhat apologetically kick out one of our employees who had taken up occupancy in my room along with their child. But I had booked the room and I needed it for what had to be a very private conversation.

I felt sorry for Larry in some ways. God knows the poor bugger was genuinely trying to change his behaviour and save his job, but it just wasn't working and he knew it deep down. I was open with him that, at this stage, based on his current lack of progress or success, I didn't see this having a happy outcome for him, but that I'd continue to support and counsel him as much as possible and we'd reach a conclusion one way or the other before the end of the year.

I wanted to give him as much time as possible, not so much to turn things around anymore as that was really becoming a foregone conclusion, but more to enable him to deal with it and find himself another job. In the background I continued to fend off our HR Department, who were constantly asking for updates while they watched from the sidelines, offering no real help or support for the process. Typical.

Shortly after I finished the session with Larry, I had a call from Stephanie in HR. As I answered her call, I figured that perhaps she wanted an update on my progress with Larry. So the timing was good, I thought. But no, that wasn't the case at all.

After confirming for her that I was in a private place and couldn't be overheard, she went on to say that there had been some serious allegations made against one of my colleagues and that she needed my account of what had occurred. I was perplexed as to what this was all about, but assured Stephanie I'd help if I could. Stephanie then told me that Dexter had made a formal complaint against Jonathon for inappropriate behaviour.

She said, 'Michael, these allegations are quite serious, so I need you to tell me exactly what you saw and heard in the Project Gravity status review meeting last Tuesday morning.'

'You mean right before Dexter seemed to storm out of the room in a huff, Stephanie?' I asked.

'Precisely. Dexter says that he left the room after Jonathan called him the "c" word in a heated exchange. What's your recollection, Michael?' she asked in her formal tone.

Wow! Clearly this was a very serious matter for Stephanie, but I couldn't quite stop myself from having a quick dig back. 'You mean, like what they reckon Christiaan said in Brisbane last year, eh?' I said somewhat sarcastically.

'Michael, that is a scurrilous rumour and not helpful or relevant right now. I need to know exactly what you heard in the exchange between Jonathan and Dexter,' was her calm but firm response.

'Stephanie, I heard no such language at all. What I heard was Dexter asking for a change of the project codename and Jonathon responding by saying something like "you can't change that now, we don't have time". He certainly didn't call him the "c" word. He used the word "can't".'

'And you are completely certain of this, Michael?'

'Absolutely,' I said. 'I definitely would have noticed if Jonathon had called him the "c" word. Besides, I was sitting with Tony Davidson and he would have certainly said something to me if that had actually happened.'

Stephanie sighed and said, 'Thanks, Michael. You are now the third person that's confirmed this. It's just that Dexter and his boss Rudy won't let this thing go and are demanding action.'

'Steph, even if you want to me sign a Statutory Declaration on this, I happily will,' I responded, since I was sure about what I'd heard.

'Let's hope we can make this go away and it doesn't get to that, thanks, Michael,' she closed out.

After that little exchange I spent the rest of the day before my flight to Sydney drafting the Commercial document that had been assigned to Kieron. I simply had no faith that he'd come through with the goods and I needed a contingency plan. Or at least a starting point for him once he did get engaged, as he'd not answered my call earlier today and hadn't responded to any of my previous emails yet either.

## Chapter Thirty-Two

# False Hero

Tuesday went by in a blur as we worked frantically to get all of the solution and content elements we needed together and in a fit state ready for review. At around midnight on Wednesday night we got the final approval on the Solution and related pricing agreed by both the offshore and local approvers. So whilst there was a stack of work still to do to bake it all into a nice response to Utility Co before submission on Friday at noon, we at least had all the raw ingredients ready. Tony had done well wrangling the Solution people to get us to this point, and Lu Lu was her usual responsive and reliable self with the pricing inputs. Which left us with the Commercial part. The elusive Kieron had told me that afternoon that he was onto it and would definitely be in the office on Thursday to meet with me and share where he'd got to. I didn't tell him that I'd already more or less drafted the entire document and that it was being reviewed for alignment by Tony and the Solution leads.

Kieron finally swaggered into the war room at about 10 am on Thursday with much self-generated fuss and fanfare. Having not been previously sighted at all, he was doing his level best to ensure that everyone knew he was there now.

There seemed little point to me, since we'd already completed his part for him; and the whole document was due to be locked down for final printing and production at 10 o'clock on Friday morning for submission at noon.

I had no intention of putting up with his bullshit excuses so I told him politely but straight up that, since he'd clearly been otherwise occupied, we'd already written up his document and that he was no longer needed on the deal. This seemed to dent his pride a little and he soon skulked away, although I saw him soon after talking to Jonathon in the corridor, probably complaining that I called him out.

We continued to scramble to finalise everything else that was required for the rest of the day and into the evening. In a deal as complex as this, there was always the chance of something being overlooked. Plus, there were inevitably last-minute changes as various approvers insisted we adjust something or make some alterations to wording.

The team were no doubt all pretty exhausted by the time the 8:30 am status call came around on Friday morning. But much to my surprise, when I arrived that morning the most exhausted and dishevelled looking person in the war room was Kieron. He was sitting next to Jonathon, looking rather unkempt and wearing what looked like yesterday's clothes. What the fuck?

Jonathon launched into the status call, thanking the team for their hard work and dedicated effort. None more so, he said, than Kieron, who had pulled an all-nighter in order to save the deal and ensure that the Commercial submission was completed on time. A few in the room burst into spontaneous applause for Kieron while the rest of us sat in stunned disbelief.

This arsehole, who had not met a single commitment or responded to a single request, was now being lauded by some as the hero of the team. What a crock of shit! And why was Jonathon buying into this BS? I was fuming.

Well, as I found out later that day after the submission went in, Jonathon and Kieron went to University together and had been mates for a long time. No wonder Jonathon showed such flawed judgement.

The story that Kieron himself was spruiking about his all-nighter heroism was that he needed to review the Commercial document and in doing so found some serious flaws that had to be corrected. So being the devoted company man that he is, he worked right through the night to fix it all up. I wasn't copping that clearly false crap, so I had Lu Lu run a document comparison for me showing the before and after snapshots of our final document version and Kieron's. I'm not sure what he had actually done all night, because the sum total of differences between the two document versions were three minor word changes and some small formatting changes to the paragraph numbering. And the time stamp for the changes showed that his last change was at 10:35 pm.

So before I left for the airport to head home, I sent the following email:

**From:** Michael Mansfield – 18/10/2019 2:29pm

**To:** Jonathon Davies

**Cc:** Dianne Johnson

**Subject:** Kieron's Commercial Document Updates – the Reality

Hi Jonathon,

I understand that Kieron is an old mate of yours, but all the same it is important that you understand the real facts around the supposedly heroic all-nighter that he says he pulled to save our deal submission.

Fact 1 – As you can see from the attached Document Comparison Report, Kieron made just three minor wording changes and some very minor updates to the paragraph formatting.

Fact 2 – The last of these changes was made at 10:35 pm on Thursday night.

So clearly, if he did in fact pull an all-nighter, it wasn't to save this deal and the changes listed above remain his sole and net contribution to this deal.

Regards,

Mike

ATT: CommDoc_Comparison_Report.pdf

## Chapter Thirty-Three

# Internal Crap

BY THE START OF NOVEMBER, it really felt like we were rocketing towards Christmas. The rush to get deals done in the quarter was well and truly underway. On some review calls, the point of view on a particular deal closing or not swung from one extreme to the other. One minute we were being fed wildly optimistic predictions that it was a 'done deal' and we just needed to finalise the paperwork. Then a minute or so later, after some further discussion, we were told that it 'was definitely not going to happen' because the client had actually de-prioritised doing the work this year. All in the matter of a few sentences and depending, of course, on the personal viewpoint of whoever was contributing the opinion and how well informed they were. Sometimes it was amusing, at other times it was just demoralising.

I was also losing all hope of receiving my deal bonus for the Simple Extension deal by the end of this month, since there had continued to be more questions asked about the deal, its timeline and my engagement on it over the past few weeks. Dianne continued to reassure me that all would be well, but I smelled a rat with the Payment Prevention Police in our Sales Admin team trying to stitch me up somehow for Christiaan.

Interestingly, Lu Lu had already been paid her due bonus for the deal, which was good news for her and also for me, as it meant she was no longer calling me on a daily basis asking for updates on the status of the payment. I was really hoping to receive this bonus before Christmas so that I could surprise Emily with it, but I was now beginning to think about how to tell her that it appeared that I was once again being shafted.

The best thing for me right now was to keep my head down and soldier on with whatever the next priority action was. Increasingly, it was all internal Company actions that were taking up my time, rather than clients and deals. The internal administration was primarily because there was just so much to get done in these couple of months, what with Annual Performance Reviews to prepare for each of my team, constant forecast adjustments, the start of planning around the target numbers for next year, regular information demands from Global, still trying to recruit some good resources to fill out my team, plus all the usual deal stress that goes on this time of year. I'd be very happy to take a nap and wake up post January $1^{st}$ if I could.

It also didn't help that I'd lost access to The Company's Annual Review system, and hadn't been able to start that process properly yet. For some reason I just couldn't get into the system, so I had to confront the horror of contacting The Company's internal Tech Support Team. You see, IT Services companies are a lot like the proverbial plumbers' taps: seldom do our own systems get the care, attention and level of support that they need to function effectively.

First up I spent 30 minutes trying to find the phone number for Tech Support so I could call someone; it was no easy task, since the last thing that Tech Support wanted was for someone to actually call them. I had to revert to this since my instant chat messaging seemed not to be working - either that or Tech Support were choosing to ignore my pings. Once I finally located the contact phone number and immediately stored it in my phone for future reference, I called them.

After another 15 or so minutes navigating the Automated Call Distribution system, which appeared to not understand most of what I was saying, I miraculously got through to speak with a real Tech Support person, only to find out that they needed to transfer me to another section to deal with my issue. Two more transfers later, I managed to outline my issue for the fourth time to someone who seemed able to assist me. He raised a ticket for the issue, which he assured me would be dealt with 'by the next business day, in line with the service level target'.

After I hung up the call, feeling relieved that it should hopefully be fixed by tomorrow giving me the access I needed, I saw the email confirmation that the ticket had been raised. It was immediately followed by another email showing that the ticket had now been closed.

So I checked my Annual Review system access, thinking that it would be too good to be true if they'd managed to fix it this quickly. And I was right. They hadn't fixed it at all. But the ticket had been closed and I'd now also been sent an email survey from Tech Support asking 'how was our service'. Probably best for them if I don't respond to that right now...

Recruiting a couple of new team members was also taking much longer than I had hoped. It was a tough, time-consuming process sifting through the masses of mediocrity to find some good, experienced sales talent to add to the team. I still had two vacancies on the team to fill. One was one of the original vacant positions I'd inherited when I took on responsibility for the team. The other was for Amber's role on my team, which necessitated additional pain as I went through a whole process to get a new position created, since her position had effectively transferred with her when she was moved. It was pretty tough going because, despite having a fairly substantial and well-staffed HR Department, The Company had implemented a 'self-service' process for all new hires.

This meant, essentially, that you had to do it all yourself. Whilst this was painful, and also painfully slow, at least it meant that I could be choosy about who I recruited - unlike the new hire 'gift' that I had already received for one of my vacant positions, over which I had no say whatsoever. This particular new employee was injected into my team directly by Dianne. The individual used to work for one of our Partner organisations, and their MD and Christiaan apparently played golf together occasionally. Christiaan basically told Dianne to hire him to join our Sales function and, having nowhere else to place him, she plonked him onto my team.

I quickly worked out that the other MD had sold Christiaan a pup. This new chap presented himself reasonably well, and in casual conversation you'd think he was a solid enough IT professional. However, some challenges very quickly became apparent.

Firstly, this guy had never worked in Services sales, but rather he had spent his entire IT career in the consumer hardware business. It is a completely different beast, since flogging the latest model laptop is a whole lot different from putting together a complex, multi-year, multi-million-dollar deal to design, build and support a new business system.

The second problem was that I couldn't confirm, either from his very detailed CV, or by speaking with him once we met, that he'd ever actually been engaged in a sales role of any sort. Rather, it seemed he was more of a back-room guy who simply provided order fulfilment services once someone else had sold something.

Dianne had worked this out too, so I managed to get her agreement to move him elsewhere early in the New Year. In the meantime, though, under the self-service recruitment policy, I'd have to induct him into The Company and get him up to speed.

The only external light in the tunnel amongst all this internal Company crap was that we'd continued to get a trickle of clarification questions from Utility Co in relation to our proposal to them. There were some good questions too, showing not only that they were taking the process seriously, but also that it seemed that we were well and truly in the hunt for this business. At least, that's what we hoped.

## Chapter Thirty-Four

# Shortlisted

I'D JUST HAD A RARE full week spent in Adelaide without the necessity to travel anywhere, which made for a pleasant change and a slightly more relaxing weekend than usual. I also had no firm plans to travel this week either, which set the scene for an almost mythical full fortnight without going away. Since she wasn't used to having me around so much except when we were on holidays, even Emily was starting to joke with me, saying things like: 'Haven't you got somewhere you need to be?' I was getting the distinct feeling that I was interrupting her well-practised routines to get the kids organised, get her own job done, and also maintain household order. Oh well, at least I was doing my bit as part of The Company Q4 spending constraints by not travelling, I thought.

I went into the Adelaide office on Monday morning to spend some time with the wonderful and effervescent Amy, as she helped me to fix up a bunch of Q4 and Q1 deal entries in the Sales Record System. I tried to return the favour by helping her with some thoughts and ideas for an impending services opportunity in one of her accounts that the client had just told her would be released before Christmas. The client's procurement section had very kindly informed her that it would hit her inbox on Thursday 19th December and the response was due back to them on Friday 10th January.

This is increasingly typical of so many clients. They throw an RFP or Tender over the fence for us to respond to over the holiday period, while they all piss off and have their holidays. That way, when they get back in the second week of January they'll have a bunch of proposal responses ready and waiting for them to review; and they don't give a rat's arse that it forces a whole bunch of people in the IT services companies competing for their business to work on over the Christmas and New Year's Eve period.

What they don't seem to comprehend is that by doing this they are far more likely to get a half-arsed, second-rate solution proposed, since most companies have a shut-down period and will often just deploy a skeleton or second-string team to work on these types of deals. In any case, I suggested to Amy that she reach out to Tony to see if he wanted to help with the deal, since he always seemed pretty keen to work over the Christmas period and avoid as much contact with his wife's family as he could.

Early Monday afternoon I got a call from Jonathon about the Utility Co deal. My heart was always in my mouth when I answered these calls, because they are usually completely binary in that you're either still in the hunt or you are out of contention; and when you have invested a significant amount of metaphorical blood, sweat and tears in an opportunity, it really hurts to lose. Fortunately, Jonathon being the no-nonsense, time-poor, cut-to-the-chase guy that he is, he told me straight up that we'd been shortlisted and were through to the next stage. Woo-ho! That's awesome. We were still in the game and got to continue the pursuit of this one.

With the good news dispensed with, Jonathon told me the less than good news. The deal remained competitive and we had three days to submit our best and final offer (or BAFO as we called it) to Utility Co. So I needed to get my butt and my team's butts back to the war room in North Ryde ASAP. So much for a fortnight without travel.

'No worries, Jonathon. I'll fly down this arvo and we'll be there first thing Tuesday morning,' I said.

'Thanks, Mike, I appreciate it. By the way I did see your email about Kieron's work on the commercial submission and I completely understand your point of view, so let's just move on and win this sucker!'

By 8 am on Tuesday morning, Tony and I were in the war room as the rest of the deal team started to assemble. Jonathon arrived just before 8:30 and proceeded to tell a bunch of people that they weren't required for this BAFO phase. He said that instead, we were going to use a smaller, core team of expertise to ensure that we focused fully on the task of refining our proposal into the winning solution by the BAFO submission close at 5 pm on Thursday.

A few people were a bit miffed by this, but Jonathon wasn't exactly going to engage in a discussion on the merits of his selected team. As the protests continued, he picked up a whiteboard marker and started to write a handful of names on the board, including Tony's name and mine. He put the pen down and turned back to the throng gathered in the room, and said: 'Those of you whose names are on the whiteboard are part of the BAFO team and can stay.'

He then pointed to the door and said, 'To the rest of you, thank you for your contributions to date, but you can fuck off now, please.'

Subtle as a sledgehammer, I thought. But some bluntness upfront would no doubt help us get the focus that we needed over the coming days.

Once the room had cleared, Jonathon launched into a briefing to share what he knew about the state of play on the deal. He was fairly confident that it was down to us and just one other short-listed competitor, and he'd had some good 'off the record' advice from the client on how we needed to tweak our proposal to align better to the future directions of Utility Co. So he wanted to start with us all reviewing Utility Co's current strategic plan and key business initiatives.

He asked the Graduate who'd been assisting on the deal to connect his laptop to the flat screen in the room and pull up the Annual Report. We were chatting about the other potential competitor for the deal as he did this; and once he was connected, the Grad Googled 'Utility Co Annual Report'.

It was at this point that Jonathon asked the Grad, 'What exactly have you been using your computer for lately?'

'Why are you asking me that?' naively responded the Grad without looking up from his keyboard.

'Because the ads popping up in your browser appear to be for "hot Asian girls", lad!' was Jonathon's dry response as he stared at the flat screen. The poor Grad turned a beetroot shade of red as we all pissed ourselves laughing.

Clearly Jonathon, who came across as a hard task master, did actually have a good sense of humour. But our mirth at the poor lad's expense was short-lived before Jonathon called us back to order, as we needed to get on with it.

By 10:30 Tuesday morning we'd finished this refresher background research on Utility Co and had agreed the plan for the next three days. It essentially started with the end in mind and worked backwards over what we needed to do from a solution, pricing and commercial perspective, along with the approvals we'd need for our final pricing offer to Utility Co. We also settled on our target price to win, which gave us a shared reference point as we worked through all that was required over what promised to be a very full-on few days.

And those few days certainly proved to be manic. We worked through until well after midnight on Tuesday and Wednesday, getting the offshore teams to agree to the changes we needed. Thursday was just a mad scramble as we frantically provided briefings and sought the internal approvals that we needed to release our BAFO proposal to the client. In parallel we had some of the team re-crafting the written submission, to ensure that we achieved the alignment with Utility Co's strategy that Jonathon had been coached on by the client.

We got our BAFO response in at 4:53 pm EST, according to the time-stamped receipt that we got back from the online submission application. It was a little too close for my liking; but Jonathon seemed unfazed and was actually delighted that we got what he regarded as a winning solution, in before the deadline. I was exhausted when I got back to my hotel room that night, having decided to stay in Sydney as a contingency in case Utility Co granted, or we needed an extension.

I caught up with Dianne in the city office the next day before I flew home that evening. She was pleased with what we'd done on the deal and thanked me for again pitching in, as she was 'certain that we wouldn't have got this far without you on this, Mikey.'

While I had her attention I followed her up again on the Simple Extension deal bonus; and whilst acknowledging that Sales Admin were causing grief on this one, she remained quietly confident that we'd get Christiaan's approval on it and all would be good. I was far less confident on that one than she was.

While we were chatting Dianne also asked me about a conference that our partners T9One were holding. I told her that Neville had raised it with me briefly last month, but that I'd politely declined his invitation as I understood it was in the US, and with our Q4 travel and spending restricted it simply wouldn't be possible to get it approved. Besides, the timing of the conference in late November was terrible, with the focus we needed on closing out the Q4 deals and The Company fiscal year strongly, as well as all the other stuff that had to be done around Annual Performance Reviews and planning for next year.

Dianne understood and agreed with my view, and said that Neville had also approached her to attend as well. She would go back to him and let him know that it simply wouldn't be possible this time around for us to send a representative from our region.

Thank God, I thought. I needed a trip like that like a hole in the head right now.

I was unwinding with a cold beer in the Qantas lounge before my flight home that evening when Dianne sent me an email confirming that she'd dealt with the T9One conference. Or at least, that's what I thought until I read it.

**From:** Dianne Johnson – 15/11/2019 4:55pm

**To:** Michael Mansfield

**Fwd:** Company representative – T9One global conference

Mike,
I'm sorry, I tried my best to talk him around but he insisted... Give me a call on the weekend if you can't attend for some reason.
Thx,
Di
Sales Director


**From:** Christiaan Joubert – 15/11/2019 4:47pm

**To:** Sebastian Petersen <CEO@t9one.com>

**Cc:** Dianne Johnson; Neville Thomas <nthomas@t9one. com>

**Subject:** Company representative – T9One global conference

Seb,
Confirming that Michael Mansfield will be attending your global conference as our regional representative and I have provided travel approval for same.

Christiaan Joubert
**Managing Director**

Shit. There's nothing like being volunteered for something that makes no sense at all in terms of real priorities. Clearly,

Christiaan was just bowing to political pressure from our colleagues at T9One and I was the sacrificial attendee from our region. And the prick doesn't even have the decency to copy me in on the email directly. Mind you, I'm surprised that he even spelt my name right.

I quickly pulled up the conference details via the link below the emails as my plane was being called. Bugger! It was in Vegas, which was quite possibly the last place on the planet that I felt the need to visit again. And it was the week after next, meaning I'd have to scramble to get my flights and accommodation organised quickly, and also reorganise my schedule for the coming weeks.

## Chapter Thirty-Five

# Taking the PISS

EMILY WAS IMMENSELY AMUSED AT me being directed to drop everything and head halfway around the world to Las Vegas for some conference, at what she knew was the busiest time of year for me personally, and certainly for The Company. I tried to explain the politics of it all but I couldn't even convince myself it made sense, so I had no chance of convincing her.

'Still,' she said. 'Look on the bright side. At least you'll have about 30 hours of travel time that week to catch up on the backlog of work you keep complaining about.'

Having digested Emily's coded advice not to spend too much time working that weekend, I decided not to waste half of it making travel arrangements for the conference the following week. Instead, I spent just a few hours updating my forecast for Q4 signings, which I had to submit to Sales Admin before Monday.

So having temporarily deferred the travel booking anguish, I ended up spending all of Monday morning wrangling with The Company's online travel booking portal, trying to get some half-sensible flight options that would get me to Las Vegas and back as painlessly as possible. Alas, it was all in vain. After finding neither suitable flight options nor accommodation choices near the conference venue, I gave up and rang The Company's Travel Booking Agency for help.

After only 20 minutes on hold, I got put through to a Travel Consultant named Lisa, who tried her best to help me out within the ridiculous travel policy constraints. After eliminating some low airfare options that would see me take almost three days and two overnight stops to get to Vegas, we settled on the least worst option of flights from Adelaide to Sydney to LA to Vegas. The issue was that these involved a 10-hour layover in LA after an almost 14-hour flight from Sydney in Economy class, which didn't thrill me at all.

'Lisa, that's a very long layover in LA - are there any other options within policy to get me onward to Vegas sooner?' I asked.

'I'm sorry, Mr Mansfield, but there is nothing else coming up within the policy guidelines for lowest logical airfare. Can I suggest that you lock these flights in now and then maybe call us back when your plans change, perhaps?' she said, with a strong emphasis on the part about when my plans change.

For once I took the hint immediately and asked Lisa to confirm these flights for me, thanking her for her assistance and suggesting that I would need to confirm some other details before calling back to arrange my accommodation in Vegas.

I hung up and called the Travel Booking Agency straight back. As serendipity would have it, and against all the call-centre odds, I was connected straight through to a familiar voice saying, 'Good afternoon, this is Lisa speaking. Can you please provide your employee number so that I can assist you?'

'Hello, Lisa. This is Michael Mansfield, employee number 6751937. I believe you may have just assisted me with my flights to the US next week,' I said.

'Hello again, Mr Mansfield. How may I assist you, sir?'

'Well Lisa, I just found out that I have some additional business commitments in Las Vegas before the conference starts, and I need to be there just a little bit earlier than I anticipated. So I need your help to change me to an earlier flight from LA to Vegas that will see me arrive by around 1 pm that day. Can you please see what options we might have for this?'

'Certainly, Mr Mansfield. I can see from your booking that you arrive at LAX at 6 am. There are some onward flight options to Las Vegas available at 8:11 am and 8:35 am with American Airlines. With your change of plans, I'd probably suggest the 8:35 flight, sir, so that you have ample time to clear customs and immigration and change terminals. That flight will get you into Las Vegas in plenty of time for your 1 pm appointment. Would you like me to make that change, Mr Mansfield?'

'Yes please, Lisa. Thank you, you've been very helpful.'

Way to work the system, I thought as I hung up, feeling very self-satisfied that I'd avoided a 10-hour layover at LAX. Given that I was spending my Sunday travelling to this conference, I sure as hell had no intention of wasting the best part of a day hanging around LAX if I could move on much more quickly.

Then I remembered that I'd forgotten to book the accommodation, so I had to call back again. This time I didn't get Lisa, unfortunately, but instead was connected to a less than helpful Travel Consultant who, as it turned out, had never been to Las Vegas herself. She couldn't possibly get me into the actual conference venue at the Cosmopolitan, as there were no rooms in line with Company policy available there. Instead, she seemed to think that putting me up in some 2-star off-strip dump about four kilometres away from the Cosmopolitan was OK, since that was the lowest-cost accommodation showing in the system.

I had Google maps open as she fired off that option, so I was ready to argue it down; and eventually after some push and shove, I convinced her to book me in at the cheapest possible rate at Planet Hollywood, just across the road from the conference venue. As always, self-service travel arrangements drove me nuts and occupied far too much time, but at least I was getting the most palatable options possible for a trip I really didn't want to do.

Once I got off the phone, I realised that I was slightly late dialling in to the Sales forecast call, so I quickly dialled in and started to listen to the usual roll call of self-serving bullshit about deals. Dianne was running the call today because Christiaan, who usually ran it, was otherwise disposed somewhere else. This generally made for a smoother and quicker call involving much less swearing.

About an hour into the call, my turn came. When Sales Admin put up my forecast details on the screen, I immediately saw that there was a problem. These were not the numbers I'd sent in over the weekend, but were several million dollars higher. I queried this straight away, to be told by Sales Admin that these numbers represented my forecast numbers plus some 'stretch' deals that they had added, based on some data that Global had sent them.

It turned out that Global had ever so helpfully done their own analysis of the information in the Sales Record System and, without any actual knowledge about the specific opportunities themselves, recommended to Sales Admin which deals should be included in my Q4 forecast.

What a crock of shit, I thought! So I told them that they may as well forecast whatever the hell they liked, as these were not my numbers but were just some made up crappy wishful-thinking numbers. Sales Admin tried to tell me that it was too bad; these were now my 'locked in' forecast numbers and I needed to report against them. As I got even further wound up and proceeded to explain that I was not being put on the hook for someone else's bullshit numbers, Dianne interrupted me to suggest we take the discussion to confirm my forecast offline, and move on.

Bloody Sales Admin! Not only were they trying to shaft me on deal bonuses, but now they were dictating to me what my forecast numbers should be. They could get stuffed as far as I was concerned. After all, it was me who was accountable for meeting the forecast numbers, not them. They are just supposed to report on them. I was already penning an email to Dianne to say that I was not accepting responsibility for any forecast numbers other than those I'd submitted, when the forecast part of the call finished and we moved on to other business.

The first item here was about the Annual Performance Review cycle. Thankfully I'd finally resolved the issue with my access to the Annual Review System and could get into it again to start the process for my team. In fact, I think the access problem just resolved itself in the end since Tech Support were of no value and just kept closing my tickets whenever I raised one to report the problem.

Anyway, on the call it was announced that Sales Admin were introducing another new system as part of the Annual Review process. Apparently, we had to use this new system to provide the performance data on what each salesperson had achieved throughout the year. OK, that sounds helpful, I thought. This new 'Performance Indicator Sales System' would collate all the information about signing achieved, bonuses paid to date, etc.

Hang on, I thought, wait a second... The 'Performance Indicator Sales System'? Are they taking the PISS or what?

At about exactly the same time, the instant chat window for the conference call lit up as most of the other 40 or so people on the call figured out the same thing about this rather unfortunate acronym and proceeded to take the proverbial piss out of the Sales Admin team, who clearly hadn't - at least until now - realised that they had given their new system such a memorable moniker. After we had our five minutes of fun at their expense, Dianne wound the call up with the news that going forward, at least for the rest of the year, we'd be moving to a combined forecast and deal review call and that attendance was compulsory. That news, whilst inevitable for this time of year, still managed to take the mirth out of everyone on the call.

## Chapter Thirty-Six

# Vegas

I ARRIVED IN THE IMMIGRATION HALL at LAX at just after 6:30 on Sunday morning after my thirteen-and-a-half-hour flight from Sydney. I'd actually left Adelaide on the red-eye at 6 am, as this was the only flight that would allow me to get my connecting flight to LAX on time. I'd then had to endure my second least favourite part of international travel from Adelaide, which was the Sydney airport domestic-to-international transfer bus (the transfer bus back to domestic on the way home is my least favourite…). Still, as a Platinum Frequent Flyer I got to relax briefly in the awesome Qantas First Class Lounge in the Sydney International Terminal, and the flight from Australia to the US had been relatively comfortable. I'd been fortunate enough to have the next best thing to an actual upgrade, which was a rare spare seat next to me; and I'd managed to watch a couple of movies and grab a little sleep, so I was feeling OK so far.

I got through to Terminal 5 for my flight to Vegas with about half an hour to spare before boarding the next flight, so I had time to head to the AA Admirals Club lounge for a quick snack and a breakfast bourbon. That's one thing about the disconnected, bubble-like world of global travel across time zones. The usual rules about morning drinking don't apply and no one really looks twice if you pair a bowl of breakfast cereal with a bourbon on the rocks.

Thankfully, I didn't have another eight or so hours to kill there, which was what the original booking entailed before my 'change of plans'. And thankfully, a couple of hours later, my room was already available in Vegas when I checked in to the hotel. So I could take a refreshing shower before I got stuck into some work ahead of the conference welcome function that evening. There was no way I was going to take a nap, as that would be the death of me. I had to stay awake until that night, and I'd be fine from then on until the end of the conference on Wednesday night, before I headed off for the long flight home late on Thursday afternoon. In any case, it was rapidly heading towards Monday morning back home in Australia, and I had a forecast to update and some deal status information to submit ahead of the new round of Sales forecast and deal review calls starting that morning.

As I headed over to the Cosmopolitan for the 6 pm Welcome Reception, I flicked Neville a message to say I was on my way. After T9One's escalations to Christiaan, I sure as hell was going to make sure they knew I was here!

Sunday 6:05pm

Hi Neville, just to let you know I've arrived in Vegas and am heading over to the reception. Cheers, Mike

Thanks Mike. See you there soon! Nev

I got my name badge and welcome kit at the Registration Desk out front of the Welcome Reception room. It was quite a nice T9One branded backpack full of the usual tacky merchandise and conference program information. There were a few hundred people at the welcome reception already, but I spied Neville just near the entrance on my way in. He greeted me warmly and took me over to meet their CEO, Sebastian, straight away.

Sebastian was clearly of South African descent, the same as Christiaan, but he seemed a far more charming individual. He thanked me for making the long journey over for the Conference and told Neville to make sure that he looked after me as their guest over the coming days.

After meeting Sebastian, I took Neville aside and explained that I had quite a bit on over the coming days so I was likely to miss a couple of sessions, but would attend whatever sessions of the Conference that I could. He was fine with that and said he'd be quite 'selective' about what he attended over the coming days, too. He then took me over to meet Doris, who was the Marketing lead from my Company in the US that was attending the conference, since I hadn't previously met her. Neville then left me with Doris and the rather extensive marketing team that she had at the event, and made his apologies as he headed off out somewhere else.

As I got to know Doris and the team from The Company, who were all here at the conference to help strengthen the relationship between our Company and T9One, it became apparent that I was the only person from the Sales function attending. Everyone else was from Marketing. It seems that despite the pressure put on me to be there, no one from the

Global Practice had bothered to turn up, despite the conference practically being in their own backyard rather than 20-plus hours of travel time away.

Oh well. It meant I didn't have to spend time with people from the Global Practice and I could be very selective about what I needed to attend, spending time as needed on business matters arising back home. As I had a couple of drinks with the friendly team from Marketing, I also found out that they were all staying at the Cosmopolitan, having been given exception approval by The Company to do so because it was important that they be 'right where the action is'. Typical, I thought as I bade them farewell and trudged back across the strip to my hotel, to fall into bed and get some much-needed rest.

Rookie mistake number one when travelling internationally is to forget to put your phone on mute or flight mode at night. So after only two hours of blissful sleep, I was abruptly woken by the sound of a phone call from Sydney, where it was now about 6:30 pm.

It was Dianne, who was surprised to hear me answer as she had been fully expecting to get my voicemail. She was calling to give me a heads-up that Christiaan had cracked it on the daily call today because I wasn't on the call to give my update first-hand. She said when she told him I was in Vegas, he bellowed: 'What the fuck is he doing in Vegas?' She replied that I was representing him and The Company with T9One, as per his specific request. So he quickly moved on, but she found it rather amusing, and I think she enjoyed giving him one back for a change, and in front of a substantial conference call audience too!

She also told me that the deadline for draft Annual Performance Reviews had been brought forward to this Thursday. This meant that I now had just two days to gather a shitload of input from my colleagues as well as the PIS System, and get my draft ratings in. I was too tired to plead for a deadline extension so I just said I'd do my best to get it done before I hung up the phone and went back to sleep.

I did manage to get to a couple of Conference sessions over the next couple of days, but by and large I was on the phone or my laptop, working either from my hotel room or one of the many breakout areas at the Conference venue. At least at the Conference venue I could help myself to the never-ending flow of snacks and crappy American coffee. The irony of travelling halfway around the world to largely do exactly what I could have done from my home office in Adelaide wasn't lost on me; but at least I'd ticked a box for The Company by attending. In between dealing with various work emergencies and getting the Performance Reviews done, I'd messaged Neville a couple of times but he hadn't responded. I hadn't seen him around the venue at all, either; but then again, I wasn't too fussed as I had plenty to do without having him feel the need to look after me.

Tuesday afternoon I had a call from Jonathon with some news on the Utility Co deal. We'd been invited to present our BAFO proposal to them next Wednesday, which was awesome news. I quickly did the time zone and travel sums in my head to work out that I should be back in Australia in plenty of time to get to Sydney the day before the presentation. I'd just have to do whatever preparation was needed from here and while in transit on the way home. Once I'd confirmed with Jonathan what he needed from me over the next day or so to help prepare, he told me that he was having some robust discussions about our presentation team.

'How so?' I enquired.

'Rudy from Consulting has gotten in Christiaan's ear about the lack of diversity on our pursuit team. So I'm being told to ensure our presentation team is a broadly diverse representation of The Company,' he responded.

'What the fuck has that got to do with Rudy, Jonathon? There's no Consulting content in this deal anyway, especially since Dexter spat the dummy and buggered off. Besides which, isn't it better to have people attend who can actually talk to the proposal with some depth?' I rattled at him.

'I know, Mike. Don't you worry about it. I'm fighting the fight to ensure that sanity prevails. You just get me my content before you head for home and I'll deal with this shit.'

'No worries, Jonathan. Will do.'

So rather than attend the Conference social function, I worked all of Tuesday evening and well into the night Vegas time, to get my draft presentation content ready for Jonathon as well as finalising my draft Performance Reviews for the team. I fell into bed at around 2 am local time and didn't set an alarm for the morning.

I woke up at just after 9 am feeling a bit refreshed. There were several missed calls from an American number that I didn't recognise, as well as several voice messages. I checked my emails too, and Jonathan had confirmed that my presentation content was good and they'd run with it for now at their end.

The calls and messages were from Doris from our US Marketing Team, so I called her right away. She told me that she'd had a tipoff from the local T9One Marketing people that The Company was a very good chance to win an award at the Gala Awards and Dinner that evening. And she wanted to make sure that I was there to accept it, since I was in effect the most senior Company representative there.

'Sure, Doris. I was planning to be there and I'm happy to accept it if we do win. I'll drop by our booth in about an hour to see you and the team and confirm the run of things for the dinner tonight,' I said.

That night I joined Doris and The Company team on our table at the Gala dinner. There's nothing that a marketing team seems to enjoy more than getting frocked up and attending these types of award functions, so Doris and the team were in fine form and made for great company that evening. After being pretty much locked away working on my own for two days, it was nice to socialise too. I still hadn't sighted Neville since the first night so I messaged him again to let him know I was there.

After the main course was served, the awards ceremony began. The third award was for 'Innovative Solutions Partner of the Year' and this was the one that Doris had been tipped off on. The MC duly read out the nominees and announced that the winner was 'The Company'! Our table went nuts and there was much hugging and high fiving as the MC announced, 'Accepting the award, all the way from the land down under, is Mr Michael Mansfield, Sales Director for The Company.' Sebastian was handing out the awards, and by the time I got up on the stage to shake his hand, another familiar face was standing next to him. It was Neville, who had finally re-appeared, materialising from out of nowhere.

Well, that kind of made the whole trip worthwhile, I thought as I returned to our table with Neville in tow. The Marketing team, whilst still celebrating, turned their attention to what they do best, that is, posting the good news on every social media platform known to humankind. I flicked off a quick message to Dianne to let her know as well.

In no time flat, congratulatory messages started flowing in. It's weird how quickly positive news can travel. Soon we'd all settled down and had another drink or two. As the awards ceremony concluded, Neville suggested that he and I skip dessert and head out to celebrate. It was a suggestion I happily accepted, as long as we went to a proper bar, not a strip joint, which was his usual favourite type of post-dinner hangout. So I left the award trophy in Doris's safe hands and headed out into the very crisp Vegas night with Neville.

I woke up to the sound of vacuum cleaners in the corridor at around 10am the next morning. Good thing that I'd arranged a late checkout time, was my first thought before I realised how much my head was pounding and how dry my mouth was. Shit, that had been quite the big night, I thought as I guzzled several glasses of water.

I was trying hard to recall exactly what had transpired. I remembered the awards and heading out with Neville afterwards for a couple of celebratory martinis. I could remember turning down Neville's requests to head to a topless bar a couple of times, before I told him that I'd be fine and he should just head there by himself if he wanted to. I then vaguely remember gambling on a roulette table, which is something I didn't do at all often.

I checked my phone to find several missed calls, a mountain of social media updates, mostly about the award, and some blurry photos from the night before including one of me with two faux Las Vegas showgirls in front of the Bellagio Fountain, presumably taken by Neville earlier in the evening. Best I delete that, I initially thought, before deciding to keep it to show Emily. She would no doubt be amused and probably say something about me looking like a pathetic dirty old man who was deluding himself.

As various bits and pieces of recollection came seeping back, I checked my jacket pockets for other evidence of the evening. I was relieved and very pleased to see that the amount of US cash in my wallet was somewhat more than I had started with that evening, and I also found a couple of $50 chips from the MGM Grand.

So apart from a rapidly developing killer hangover, I thought I'd had a successful and safe night out in Vegas. Time now to head out for some fresh air, to get some food and do some shopping before I had to head for home.

After walking about 15 minutes north down the strip, I stumbled across the Holy Grail of hangover cures, an In-N-Out Burger outlet. I went in and ordered a Double Double with Animal Fries, washed it down with a bucket of Cherry Coke, and almost immediately I felt better, at least for a few minutes as my body started to digest the meat and fat overload I'd just consumed. Several hours later, as I boarded the first flight for my long journey home, I wasn't so sure that I'd made the greatest brunch choice before flying.

After a delayed and completely packed flight from LAX back into Sydney, the dreaded bus trip between the International and Domestic airports, and a rescheduled flight to Adelaide, I finally made it home, feeling much the worse for wear. I'd left Vegas mid-afternoon on Thursday and arrived home late afternoon on Saturday, after more than 28 hours in transit. After hugging the kids and handing over some moderately tacky Las Vegas t-shirts and other souvenirs, as well as gifting Emily some duty-free perfume and a bottle of her favourite gin, I fell into bed unable and unwilling to stay up any longer.

## Chapter Thirty-Seven

# The Presentation

AFTER A DAY AND A bit back home with the family, most of which I spent sleeping off my jetlag, I boarded another flight to Sydney to prepare with the team for our all-important final presentation to Utility Co. I messaged Jonathon as soon I hit the ground in Sydney, as I was keen to have a one-on-one coffee chat with him to understand the latest thinking on the make-up of the presentation team.

'Hi, Mike. How was Vegas?' Jonathon greeted me at the coffee shop.

'Tacky as usual. We won an award at the conference and I had a win playing roulette, though. So it wasn't a complete waste of time going there,' I responded, already sensing that my answer was too long for Jonathon's straight-talking, time-poor approach to life.

Sure enough, he was immediately onto the topic at hand.

'Mike, as I mentioned while you were over there, I've been getting enormous pressure from Christiaan to take a more diverse team into this presentation. I know that Utility Co have two women on their Selection Panel, and the other six members are men. But for some reason, and with that dickhead Rudy goading him on, Christiaan is insisting that we have at least three women on our team of five for the presentation. They've told me that I should be going in with Dianne, Shayna from Marketing, and this Chloe Lovett person from Consulting, with you and I making up the rest of the team, Mike.'

'Well,' I said with a smirk, 'at least you and I get to be there'.

'Don't laugh, Mike. At one stage I was the only pursuit team member that was going!'

'This makes no sense, Jonathon. We need people who know about the proposal and can add value to the presentation, not people who are there as window dressing. What's Dianne's opinion on this?' I asked.

'She said she's happy to attend and support us. I don't think she wants to fight Christiaan on this at all. Do you know this Chloe woman, Mike?'

It was at that moment that Dianne walked in and came over to join us.

'Morning, gentlemen. I bet I know what you two are talking about,' she said as she pulled up a chair. 'Perhaps I can help you resolve this and get our team locked in for Wednesday,' she said, clearly not as a question.

'Thanks, Di. We'd appreciate your help,' I said. I looked over at Jonathon and he nodded slightly in a way that said to me: you take this and see what you can work with Dianne.

'Di, I understand from Jonathan that we've been told to balance the team with at least three women. I assume that that's a not-negotiable?'

'Correct, Mike. I'd suggest we fall in line with that and get the best team formed that we can, within that constraint. Christiaan is really using this presentation as a test case to drive his broader diversity agenda, so I don't see any way out but to follow his wishes.'

'OK, Di. And you are OK to be part of the presentation team yourself? Perhaps as the Executive representative for The Company?' I asked.

'Sure, Mike. I've told Jonathon that I'll support you guys however you wish me to,' she responded.

'Great, thanks, Di. So that leaves us with two more participants to agree. Now, nothing personal here, but I see no value in having Shayna attend. She'd be completely content free, and I don't think it sends the right message to have a Marketing lead there,' I said. Both Dianne and Jonathon nodded in agreement, so I continued, 'So I'd suggest that we swap out Shayna and include Lu Lu. She has actually contributed to the deal and understands the proposal. She knows the pricing inside and out if we get any questions around that, and she also ticks more than one box from a diversity perspective, if you get my drift.'

'Great idea, Michael,' responded Jonathon, and Dianne agreed also.

'OK, I'll line up Lu Lu. Now let's talk about Chloe Lovett,' I said.

'I've not encountered her before. Do you know her, Mike?' asked Jonathan.

'Sure do. Whilst there is no Consulting content as such in the deal, I think Chloe could present quite well, provided that we can find something specific for her to contribute in the session. She seems smart and very articulate, so I think we can ask her to perform a role on the day,' I offered. 'Besides,' I said, looking a little sideways at Dianne to gauge her reaction to what I was about to say, 'she dresses immaculately and is a very attractive woman.'

Dianne smiled at me and added, 'Mike's right. She's one of our brightest prospects, so we should be putting her in front of clients wherever possible. And the fact that she's quite hot doesn't hurt either.'

With that it appeared that we had our 'diverse' presentation team agreed. We now had a day and a bit to finalise the presentation deck, brief the team, and rehearse our winning presentation that would knock the socks off the selection panel at Utility Co.

The next 48 hours were a bit of a blur as I continued to fight a bit of lingering jet lag and we frantically prepared for the presentation on Wednesday afternoon. From piecing together a couple of snippets of intel from Utility Co, we understood that we were the second of two organisations presenting to them that day, which I thought was a good position to be in. Lu Lu was very reluctant to participate at first, as she much preferred to be a back-room kind of person. But once I got her confident with the five-minute pricing summary piece that she would talk to, she came around to the idea.

Chloe had proven to be a bit of an ace in the pack. She seemed very comfortable at being pitched in late to presentations such as this, so clearly she'd been called upon for similar needs before. She was a flawlessly presented and very striking woman, who came across as credible and confident. Chloe quickly came up to speed with the proposal and we gave her a presentation role to summarise the benefits and value of our proposal, which she was very well suited to do.

Dianne would top and tail the session, introducing the team and providing Executive commitment on behalf of The Company, with Jonathan and myself doing the rest of the content. We only had one hour to present, with thirty minutes of questions to follow, so we needed to be crisp, precise and on message. I always found that it was easy to prepare loads of content or slideware. The hardest part was to distil it all down into a nice, simple and convincing story about why us and not the competition.

During the preparations Dianne pulled me aside to chat about my bonuses. She was apologetic that the Sales Admin team was still continuing to stall on the Simple Extension deal bonus, and levelled with me that they were actually trying to find loopholes to minimise my payment or avoid it all together, which confirmed my fears and pissed me off at the same time. She continued to weigh in on my side and told me that she'd written a response to their latest point of view on the deal and was planning to raise it again with Christiaan.

Additionally, Dianne did also have some good news for me, in that the Telco deal bonus had been approved by Christiaan and was going to be paid in the December pay run. About bloody time, I thought! We'd only closed that deal in March and now some nine months later they'd generously decided to pay me and the rest of the team for our contributions. This would be a much smaller bonus for me than the Simple Extension deal, but at least it was something.

When we had a quick chat late on Tuesday night, I let Emily know that at least I was getting some bonus payment before Christmas and to keep her eye out for a payment of about $20k, which was what I'd worked out my share would be after tax. I levelled with her too about them stuffing me around on the much larger extension deal bonus, and as usual she encouraged me to stick up for myself and fight for what I was entitled to. She also asked if I was ever going to see anything for the Canberra deals I did in the middle of the year.

We had a final rehearsal session for the presentation on Wednesday morning. Jonathon had invited a couple of his colleagues from the complex deal team to observe, and play devil's advocate on our content and readiness to respond to questions from the client. Done well, this can be of great assistance to a presentation team. Done poorly, it can tear down the confidence of the team members, so I'm not a great fan of this approach, especially so close to the actual session. Indeed, Jonathon and I had to intervene and put a stop to one of his colleagues, who was starting to rip into poor Lu Lu, who certainly did not need her confidence dented ahead of some rare client interaction for her.

Our diverse five-person team headed into the city to Utility Co's offices an hour early to allow us to grab some lunch and calmly eat beforehand. As we arrived at the café across the street from their office, we observed our competitors leaving the building following their session. It seemed that our intel was correct, as both Dianne and I recognised a couple of people from their team. They clearly hadn't got the diversity message, as they appeared to have gone with an all-male presentation team.

Our presentation seemed to go very well. Everyone from our team played their part and contributed. Dianne provided appropriate executive gravitas to convince them that they would be a top tier client for our organisation. Jonathon's and my parts seemed to resonate with the panel and we were getting plenty of positive nods. Lu Lu was solid and her answers to questions were confident and definitive. But Chloe was the star. Her presentation on the benefits of our proposal was compelling and slick. Dressed immaculately in her fitted black power suit, she completely held the focus and attention of the six men on the Utility Co selection panel. You see, in their introductory remarks the client had commented that 'it was nice to see such a diverse presentation team' and also apologised that the two women on their selection panel team were not able to attend the presentations today.

## Chapter Thirty-Eight

# December Madness

NOW THAT WE WERE WELL and truly barrelling into December, the end of year madness was reaching its zenith. I had to prepare a report for Dianne and HR on our plans for each and every team member over the compulsory shutdown period. I was told to include Larry even though I was about to exit him for poor performance. Somehow counting him even though he wouldn't be an employee by the time the shutdown came around seemed to matter for someone's KPIs. I was also told to include Amber, who doesn't work on my team, and hadn't since her little episode in the middle of the year. Shortly after I'd submitted the plan, it came back to me with some changes showing that Amber had exception approval to work during the shutdown period. Fucked if I knew why, but I wasn't going to argue as she wasn't on my team, anyway.

Of course, it was extremely difficult to get exception approval for the people I really did need to work over the shutdown, justifying the need for a couple of them to work through this period in order to help deal with the increasing number of RFPs being thrown at us by clients planning for us to respond while they sat on the beach themselves. The continued ebb and flow of these 'pre-Christmas special deals' meant that we never really locked in the list of who needed to work through and who was taking leave, until right before Christmas, or in some cases after the event. Nothing like allowing our employees to plan their family time ahead of the holiday season. It was clear that this didn't enter into the minds of our clients; and it certainly didn't enter the minds of our executives, who were far more interested in the top and bottom line impact of leave balances being taken.

One positive trend during the lead-up to Christmas in recent years, at least in my view, was the decline in the number of Christmas functions one was expected to attend. This included both functions for The Company and those put on by our various business and industry partners. In not-too-distant times past, there would be at least two Company functions to attend, one for all employees and their partners and one for our clients. The employee and partners soirée seemed to be very much a thing of the past, driven by the tight-arse bean counters who decided that it was a smart move to save fifty bucks a head by not including and thanking long-suffering employees' partners for their support of The Company over the past year.

Still, it didn't bother me and I sure as hell knew that it pleased Emily to not have to suffer through such events anymore. Nowadays, employees of most companies seemed to think themselves lucky if they scored any sort of Christmas event that involved company-supplied alcohol. Served, of course, by an appropriately accredited Responsible Service of Alcohol host. No more would Reggie from Accounts Payable be the volunteer from the Social Club behind the bar, dispensing drinks at will to the assembled throng of employees who themselves were desperate to get one back at The Company by drinking way more than their fair share.

For loyal and hard-working employees looking forward to some sort of end-of-year shindig, there is probably only one thing worse than an announcement early in the year that there will be no staff Christmas party that year; and that is when a bunch of Executives, desperately implementing any and all measures possible to try and rescue their executive pool bonus, decide to cancel the much-hyped Christmas party just a week before it is due to be held. What a great way to kill off any remaining shred of staff morale, you geniuses.

It seemed that many of our business and industry partners had also had their belts tightened in recent years, and the days of free-flowing French Champagne and cocktails at a swanky rooftop bar were bygone traditions. Sure, there were a few start-ups still displaying the type of extravagance that was common pre-GFC, but it was less and less the case. It also suited me fine these days, as I'd much rather share a couple of quiet drinks with the people I've really worked with during the year instead of feeling compelled to make an appearance at some partner or industry event for the sake of it.

I headed down to Melbourne in the second week of December, as I really needed to pull the trigger and finalise Larry's exit from The Company. I'd given him every opportunity possible to turn his performance around, but it clearly wasn't working for him or for The Company. I arranged for a meeting with Larry and asked HR to provide someone to be there as well, just in case Larry needed any additional support from them. From our previous quite open discussions as part of the Performance Management Process, Larry was well aware that he was on a pathway out of the organisation, so I didn't expect this to be a surprise or to be too difficult for him.

That was the way it played out as well. I think Larry was more grateful to get it over and done with so that he could move on with his life. The chap that HR sent along to sit in the final meeting with Larry and me was more of a problem. He'd never been involved in exiting someone before and was completely clueless. He actually made it worse for Larry a couple of times by trying to empathise with him, which really only served to take us back over emotional territory that we'd previously covered. In the end I shut it down and let Larry head off to say his goodbyes while we closed out the paperwork. I'd done my best to genuinely help him and I knew that I was really doing the right thing by The Company. I still felt like a bastard for moving him on before Christmas.

By mid-December the daily sales forecast and deal review calls had become twice daily calls. So at 8:30 every morning and then again at 4:00 every afternoon, I had to dial in to listen to the latest insights and fantasies about which deals were closing and which ones had challenges, as well as giving my own updates on the remaining two deals that I had in Q4.

On top of this, the Global team had decided to have review calls twice a week, so I now had a Friday night call as well as the regular Wednesday night one. That meant twelve separate update calls a week, not counting the incessant ad hoc requests for information on the next steps or the latest status on a deal. Of my two deals, one was the Utility Co deal that we were all waiting on with bated breath. They'd told us that they were likely to have a decision the last week before Christmas on that one. I was just leaving it to Jonathon, as he didn't need me pestering him for updates as well. My other Q4 deal was going through the client's signing process and was a sure thing to happen. It just needed their Head of IT to sign the contract. So I was checking in with my connection there twice daily to see what was happening, apologising that I seemed to be stalking her. But she understood the importance to us, so all was good.

Assuming that this deal would close along with the other committed deals that my team was still targeting to sign, I would finish the quarter and the year bang on, exactly as I had forecast back in October. So true to expectations, none of the stretch deals that Sales Admin insisted should come in to my forecast would happen, just as I had argued at the time.

That week, Sales Admin sent me an email with the heading of 'Good News', which I opened immediately under the false hope that perhaps they were going to pay my Simple Extension deal bonus or confirm that my Telco deal bonus had been paid. Unfortunately, the note was just to let me know that they had finally adjusted my forecast in the system back to what I'd told them I'd commit to in October. Nothing like being timely in their updates! Still, at least with this adjustment made I could stop having to justify being 'short' against forecast several times a week as our Executive Leadership Team continually forgot what I'd previously told them.

It was also a good thing because Sales Admin in their immense wisdom had planned for an upgrade of the Sales Record System for the first week of December, in what is the lead-up to undoubtably the busiest time for the system all year. That upgrade didn't go so well and they ended up having a major outage before they backed out the changes and reverted to the previous version of the system.

Soon after reading the note from Sales Admin regarding my forecast adjustments, I received a message from Emily to let me know that our bank records showed a $9,900 amount had been paid in to our account by The Company, and she assumed it was my Telco Deal bonus, but it wasn't around the $20k I'd told her it would be. What the fuck is going on here, I thought as I searched for my calculation sheet in my files to double-check what I'd calculated against the deal bonus policy guidelines. Surely they've got something wrong here. I checked my spreadsheet and sure enough, based on the deal metrics I was due a post-tax bonus of $19,800.

Hmm, something was smelling really rotten here. Before I reacted and fired off another please-explain note to Sales Admin, I thought I'd better triple-check with the best of the best in the business at these calculations, which of course was Lu Lu.

Lu Lu quickly confirmed that my calculations were correct and also that she had received her correct payment for the deal, so something no-good was definitely going on here. I called Sales Admin to thank them for the payment and to ask, as politely as I possibly could, for clarification on the payment amount. The relatively junior fellow that took my call was trying hard to be very helpful, and he actually read out to me some extracts from the approval email from Christiaan, where he had instructed Sales Admin to split my component in two, to ensure that Dexter from Consulting received an appropriate bonus payment for his work on the deal, since he wasn't actually on a Sales Plan as such.

Drawing a very deep breath, I thanked the young chap for his help and left to take a long walk around the block before sitting back down to pen an email to Dianne on this latest shafting I'd received. I had to resist the urge to just resign; but these pricks owed me too much money now for me to just walk away, so I had to stay and fight for my rights.

## Chapter Thirty-Nine

# Normalisation

B Y THE LAST WEEK BEFORE the Christmas shutdown, I'd calmed down a little and had managed to get my other deal signed. So I was no longer needing to stalk my contact there, much to both her relief and mine. I was in Sydney for another of my least favourite things to do in life, which was to attend what was referred to as a 'Normalisation Session'. This was a part of the Annual Performance review process, where all of the Sales Managers got together, along with Dianne and Stephanie from HR, to compare and review the performance ratings proposed for each individual employee on their team. The process was meant to promote equity in the ratings, to even things out if one manager was a bit softer on their team and gave more generous ratings versus another manager who dealt with his or her team more harshly than others. At least, that was the principle. But when you threw into the mix the requirement for each team, and then the sales team overall, to issue performance ratings in line with a Company pre-ordained bell curve, it became rather a heated process with more attempts at manipulation and back-stabbing than an episode of Survivor.

You see, as managers we were expected to align our teams' ratings to this statistically defined bell curve. So if you had five people on your team, you'd be expected to rate maybe one as 'excellent', two as 'solid', one as 'needs some improvement', and one as 'needs significant improvement'. The latter category supposedly being the pathway to a Performance Management Process. At the very top of the scale was 'outstanding', and statistically we were only meant to have about one in around twenty employees rated as outstanding, representing the top 5% of our employee cohort.

So inevitably these Normalisation sessions descended quickly into slanging matches, as each Manager tried to justify why their people were worthy of being rated 'excellent' or even 'outstanding' whilst the rest of us had teams comprised of people that needed to be rated as 'needs some improvement'. Stephanie from HR did a good job in chairing the session and giving it an even keel; but even she struggled at times, as it became more of a shit fight than a structured debate.

It was also one of those sessions where everyone had an opinion on everyone else's people, no matter how little they actually knew about the individual. Why let the facts get in the way of your preference for a bell curve spread that benefited your team members? Not that the ratings themselves meant that much anymore, anyway. For people on sales bonus plans like everyone on the Sales team, the ratings didn't actually directly affect your deal bonuses. All they potentially impacted was the opportunity for a base salary increase, and since The Company hadn't offered any salary increases for several years now and there was no real prospect of them returning any time soon, it seemed to me to be a moot argument. But, of course, I had to go in to bat for my team, lest some other boofhead managed to convince the Normalisation meeting that one of my better performers was really a dud that deserved to be rated as 'substantial improvement needed'.

I'd just managed to gain agreement for the ratings for my team when my phone lit up with a call from Jonathon, so I quickly excused myself to take it and stepped outside, signalling to Dianne as I left the room that this was Jonathon calling. I knew he had to have an update on the Utility Co deal so my heart was racing just a little as I answered.

'Hi, Jonathon. What's the news?'

He paused and drew breath, which I didn't like, then blurted, 'We won, Mikey, we fucken well won!'

'That's awesome, mate. Fabulous news!' I said while I fist pumped the air.

'If you're in Sydney, Mike, we are gathering to celebrate after work at Hotel CBD for a drink.'

'I am indeed in Sydney, Jonathon, so I will see you there later today, mate. Cheers.'

As soon as I walked back into the room, Dianne held up her hand and interrupted proceedings to ask, 'Well, what's the news, Michael?'

I couldn't constrain my grin for more than another second, so I raised my arms in triumph and blurted out, 'We won!'

There was spontaneous cheering in the room as everyone knew about the deal and how important it was to The Company. Dianne raced around and gave me a big hug, then disappeared herself, presumably to share the news with Christiaan if he didn't already know.

It was hard to concentrate for the rest of the Normalisation meeting. As soon as it finished, I called Tony and Lu Lu to let them know the happy news and invite them to come into town if they could, for a celebratory drink. In yet another demonstration of how quickly good news travels, they'd both already found out and Tony was already on his way in.

I then had to make a few quick calls myself before I could head over to the celebrations. I'd just got wind of a client dropping a Request for Proposal on us today, with the response due at the end of the first week back in January. This was after their Procurement lead on the RFP told me last week, when I rang him to check on the timing, that it would not be released until February. And now, here it was with a ridiculous response time frame; and I needed to assemble a team to do this over Christmas, since qualifying it out was not a realistic goal, as much as I was tempted to try.

When I sent an email to the Procurement contact listed in the RFP to confirm who our contact point for the RFP process would be, I was even more staggered when I received an out-of-office notification indicating that he was now on annual leave until the day after the response was due in.

What a fucken joke! I mean, who do we even approach if we have any questions or clarifications? We'd give them a half-arsed response by necessity; but even then I knew deep down that this meant that my Christmas break was now going to be completely compromised, all because some low-level procurement fuckwit decided it was a good idea to chuck this one out to the market before Christmas.

By the time I got to the Hotel CBD at around 6pm, the celebrations were in full swing in the ground floor bar. Dianne was there, as was Christiaan, who even said hello and shook my hand as I arrived and he departed. Most of the people who had contributed to the deal were there, along with some other hangers-on. These included Rudy, whose only real contribution was to allow Chloe to attend the presentation. Dexter was there too; it was the first time I'd seen him near Jonathon since he'd falsely accused him of calling him that c-word and he'd 'stolen' half my deal bonus. Still, that wasn't his fault necessarily, as it seemed I was the victim of a game around 'where do we find some money to throw his way' that was no doubt led by Rudy and decided by Christiaan. I certainly hadn't given up that fight yet, anyway, and Dianne was looking into options for me.

Naturally - being an accolade thief - Kieron was there too, stealing glory from the real contributors to the deal without any shame whatsoever. So was Rudy, who was loudly proclaiming that Chloe's outstanding performance at the presentation was the only reason we won the deal. Sure, she was very good at the presentation; but in the scheme of the overall pursuit it was disrespectful to her and to the rest of the deal team who had worked hard on this for several months to suggest that she alone won the day. If she had actually been there at the hotel, I don't think she would have let him get away with that, as she seemed to me to be a person of integrity.

Once I'd had a drink and a toast with Jonathon and Dianne I decided to cut and run from the celebrations, since I didn't really want to hang around listening to some of these pretenders or to dampen my positive mood following what was a really awesome and hard-fought deal win.

I grabbed Tony and said, 'Hey mate, how about we split and I'll buy you a whiskey or two at Baxters?'

'Sounds like a great idea, Mikey,' he replied as he downed his beer in one and we slipped out the side door.

'By the way, Tony, since you are working over the shutdown period, I've got another deal for you to help on, mate,' I said as we headed off down Clarence Street.

'Always happy to help you, Mikey. And as you know, any distractions I have to help me get away from Renee's mob at this time of year are always welcome, mate,' Tony answered with his trademark grin.

# Part III

## Chapter Forty

# Happy New Year

THE CHRISTMAS HOLIDAYS, ALSO KNOWN as the shutdown period, seemed to fly by at breakneck speed, apart from the numerous work interruptions, some of which could be dealt with via a simple message response, others requiring me to breakout the laptop for a few hours of analysis or updates or emails, or all of the above. Coupled with this was the fact that the rest of the global business world doesn't shut down between Christmas and Australia Day like we do Down Under, so there was still the expectation of attending several late-night conference calls. One of these calls was particularly amusing, as I tried to give an update on some deals to the US guys while a few early volleys of New Year's Eve fireworks were dispatched not far from where I thought I'd found a quiet spot away from the party Emily and I were attending, to discreetly do the call.

There was, however, still the chance for some good family time with Emily, the kids and the extended family over the break. The weather was hot, the beers were cold, and even with interruptions, the pace was so far off the normal frantic work day extremes it was tolerable. I also believe that a good game of beach cricket melts away stress more than virtually anything else.

The business was pretty much back in full swing by the time my 'break' finished officially on January 6th. There was the inevitable raft of announcements about new appointments and structural changes from Global for the new year, to be skimmed through to see what, if any, real impact these might cause for my part of the business. Mostly it was just announcing with much fanfare the names of people I didn't know and would never meet, into roles I didn't understand or, in some cases, even comprehend the need for. I mean, what the fuck is a Global Innovation Evangelist anyway? I'd sure like to see their KPIs for success!

There didn't seem to be any major changes of note within our region. There had been some rumours pre-Christmas that there would be quite a shake-up with some very significant restructuring. Unfortunately, as much as some of us had wishful-thinking moments about how this might unfold, and whether Christiaan would stick around, nothing of the sort occurred. Rather, a few members of the Executive Leadership Team were given some expanded or changed responsibilities, such as Clyde taking on Transport as well as Industrial, and Mining being handed over to someone else. Amongst these minor reshuffles Dianne's role seemed to be unchanged, which was probably a good thing for now, at least until she helped me resolve a few issues from the last year. Not the least of these involved a fairly significant backlog of incentive payments that I was still owed.

There were, however, a few promotion announcements buried towards the end of the note. All, not surprisingly, related to Rudy's Consulting team. Rudy himself was announced as 'Vice President of Strategic Consulting' which apparently was a promotion from 'Director of Strategic Consulting'. Chloe Lovett had been promoted from Associate Director to 'Director of Strategic Consulting'. And Dexter Bartholomew had been promoted from Chief Architect to 'Senior Chief Architect and Associate Director of Consulting'. Whatever. Perhaps Dexter's promotion was the hush-money that made his claims of being called a nasty name by Jonathon go away quietly too, even though they were baseless. Regardless of whether these were real promotions or not, Rudy had obtained a few titular upgrades for his favoured people to something more grandiose. Style over substance seemed to be his consistent way of doing things, so it wasn't really surprising.

There were also a few policy updates sent out in the first couple of days of the new year. One that was quite amusing was around the dress code for casual Fridays. As the dress code in the industry had changed quite a lot in the past few years to a more casual look, away from all the guys wearing suits every day, the tradition of going even more casual on a Friday seemed to accelerate, to the point where a reminder had to be issued to staff by HR about what was acceptable, since apparently people had started turning up in client-facing areas of the business wearing shorts and t-shirts. So the policy guidelines were re-issued stating that men were expected, as a minimum, to wear long trousers ('neat jeans OK') with a collared shirt and enclosed shoes. Naturally, this sparked a few smart-arse clarification questions on The Company HR Q&A forum.

There was also an announcement buried deep in a regular Sales update email about the Sales Incentive Trip for last year's highest achievers. This involved an annual trip away to some-where exotic for the top 10% of Company Sales people world-wide, accompanied by their partners. It was called the 'Inner Sanctum' and was eagerly anticipated by the generally highly egotistical and greedy Sales people. It gave them great personal status in The Company as well as an all-expenses paid free trip with absolutely everything laid on. Plus, of course, their spouses usually coveted these trips, since these junkets were really designed to keep the spouses happy with the workload and demands from The Company on their partners who (let's face it) were in a form of servitude to The Company, being consistently required to work ridiculous hours in order to achieve the results that got them on the trip.

Emily had been to a couple of these with me before and had quite enjoyed them. She was looking forward to me hitting the mark to get to this year's trip since it was going to be in Fiji, somewhere she hadn't been before and was keen to see.

It had been rumoured back in December that the Executive Leadership team had been looking at the trip in their cost-cutting quest so they could hit their profit numbers, but no one really thought that they'd change it in any major way, especially since the Executive Leadership Team members generally all got to attend these junkets as well. The announcement on the Sales update email confirmed that the trip would be held in Fiji in early April, and it crowed about some exciting changes to this year's approach. The trip had been extended by an additional two days to allow 'additional training opportunities', which was generally Sales code for more time spent drinking, playing golf or sightseeing. However, it then went on to say that a further 'enhancement' this year was to restrict the trip only to the individual eligible Sales employees of The Company, with partners now excluded.

Wow! That would go down a treat with Emily and the other long-suffering spouses and partners. Most of them only put up with the never-ending work demands heaped upon their other halves for the financial rewards and the chance to maybe head off once a year on The Company coin to a glamorous insta-worthy location somewhere far away from their kids. What a genius motivational move this would turn out to be for The Company, I sarcastically thought. I also pondered how I'd break the news to Emily and to my Sales Team if, as usual, they hadn't read the Sales update email. I also began to wonder how they might further 'enhance' the trip for next year? Perhaps they would scale it back to a single night at some three-star training venue in Paramatta. I wouldn't put it past the pricks.

On my second morning back, I awoke to see a series of emails requesting urgent updates on the status of the pipe-line for the coming year. There was one from the Global Practice Leader from late the night before, another from the Regional CFO, one from Dianne, and a final request from Sales Administration. All were essentially asking for the same urgent information updates with a few subtle variations. Surely they couldn't be this badly coordinated and they'd realise soon that they had all asked for the same thing? No, as it turned out. I went ahead and prepared the requested data into a single submission and then attached each of their email requests and copied them all in on the same response.

Along with it, I sent a separate note to Dianne suggesting that we could do better and perhaps coordinate all of these requests via a single entity such as Sales Admin. It was met with silence. Not even a single thank you email for my rapid response. Later that day I got a fifth request for the same thing from someone in Global Finance, followed soon after by a sixth as someone from our Indian-based Operations Office who had helpfully forwarded on the request from Global Finance. I thought for a moment that perhaps the best thing to do was to set up an out-of-office-type email response to any email I received that mentioned forecast update in the heading, so that it just automatically forwarded the earlier response to anyone who emailed me again for the same stuff.

The next day there was a similar flurry of email requests for updates to the full year Sales outlook. The day after that it was for final signing results by each Sales executive and by each practice line. While the sun was shining outside and most people were still in holiday mode, it was all a bit soul destroying. But it was best to provide the information as accurately as possible, lest some ill-informed bozo elsewhere in The Company made it up for me.

The first week back did close on a high note, though. On Friday I received a What's App message from a mate in our Brisbane office with a couple of pictures attached. It seems that a few of the Tech Support team based there had taken exception to the new Casual Friday guidelines from HR and had turned up in full-blown clown outfits! As his message said, they were fully compliant with the policy as they had long trousers, collared shirts and fully enclosed big floppy shoes. Touché, I thought.

## Chapter Forty-One

# The Game Changing Deal

B Y THE END OF THE second week back, things had very much ramped up to nearly normal pace from a business perspective. We'd managed to submit the couple of 'Christmas present' deals that had responses due in the first two weeks of January. On one that was due the first week back, our Bid Manager forwarded me the updated out-of-office email response from the client Procurement lead that she had received when she submitted our proposal. Whilst we'd had a team working away on the deal over Christmas and New Year, it seems that he'd decided to extend his vacation by another week and wouldn't now be back to start to assess the submissions until a full week after they were due in. I truly hoped that this fuckwit would one day lose his cushy procurement job and have to work in a deal team on our side of the fence.

Late in the week I had a catch-up scheduled with Dianne, to follow up on a few outstanding issues. During the call she assured me that she was batting hard for me on the deal bonus issues, including addressing the shafting I'd received on the Telco deal, as well as progressing the Canberra deal payments (now owing for more than six months) and the Simple Extension deal. During our chat she let slip that part of the reason for them stalling on some of these payments was that Sales Admin had overspent their budget on deal incentives for the previous year. I politely let her know that this wasn't my problem, and wondered out loud how the hell that could happen when most of the Sales Executives I knew were being short-changed on incentives or having their payments delayed. Surely someone stuffed up big time in the budgeting cycle and must have planned for a very poor year of signings if we'd run out of budget. Especially since we all knew that The Company overall was well behind on its signings target.

Dianne then changed gears on me to tell me about a new opportunity that they'd just got wind of.

'Mike, it's a huge opportunity with a client in the transportation sector out of Melbourne. It could be a ten-year deal across all of our service areas. It's a full system design, roll-out and ongoing managed services, with lots of additional service opportunities for consulting too. We believe that we will be one of just three organisations invited to compete for the business. This one is a true game-changing deal, Mike, and I want you to play a leading role on it,' she said.

Very interesting, I thought, since I needed a new meaty deal to get stuck into and distract me from all of the other internal Company crap. 'Who is the client, Dianne?' I asked.

'It's Transport Co, Mike - the biggest transportation conglomerate in the country. Assume you've heard of them?'

I pondered for a moment before responding, quickly weighing up in my mind how much or how little to disclose before I played my cards. 'I sure have heard of them, Di. In fact, one of my good mates happens to be the CEO there,' I said, before quickly adding, 'But I'm sharing that with you in complete confidence, Di. You know how this type of insight can quickly get out of hand. I need you to promise me that you won't share that with anyone else.'

I could hear Dianne drawing breath to contain herself. 'Mike, that's fantastic. And all the more reason for having you on this deal. I won't tell a soul, promise,' she responded, clearly very pleased at hearing this little nugget of information. 'How do you know Brad?' she continued, obviously having already done some research into the client and opportunity to the extent that she knew the name of the CEO.

'He's an old personal friend. We were mates at high school and played footy at university together. His wife and Emily are good friends, too. We catch up a couple of times a year in Melbourne or when he's back in Adelaide. We only just caught up with them over Christmas while he was down here visiting his family,' I said. 'But I need to be clear, Dianne. Brad is a very straight shooter and a complete professional. His reputation is paramount to him. He will make absolutely sure that we don't get any unfair advantage because of my relationship with him. So we need to tread very, very carefully if I'm to be involved in this one.'

'I understand and completely agree, Mike. We don't want to screw this one up and get excluded from a probity perspective, so let's keep your relationship between you and me for now,' Dianne said.

'When do we get notified formally of the opportunity?' I asked.

'Next Monday. There is a briefing with the client that we think will happen mid-week so it will be best if we get you down to Melbourne early next week to be ready,' she responded.

'No worries, Di. I'll plan for that.'

This was a very interesting development, I thought as I disconnected the call. Apart from the opportunity itself, which would be great to work on, my relationship with Brad, now that Dianne was aware of it, gave me some additional currency within The Company. Not that I was going to use the relationship overtly to either my own or The Company's advantage. However, the mere fact that it existed and Dianne now knew about it should make them think twice about stuffing me around or trying any further shafting manoeuvres around my bonuses.

## Chapter Forty-Two

# The Numbers Game

I FLEW INTO MELBOURNE ON MONDAY morning to start preparing for and assembling the rest of the team for the hopefully imminent Transport Co opportunity. I'd resisted all urges to call Brad and ask him about it, as that would be downright stupid. I'd also played back over and over in my mind the conversations from when Emily and I hosted Brad and his wife and their kids at our place for lunch a couple of days after Christmas. All I could recall that might have been a hint was his grinning comment as he left, that he expected to perhaps see me again early in the new year. Bastard! He would have known this was coming and that my employer would be invited to be part of it. But being the consummate professional that he is, he chose not to say a word.

There already seemed to be a growing excitement within The Company around this deal, judging from the flow of emails over the weekend. It appeared that word was spreading fast about this potentially game-changing opportunity, and everyone wanted in on it. What started as a quite closed email chain between Dianne, Rudy from Consulting, Clyde the newly appointed Industry Lead for Transportation, Mario the Bid Manager, and two other Practice Leaders, had

rapidly expanded to include around 40 people as each individual leader sought to appoint their best and brightest to
the deal. All before we had actually seen any formal confirmation from Transport Co that we were being invited to
participate. Dianne and Clyde were both doing their best
to bat away numerous well-intentioned colleagues who
wanted to be part of it until we'd at least got the scope and
timing confirmed.

By the time I arrived in the Melbourne city office mid
Monday morning we had, thankfully, received the formal
notification from Transport Co that The Company was
being invited to participate in a selective sourcing program
for their 'Generational IT Change Initiative (GICI)'. Once
that confirmation note started to circulate within The
Company it did nothing to dampen the enthusiasm for the
opportunity. Rather, it wildly accelerated the mad scramble
of people wanting to be part of the team and demanding that
they attend the briefing session, even though the notification
from Transport Co was short on detail and didn't contain
the requirements of the opportunity yet. It merely confirmed
that we were being invited to participate and that there was
to be a briefing session on Wednesday, with further details
around the specific time, place and intent of the briefing
session to be provided by noon on Tuesday. It also included
some probity guidelines about their sole point of contact for
the opportunity and a Non-Disclosure Agreement which
was promptly dispatched to Legal to review and agree.

The timing of the briefing session suited me fine as I had
to fly home Wednesday night for a family commitment.
Besides which, I couldn't actually care less whether I attended

the briefing session or not, since those things were usually dry, boring affairs where a bunch of procurement folk went through slide after slide in excruciating detail (all of which could be read from the pack to be distributed following the session) and offering no real valuable insights into the deal. Any questions from vendors were often just pushed aside as well, so I saw limited value in attending. But I would do so if it made sense for The Company.

In the meantime, I sat back and enjoyed the escalating demands from different areas of The Company that they have their key people included in this key opportunity, including attending the briefing. Poor old Mario the Bid Manager was already looking very flustered and it was only effectively day minus two on the deal! I reckon that by mid-afternoon he'd already taken about ten ciggie breaks to calm his nerves and disappear from the constant lobbying. By the end of the day on Monday Mario had composed a 'shortlist' of ten attendees from The Company, out of the thirty-plus nominations. Struth, we'd need to make sure The Company bus was on standby to take everyone, I joked. The ten proposed attendees included six people from Consulting that Rudy had instructed Mario were his 'minimum acceptable attendance team to show the client how serious we are'. It also included Christiaan (who would never be seen dead at something like this), Dianne (ditto), Clyde and Mario himself. No skin off my nose, I thought, as I saw this recommended team submitted through to Dianne and Christiaan for endorsement.

Midway through Tuesday morning, as we continued to assemble a team for the actual response based on our best guesses of the scope, we received the briefing session instructions from Transport Co. There were to be no more than two representatives from each organisation attend the briefing, which would be held at their headquarters in the Docklands precinct in Melbourne at 1 pm on Wednesday. The email also helpfully confirmed exactly who our competitors were on the opportunity.

Strangely, all hell did not break loose when we found out that we could only have two representatives attend. Usually it escalates the arguments into all-out war, but on this occasion, it actually went eerily quiet on that front. I assumed it was because Christiaan would just make a call and send Rudy and one of his merry band of Consultants.

Meanwhile, we started to gather our intelligence on our two competitors for the deal, both of which were very well known to us, as we went head-to-head with them often. The first competitor was MultiCo Ltd, and they, like us, were a US-based multi-national IT Services organisation. For some time now they had been one of the biggest players on the planet and they had the attitude to match. They were regarded around the industry as self-interested, arrogant and cocky, full of swaggering alpha males and females; but when they actually managed to put their self-interest to one side, they were a very formidable competitor and could mobilise a team of top global experts in no time flat.

The other competitor was a company called Indirev Systems Ltd. They were also very formidable competitors for the deal. They are an Indian-based IT Services company that has had tremendous growth over the past decade. They are regarded as quite ruthless competitors who take no prisoners in pursuing the opportunities that they want to win. They have been investing heavily in technology assets and IP and have a very solid foot print of business in Australia and the broader Asia Pacific region, as well as globally. This sure was going to be a very tough deal to win, but my view has always been that to be the best, you have to beat the best. So we needed to counter them and bring the absolute top capabilities of The Company to the fore if we were to win this game changer.

Mario and I had just finished pulling down The Company 'Battle Cards', that provided advice on how to win against MultiCo and Indirev as the basis to start our competitive analysis, when Clyde appeared.

'Hey, Michael. It looks like you and I are going to the briefing tomorrow, laddie. Hope you are OK with that as we really don't have any choice,' he said with a grin.

I was a little stunned by this development, which wasn't where I thought it would land. 'Sure, Clyde. I'm happy to go. I assume that Dianne or Christiaan made the call?' I asked.

'Yes, it was Christiaan's call following a closed-door discussion that Dianne had with him. He insisted that it's me and you. No more arguments to be had and apparently he rang Rudy to tell him straight away,' responded Clyde.

'OK, no worries. Thanks for that, Clyde,' I said. 'Hey Mario, perhaps you can take Clyde over the start of the competitor analysis, as I have to step out for a quick call.'

I called Dianne immediately to see whether she'd broken her confidence with me and told Christiaan about my relationship with Brad. She answered immediately and said in hushed tones, 'Mike, I can't really talk right now, but I know what you are going to ask me and the answer is no, I didn't tell him. I'll call you back later.' Click.

Later that night Dianne did call me and explained that she had merely insisted to Christiaan quite strongly that it was in our best interests to have Clyde and myself attend. And he agreed because, in Dianne's playback of the conversation, '...he was sick of the fucken noise and didn't actually give a flying fuck who attended as long as he didn't have to and we won the deal.'

'Sure, Di. No pressure from the outset,' I retorted.

## Chapter Forty-Three

# The Briefing

CLYDE AND I CAUGHT THE tram down Collins Street to Transport Co's headquarters at Docklands to ensure that we were there in plenty of time to sign in and get to the room for the briefing session. As we exited the revolving entrance doors into the neat, sparse and somewhat understated office foyer, I saw a gaggle of suits walking out past the security screens. Within the gaggle was a very familiar face that spotted me straight away and, excusing himself from the entourage, made his way straight over to me.

'Mikey, I don't see you forever and then what, twice in three weeks! How are you, mate?' said Brad, taking my hand in his strong grip.

He didn't really wait for my answer before introducing himself to Clyde, who was somewhat dazed and confused by this rapid encounter but still managed to confirm, after Brad's enquiry, that we were here for a briefing for their Generational IT Change Initiative.

'That's great,' said Brad. 'It's a really critical initiative for us, so we need you to bring your best minds to the table on this. Now, Mikey, I've gotta run, but please pass on my thanks again to Emily for organising lunch at your place. We really enjoyed the catch-up. I'll see you later, mate, and it was nice to meet you, Clyde,' he said. And he strode off, leaving his assembled suits to follow him out the front entrance.

After Brad had departed, Clyde stared at me for several seconds before he leaned in and whispered, with more than his usual hint of Scottish accent, 'When were you gunna tell me you are pallies with the farkin CEO, lad?'

'Let's sign in, Clyde, and I'll explain it all to you on the way to the briefing room,' I said, making my way over to the security desk.

After we signed in, we found a quiet corner of the small foyer where I explained to Clyde about my friendship with Brad. I let him know that Dianne knew in complete confidence and between her and us, we needed to keep it confidential. Clyde was ecstatic that I was on such good terms with their CEO, but he was also wise enough to know that it could backfire spectacularly if misused. So he agreed to keep the confidence but warned me to be careful. Not that I needed any warning.

Once we made it up to the briefing room, we got to meet Transport Co's Program Director for this initiative, their Procurement Leader, CIO and their Probity Auditor. It was an abnormally high-powered group of attendees for a briefing like this, so I thought perhaps this one would be a little different. We also said hello and shook hands with the representatives from Indirev Systems and MultiCo.

Sure enough, the MultiCo guys came across as arrogant twats who weren't at all interested in meeting us. One appeared to be a fly-in because of his thick American accent and his power outfit consisting of a bold pin-striped blue suit paired with a crisp, white shirt and yellow tie. If he was a fly-in, it was a good effort to get someone on the ground so quickly, unless of course they'd known about this for much longer than us, which was always a fearful possibility.

The briefing session itself did turn out to be very different than the usual reading from the cue cards. They had clearly put a lot of thought and preparation into the initiative and the session was very informative about their requirements and also the selection process itself. As we had expected, the high-level requirements they presented were very broad, and they had obviously been defining these needs for quite some time, given the way they talked to them. The selection process for the deal was also quite fascinating and well thought through. Instead of the usual approach of us just responding to their written requirements and answering a bunch of questions, there would be a series of interactive workshop sessions over the coming weeks, where all three of the organisations invited to provide a proposal would participate at the same time.

Upon hearing this, the American from MultiCo interjected, saying something like 'surely you can't expect us to be in the same room in these workshops with our competitors', as he swept his arm around towards Clyde and me and the two reps from Indirev Systems. Perhaps he was a little too instructional and holier-than-though in his comments. They certainly upset the Program Director, who indicated that they expected to run an inclusive and very collaborative process, which he knew could at times be uncomfortable for us. He emphasised that that was how the process was going to be run, and if we didn't like it we were free to drop out of the race for the business.

The process also required some prototype application development, and there would still be an amount of the usual requirement response to be documented and submitted as part of our offer. So it was clear that this would be a very significant undertaking for us to be part of. They closed out the briefing with a section reminding us of our probity commitments on the deal, and emphasising that any and all communications must come strictly via their nominated contact point only.

Clyde and I had a quick debrief out the front of the building before I had to head straight to the airport to fly home for my family commitment that evening. He noted the emphasis on probity in the briefing, and reiterated how careful I needed to be. He also agreed to prepare and lead the debrief conference call that we'd scheduled for our core team on Thursday morning.

When I got to the entrance of the Business lounge at the airport, I noticed that the two guys from MultiCo were right behind me as I went in. I nodded to them but they looked through me as if they had never seen me before. Once inside the busy lounge, they seated themselves at a small table only about five metres away from where I'd found a spot. I couldn't believe it when the non-American guy put his phone in speaker-phone mode on the table and they proceeded to have a full deal debrief with their team. Unfuckenbelievable, I thought, as did a few other nearby lounge guests, who were giving them death stares which they didn't seem to notice.

I mean, I'd seen dickheads Facetiming their kids on speakerphone in airport lounges plenty of times, but to have a call about a highly confidential business opportunity takes it to a whole new level. Even though I didn't want to, I could clearly hear everything they were saying. I lasted about three minutes before I decided I simply had to move away, and in that time I heard the American complain profusely about the client's 'dumbass process' where other companies could steal MultiCo's IP. How dare they, he said. He'd be writing to Transport Co to tell them how wrong their process was and that they needed to change it immediately!

Good luck with that, I thought. The biggest joke, however, and a further sign of their sheer arrogance, came when someone on the other end of the call asked who the two competitors were. Neither of them could remember which companies we were, beyond knowing that one was an Indian company and they had no idea who the other was. They were certain, though, that neither represented any sort of real threat to their winning the business once they told Transport Co what they needed.

What a pair of complete fuckwits, I thought. I gathered my gear and moved well away to the other end of the lounge. As amusing as it was, I simply didn't want to hear any more.

That wasn't the most amusing and disturbing conference call I listened to that week, however. Unfortunately, that came later in the week when Christiaan had an all-hands Town Hall call to share The Company's results for the year. The call started well enough with some very positive and somewhat surprising news. The Company was about to announce a record profit. This news was greeted with spontaneous virtual applause in the chat window.

The euphoria was short-lived, though, as Christian went on to say that whilst we'd made our profit number, we'd missed our revenue targets and had also just missed our yearly signing targets. Therefore, since we as a Company and in the region had only met one of the three key targets, there would be no general staff bonus paid.

Like the previous all hands call, this extremely disappointing news, for most of our staff made the chat window light up with candid points of view and some words that you wouldn't use in front of Grandma. Loads of people simply dropped off the call, and I imagined that there would have been an immediate surge in Google searches for JobSearch, Seek and other employment services on The Company servers.

This would have peaked even further if more people had stayed on for the Q&A session at the end. After several questions about the lack of a general staff bonus for the year, someone had the brainwave to ask about the executive pool bonuses, to which Christiaan responded, quite matter-of-factly, that 'the executive bonuses will be paid in full as the EL Team has met their profit targets for the year'.

Dianne then helpfully added that all Sales Team bonuses for the prior year were being finalised and would be paid in full as well.

So the key takeaway message to the around 95% of our employees who were not on the Executive Leadership Team or on a Sales Incentive Plan was, in essence, thanks for your hard work last year but there are to be no bonuses for you. Oh, and please knuckle down and help us get some momentum towards our new targets for this year. Happy fucken new year, folks!

## Chapter Forty-Four

# Before the Game Starts

WE RECEIVED THE FULL SET of documents from Transport Co on the Thursday and it was agreed that the broader deal team would absorb these over the next two days, and come together in a deal war room in Melbourne from the following Monday morning. The scope was as extensive as we'd hoped and this truly was a huge, game-changing opportunity that we needed to win.

The process outlined by Transport Co matched what they had told us in the briefing and would be very collaborative, with the first workshop scheduled for the end of the next week, and then regular workshops over the four-week response schedule they had set out. It would be a mountain of work to get done, especially if we were to put The Company in a winning position on this one. We'd clearly need to work some very long hours and right through the weekends to get an A-class response together.

With that in mind, I worked from home on Thursday and Friday to ensure that I had some quiet time and space to fully take in the documents from Transport Co and to start preparing my plan of attack and gather some more background for the deal. I'd used my regular Wednesday night call with Global to urgently request some senior expertise in the Transportation sector to come down and be part of the pursuit team. I had also had several calls with Clyde and Mario, agreeing what resources we needed to line up locally so that we could get them assigned, ready for Monday morning.

I'd hoped basically to get the wheels turning on as much as possible before the weekend so that I could spend some time with Emily and the kids before taking off to Melbourne for the best part of the next month since, with the tightness of the schedule and the amount to be done, I couldn't see myself getting home for weekends while on this one.

With the forecast predicting a scorching hot weekend with temperatures in the low forties, Emily and I went for an early morning walk at Brighton Beach on Saturday morning to beat the heat before grabbing some breakfast at one of the cafés on Jetty Road. I took the opportunity to let Emily know that I'd likely be absent for the next four weeks, including the Australia Day long weekend.

'It's a good thing we don't have plans then, isn't it, Michael?' was her initial response.

It was more a commentary rather than pure sarcasm, because the fact was that we tended to make plans for long weekends and such at the very last minute. Too many times, we'd been bitten when I was called away at the last minute for some urgent thing or other, and had to cancel or postpone plans. Even worse were the occasions when we had booked a beach house away on Yorke Peninsula and, despite the looming likelihood of continued interruptions from work, I'd stubbornly insisted that we continue with our mini-holiday plans rather than cancel. And then, of course, I'd ended up tied to the laptop and on conference calls almost the entire time we were away. There's nothing like trying to help the kids pull up the crab nets on the jetty while you're on the phone trying to justify some element of the solution for a deal to one of our executive approvers. Ah, happy holiday memories…

Emily understood that much of this dysfunction went with the territory of the industry and career I'd chosen. Or rather, the industry and career that had chosen me. As our pancakes and flat whites arrived, she continued: 'I understand, Michael. As long as you are just doing your job the way you need to. And that you're not trying to rescue other people who don't put in like you do.'

As usual I knew she was right. I'd inevitably feel that I had to step in at some stage in this deal because someone else had stuffed up.

Apparently reading my mind, she added, 'Especially because I know that you'll want to have a good showing for Brad on this one.'

## Chapter Forty-Five

# Rookies in Charge

O N SUNDAY AFTERNOON I FLEW into Melbourne with a larger bag than usual. I'd booked a serviced apartment for the duration of the deal, since it was better to have a bit of space plus a fridge and kitchen, rather than just rely on room service or late-night restaurant meals for four weeks. Once I checked in, I went out to the local IGA supermarket for some supplies, grabbing some breakfast essentials, pre-packaged ready-to-cook meals, and a couple of bottles of wine, in readiness for some late nights on the job. I then proceeded to iron five shirts so that I had at least the first week covered.

Bright and early Monday morning, I was in the deal war room with Mario before anyone else had arrived. We compared notes on the shape of the deal team and some key aspects that we needed to be very focused on. He shared some rather ominous news with me as well: Christiaan had appointed Rudy as the Executive Sponsor for the deal.

Shit. I knew he'd have to be involved in this one given the Consulting content, but this appointment as Exec Sponsor could effectively give him control of the overall team and deal.

As I digested this Mario went on and immediately confirmed my fears. 'And he's being a self-important twat already, Mike, telling me who I can and can't have on the team. He's demanded that day-to-day deal leadership be run by some new guy on his team, Stefano. And he told me that we'll have a 'Marketing Lead' on the deal team. I looked her up on The Company personnel system, Mike, and she's a fucken Graduate who just joined!' he said in exasperation.

'Don't get yourself too worked up, Mario. It's not even 8 o'clock yet,' I said, trying to calm him down. 'Besides, have you had your quota of early morning ciggies yet, mate?' I asked.

Mario grinned at me and rolled up his shirt sleeve to reveal what I took to be a nicotine patch.

'Mate, surely you've not chosen this week to give up the durries?' I asked.

'No, Mike. This is just to give me an extra boost between ciggie breaks, to help me deal with these dickheads,' he said, obviously quite pleased with his stress-relief forward planning.

Over the next hour Mario and I walked through the detailed draft project plan he'd put together for the pursuit over the weekend as a bunch of people began to filter into the war room. One of the first Consultants to arrive informed us that Rudy's EA had sent out a meeting request for 10 am for Rudy to brief the team on the pursuit. Pity that he didn't include Mario, Clyde or myself on the invite list.

You could tell who the Consultants were as they arrived. The men all wore the typical modern Consulting 'uniform' of a funky sportscoat with mismatched jeans or trousers.

The women were usually very well dressed, wearing designer label suits often accessorised with some pearls, occasionally some chunky ostentatious jewellery, or some less than subtle Chanel or Tiffany & Co signature pieces.

By the time Rudy arrived at just on 10 am, I reckon there were around a dozen Consultants in the room. There was a delightful selection of sportscoats on show - royal blue, light grey, a few fetching plaid blazers, and a truly remarkable purple one. Rudy himself wore a lovely beige number with a burgundy pocket square.

Rudy positioned himself at the head of the conference room table, and called his meeting to order as a number of sportscoat and jewellery wearers fawned over him. The room was fairly packed by now, with around thirty or so people all up.

Rudy introduced himself by saying that he assumed that everybody present already knew who he was and that, given the immense importance of this deal to The Company, Christiaan had asked him to personally oversee all facets of the deal as the Leader and Executive Sponsor. He then introduced Stefano, who was the purple sportscoat man, as his second-in-charge and day-to-day leader on the deal. He asked Stefano to introduce himself to the team, and over the next five minutes we had the pleasure of listening to Stefano flamboyantly tell us his life history.

For me, the interesting takeaways were that Stefano was from a non-IT management consulting background and had never worked in an IT services company before, and that he was '… soooooo excited to have this amazing opportunity to work on his first ever sales proposal.'

From his seat next to me I could distinctly hear Mario mutter, 'What the fuck!' as Stefano finished on that not very reassuring note.

Rudy then went on to introduce some other key members of his team. This included the Marketing Lead he'd appointed, a very young and rather attractive woman named Jenni-Lee. He completely ignored introducing Clyde, who as Industry leader really had responsibility for the deal. Typical Rudy, trying to own any internal competition. He briefly referred to Mario and myself as being responsible for the administrative elements of the deal, like getting the necessary approvals, etc.

Then he looked directly at Clyde then me, and made the point that probity was critical on this deal, and that only he would have any executive contact with the client outside of the client procurement team. He added that he was on good terms with several of the Transport Co executive team, including the CEO, which I knew was complete bullshit. He finished by handing over to Stefano to provide 'guidance to the team on the next steps', before striding triumphantly out of the room. I wasn't the only person in the room to mouth the word 'prick' as he did so.

Stefano stood up and headed over to the whiteboard, where he proceeded to draw up a series of columns labelled MTWTF.

Mario leaned over to me and said, 'This should be good, given this wanker has never done a deal before.'

Stefano then started. 'I know we have an awful lot of expertise in this room, which I am looking forward to tapping into,' he said.

OK, I thought, at least he might be aware enough to know what he doesn't know.

He then said, 'But before we start to do some detailed planning for the week ahead, I think it's important that we all take the rest of the day out to read the documents from Transport Co.'

I put my hand across Mario to stop him from standing up at this point. I introduced myself to Stefano and asked him politely if he had read the documents yet himself, since they'd been available to us all since last Thursday.

He responded, 'No, Michael. I haven't had the opportunity yet, but think it's important to be fully informed before we start the detailed planning.'

'I agree, Stefano. Indeed, Mario and I have had the opportunity to review all of the documents and Mario has already put together a draft action plan for the next few weeks. Perhaps we can share that with you as a starting point for discussion, once you've had the chance to look over the documents,' I suggested with a smile.

'Michael, that would be fabulous, thank you,' he responded with a flourish of his whiteboard marker. 'I would love to take a look at this draft plan and see what use we can make of it. Now, before we break off to read the documents,' he continued, 'I'd like to briefly touch upon a vitally important topic for this team. That, of course, is the Marketing Plan. We are very privileged to have Jenni-Lee on our team to lead this crucial activity for us. I imagine that most people in the room are very familiar with Jenni-Lee's amazing reputation as a leader in social media marketing. I mean, after all, she has over one-hundred thousand Insta followers!' He then led a chorus of applause for Jenni-Lee as she stood up to address us.

Jenni-Lee introduced herself as a recent Media and Communications Graduate from Swinburne University with a major in Social Media. She stated that social media was her life's passion, then babbled on for the next ten minutes about hashtag categorisation, engagement rates, employee advocacy and a bunch of other terms I didn't really understand the relevance of. Especially since we were in a strict probity-governed tender environment with a target audience of about half a dozen senior executive decision makers at Transport Co.

Meanwhile, Mario had found her Instagram feed on his laptop, which he spun around to discreetly show me. It seems that Jenni-Lee did in fact have over one hundred thousand followers online, quite possibly because - as a quick scroll down her feed revealed - most of her posts were comprised of pictures of her in various poses wearing a rather insubstantial bikini. Looking at most of the shots that she had posted, she definitely had been blessed with some impressive physical attributes. So I assume that up to this point of her career, her target marketing audience was adolescent boys looking for hot girls and teenage girls looking for swimwear inspiration, and not the battle-hardened senior business executives looking for a comprehensive long-term IT services solution to take their operations through the next decade and beyond.

I leaned over and whispered to Mario, 'I can't wait to see what value this adds to the deal. By the way, mate, HR will come after you for looking at inappropriate content like that on your work laptop,' I added wryly.

Jenni-Lee finished her bubbly overview by introducing another young Graduate who was also new to our Company. A young, neatly dressed but shy-looking fellow named Liam, who sheepishly stood at her prompting and introduced himself as recent new hire with a background in Computer Sciences. According to Jenni-Lee, he'd been assigned as her Technical Assistant for this project. Awesome, I thought. Now the Grads have assistants too!

Stefano then closed out with some rousing statements about us bonding together as a winning team, before imploring everyone to read the documents ahead of us regrouping as a team tomorrow morning. This guy seriously had no idea what he was in for and what was really required to get us into a winning position on this proposal. We couldn't afford to waste an hour, let alone a whole day while these inexperienced slackers read some documents that they likely wouldn't understand anyway. So immediately afterwards, Mario, Clyde and I headed off to grab a quick coffee and have a chat about what strategy we needed to keep this one on the rails as much as possible.

## Chapter Forty-Six

# Consensus in a Fantasy World

L ATER THAT MONDAY AFTERNOON, MARIO and I
managed to get hold of Stefano and convince him to stop
reading for a few minutes while we took him over a quick
synopsis of the deal requirements and the draft plan that
Mario, as a very experienced Bid Manager, had put together
over the weekend. We talked him through the importance of getting the team moving across multiple streams
of activity in order to start preparing for the client workshops, while simultaneously working on the requirements
of the detailed response and the application prototype that
was required.

He was genuinely stunned when he saw the depth, detail
and sheer number of tasks captured in the draft plan. He
therefore seemed to get a better sense of urgency, but soon
quickly regressed into talking about the need to gain the
consensus of the whole team on the draft plan before we
could proceed. He also pointed out that we hadn't included
the Social Media Marketing aspects in the draft plan - a
genius observation, since we had only learned of the apparent
importance of that component this morning. Anyway, we
seemed to be making some progress with the inexperienced
Stefano, and at least had him thinking of the plan in terms of

our tried and proven template. As a next action, he agreed to show the draft plan to Rudy and discuss it with him.

The following morning the team assembled in the war room ahead of a 9:30 am kick-off call that Stefano had organised.

'Working bloody gentleman's hours, are we?' quipped Mario when he saw the invite come in, since we were all more accustomed to an 8 am daily stand-up call on a deal like this.

Today Stefano was rocking a duck-egg blue blazer paired with some very fashionable tight white trousers. It was probably a look more suited to a marquee at the polo on the weekend, I pondered. But who was I to judge? He thanked the team for their diligent reviews of the document. He knew that they'd read it because of the number of questions he had received. He'd be compiling those into a single document, he said, and would be asking Mario, as the experienced Bid Manager, to answer those on his behalf.

Mario grinned at me and pointed to where the nicotine patch was on his arm yesterday. Stefano went on to say that he and Rudy had spent the evening reviewing and updating a draft plan for the consideration of the team. As Mario went to open his mouth, Stefano added, 'Of course, with big thanks to Mario and Michael for providing such a delightful template and start for the plan.'

Once the draft plan was projected up on the screen for the team to review and 'buy into', one thing was very apparent. Rudy and Stefano had given Consulting ownership of nearly everything that had to be done on the pursuit. They were owning the end-to-end solutioning, the pricing, the response document, the workshop preparation, and even the production of the prototype application.

In the spirit of the consensus approach that Stefano was using, I helpfully asked how Consulting would deal with the technical inputs and solution elements that were clearly not their core 'bread and butter'.

Stefano responded, 'Of course, Michael, that is a very valid point. Naturally, we will need to obtain and collate these specialist inputs where we do not have that specific expertise in the Consulting team.'

'Thank you for clarifying that, Stefano,' I said, as I whipped out my phone to send a quick message to Dianne.

Tuesday 10:42am

> Hi Dianne, just wanted to let you know that the Transport Co deal is rapidly turning into a clusterf\*\*\*. Consulting want to 'own' everything & I think we will struggle to keep this one on the right track. Let's chat when you can. Mike.

> Sigh... Understood, Mike, just do your best to keep it on track as much as poss. There may be some bigger things at play which might impact... Thx, Di

Wow, an immediate response from Dianne; and a very cryptic one too. I couldn't wait to try and drill her for some insight into what she really meant. I liked her reassurance to just do my best to keep it on track, too, since that was exactly what I intended to do on this one and I had let Mario and Clyde know that too. I'd help and do the absolute best I could on the aspects that I was responsible for, but I didn't really have the inclination to save a bunch of stupid people from themselves again.

After a couple of hours of inane consensus-style discussion, on a plan that most people couldn't fully comprehend anyway, we managed to lock in version one as agreed. Along the way there were some truly insightful questions from some of the team. For example, there was much debate over the need for a task to obtain pricing approval. Why did we need this, as surely were we not going to include any pricing in this proposal? That individual must have skipped over the detailed client requirements and missed the template provided by Transport Co for our 'Detailed Pricing Response'.

Others wanted to know what a prototype was, and someone else asked whether the prototype was somehow related to the probity statements in the documents. I think education and continuous learning in the workplace is great, but it probably shouldn't be practised on a game-changing deal like this. There were many other far less important opportunities that could provide appropriate learning moments.

That afternoon we were graced with Rudy's presence for a Stakeholder Assessment Workshop. This was designed to be a session where the team provides insights and inputs so that we could map out the relationships that we might have with the key stakeholders and decision makers at Transport Co. It's done so that we can form a view of who might be supportive, and who on their team might be a detractor for our proposal, which we needed to work on. I was kind of dreading this session since I really had to declare my friendship with Brad and put that out in the open. I didn't want any pressure from Rudy to leverage my relationship for our cause since, as I'd explained to Dianne and Clyde, that simply wouldn't work with Brad.

The session turned out to be an even bigger farce than I had anticipated. The names of the key executives from Transport Co that we knew would be influential in the decision-making process for their Generational IT Change Initiative were put up on the board. To the best of our knowledge, Clyde and I were the only two people from The Company to have any level of engagement with these senior executives from Transport Co. But that clearly wasn't how Rudy saw things.

As soon as Brad's name was put on the whiteboard, he told Stefano to put his (Rudy's) name against him as the relationship owner. Clyde immediately, but rather politely, interjected and asked Rudy what the extent of his relation-ship with Brad was.

Rudy pompously responded that he had '…met with Brad on numerous occasions' and that they 'were on very good terms'.

This was news to me, since Brad would have definitely let me know if anyone from The Company had reached out to him. Besides which, knowing Brad like I did, I knew that he'd think Rudy was a complete wanker within the first 30 seconds of meeting him and would want nothing more to do with him thereafter.

Clyde looked over at me for some form of affirmation, to which I nodded. Then he said, 'Rudy, with all due respect, the only person in this room who really knows Brad is

Michael, who has a longstanding personal friendship with him.' I thought I should probably expand on this, but before I could get a word in edgeways, Rudy completely dismissed this nugget of information.

'Well, if Michael does know him, how come he hasn't raised it before? Besides, that's a personal friendship not a business relationship, so it has no value here,' he tersely said.

I wasn't actually offended by this. Seriously, if this fuckwit wanted to gloss over my relationship as being of no value, he didn't deserve to get any insights from me whatsoever on Brad or his team. He'd also forgotten a fundamental business rule, if indeed he had ever known it. That is, that people buy from people they like and trust.

And so, with that in mind I simply crossed my arms, clammed up and listened to other self-important members of the team offer their completely speculative and made-up assessments of the stakeholders. Since not one of them had actually met anyone from Transport Co, I couldn't wait to get out of the room at the end of this ridiculous, fantasy-based stakeholder mapping session.

## Chapter Forty-Seven

# Time Is Tight

IN SPITE OF THE RIDICULOUSLY tight time frames for this deal, soon after the Stakeholder session ended I buggered off from the bid room back to my serviced apartment and spent the rest of the day sulking a bit and doing some other non-bid-related tasks. There was always a never-ending supply of people management and internal company-related stuff to do, that I usually managed to put off until the last minute. So in this state of mind I decided to catch up on some of these tasks.

Deep down I must have been pretty pissed off to actually prioritise setting each of my team members their Annual Review goals for the coming year, rather than progressing with some of the deal. At least it took my mind off Rudy and his band of delusional wankers. Christ, even doing the compulsory annual online Occupational Health and Safety training seemed like a better idea at this stage. Especially when it was accompanied by wine and some favourite music playing in my earphones.

Come Wednesday morning, I was in a much better frame of mind and had steeled myself to head back in to the battle of the bid. I was still resolved to ensure that we got the best possible outcome for The Company out of this opportunity.

It wasn't just personal pride because of my friendship with Brad. It was also the fact that opportunities like this one are very few and far between in this modern world where smaller, fragmented, consumption-style deals now dominate the IT services industry.

I met with Clyde and Mario for coffee before heading to the office and the war room. The three of us had made a pact to stick together through this deal, and to collectively do our best to drive this forward in the right direction against Transport Co's process and The Company's interest. We'd therefore arranged to meet before the start of formal proceedings a couple of times a week, to regroup on priority tasks and strategise about how to play things out over the course of the day. We had a quick recap on the previous day's antics by Rudy and Stefano and co, then quickly turned our attention to the priority actions at hand. We now had less than a week before the first collaborative workshop with Transport Co and the other two competitors on the deal, so we had to really double down on our preparations for this, especially with the Australia Day holiday weekend occurring this weekend, which could be a distraction for some of the team.

For the workshop next Tuesday afternoon there were essentially three key things we needed to prepare for. We had to present our initial point of view (POV) on Transport Co's requirements, essentially at our first reading telling them if we had we seen anything they had obviously missed and to provide them with some initial suggestions to improve or innovate around their requirements. Second, we needed to provide an update on our progress on their prototype application. Lastly, this was our opportunity to ask questions and seek clarification on any aspect of the bid process and their requirements.

Whilst we had included these tasks in the project plan for the bid, the three of us agreed that our key priority for the day was to get agreement across the team that these were indeed the three key focus areas and to ensure we had a plan of attack in place over the coming six days, to prepare for the workshop. We finished our meeting with a quick wager between us to see if one of us could guess what colour sports-coat Stefano would be wearing today.

Mario had managed to convince Stefano to shift the daily Team Meeting from 9:30 to 9 am, to provide the team with more time to actually get stuff done. He'd tried for 8 am actually, but Stefano wasn't even sure that most of the team could make 9 am because, as he told Mario, 'People have personal commitments to attend to in the morning, so 9 am is a bit of an imposition really...'

Stefano arrived just after 9 am for the meeting complaining about traffic at this time of the day. I won the wager with my guess of 'white linen', which I'd speculated on the basis of the forecast for a 37° day in Melbourne.

When he started the meeting, Stefano introduced a new approach to these sessions. We would start each day with an inspirational story from a team member on a rotating basis. He'd go first himself to set the tone of what he wanted.

Mario couldn't contain himself and blurted out, 'For fuck's sake, can we just get on with it? There's so much work we have to get done!'

Stefano mistook this as Mario's blessing to start his story. Five or so excruciating minutes later, we were all 'inspired' by Stefano's teary tale about how his miniature Pomeranian dog pulled through from some mystery illness. I think the point of the story was about never giving up, but it was five minutes of my life that I will never get back again and five minutes of our precious bid time frame wasted on crap.

Once he'd finished, Clyde asked if he could please kick off proceedings around some important priority tasks, effectively grabbing control of the agenda. He proceeded to emphasise the importance of the three key tasks that we'd discussed earlier that morning and Stefano agreed, highlighting these in the project plan that he'd asked Liam the quiet Grad to project on the screen. Clyde was just saying that he felt we needed to keep the team working over the long weekend if we were to have any chance of being properly prepared for the workshop on Tuesday, when Rudy entered the room.

Never one to miss an opportunity to impose himself, and without obviously having the background context that Clyde had laid out in his argument, Rudy launched straight in with his opinion.

'That won't be necessary, Clyde. We've got this under control, and as the Executive sponsor for this deal I've told Christiaan that the team need to take a break over the long weekend. This is a long process and we can't afford to burn them out at the start,' he stated in a matter-of-fact tone. This was supported by a wildly nodding Stefano, who seemed to have rapidly changed his mind on the amount of work ahead of us over the next six days.

Clyde drew in a very deep breath, trying his best to mask as much as possible his complete personal dislike and lack of respect for Rudy. 'I'm sorry, Rudy, but I have to disagree. I think there is simply too much to get through to completely stand the team down this weekend,' he replied.

Rudy retorted with, 'Well, what exactly do you think we need to get through then, Clyde?'

Clyde walked over to the screen and started to go through the critical tasks, now prominently highlighted by Liam.

'First of all, we need to present our initial point of view on Transport Co's requirements,' Clyde started before Rudy cut across him.

'Already well underway, Clyde. What else?'

Clyde continued, 'We have the prototype application to prepare.'

'My team has been liaising with our offshore technicians, so that is underway too,' Rudy said smugly. 'Anything else, Clyde?'

Clyde drew a breath. 'The workshop is the only real opportunity to ask clarification questions, so we need to prepare for this with any questions and some insightful observations that show we understand what they are looking for,' he said slowly and carefully, emphasising the part about understanding their needs.

'Poppycock!' exclaimed Rudy. He smiled and looked around at his sycophantic supporters in the room. 'Our competitors will be in the room. Why would we ask any questions at all?' he asked rhetorically. 'We might give our ideas away. By all means, Clyde, have your team put together some clarifying questions if you feel you must. But my team will not be contributing to that at all and we will be vetting all questions before the session. And since we clearly have our tasks under control, as I have told Christiaan, my team will be taking the long weekend off and refreshing themselves ahead of the coming weeks, when the real pursuit starts.'

I wasn't sure if Clyde could constrain himself any more in this exchange, but he turned and headed back to his seat, letting the silence linger for a few moments. Once seated, he looked straight at Rudy and said, 'Fine, Rudy. No problems. We'll focus on some questions and leave your team to run with the Point of View and prototype.'

And with that, Stefano, delighted that we'd got agreement on this, suggested that we move on to any other business.

So I took the opportunity to suggest that since we had agreement on the immediate priorities and responsibilities, perhaps we could cancel the remaining deal project team meetings for the rest of the week, to allow the team to focus on their tasks, and that we'd regroup on Tuesday morning ahead of the workshop.

Rudy nodded in agreement, which was a first for me, before Stefano said, 'What a splendid idea, Michael. Agreed.' He turned to Rudy and his Consulting companions and said, 'Now, who wants to come and get coffee with me? I haven't had the chance for my fix this morning and I'm afraid I'll just die if I don't get some caffeine in me soon'.

## Chapter Forty-Eight

# Plan B

CLYDE, MARIO AND I WAITED for the room to largely empty before we clustered together down one end to make sense of what the hell had just happened. Clyde said nothing initially, but had a look of steely determination about him, while Mario just wanted to get rid of 'these fucken idiots who don't know what the fuck they are doing'.

'Christ,' he mumbled, 'this is like bloody amateur hour.'

'I know, Mario. There's too much at stake here,' I said. 'The danger is that we will fall at the first hurdle if we fuck this workshop up completely, so I think we need a counter plan,' I added.

Clyde continued to think before responding, 'You are both right, lads. We need a fallback position to make sure we give a good fist of ourselves next week. I've got no faith that Rudy and his fucken C-grade team will pull us through on this. I'd like to get in Christiaan's ear before this thing blows up around all of us, but I think we really need these fuckers to fail first before I do that.'

Clyde always was a wise head. He always seemed able to contain his fiery Scottish disposition, and he knew when to attack hard and when to roll back to a defensive position.

We quickly agreed the plan to make the best of the workshop next week. We would certainly focus strongly on clarifications and questions that showed our understanding, and Mario had already started to compile some suggestions. Clyde and I would work through them over the coming days to add some more substance, as we absolutely needed to be ready to show a point of view on Transport Co's requirements. Despite this job sitting firmly with Consulting, we couldn't take the chance that they would actually do something meaningful, especially when they were taking the weekend off. Clyde and I would focus on developing our own initial POV response, so that we at least had something as a fallback. To do this I'd need to call in some favours from a couple of other subject matter experts in The Company, but I thought I could get some good inputs from them on the quiet. Regarding the prototype, we agreed to leave this with Consulting, in the hope that their offshore team would come through with something to show before next week. If not, we'd just have to give an update on our progress and scramble ready for the second workshop. After all, the prototype part of Workshop One was just meant to be an update.

Having made our secret plan, we shifted our attention to the attendees for the workshop on Tuesday. We had five slots per company, so we needed to make sure that these were not completely hijacked by Consulting. Clyde sensed that Stefano seemed comfortable with my inputs, so suggested that I tackle that 'off the record' with Stefano, which I was happy to do.

I flicked off a message to update Dianne on our difference of opinion on the approach to preparing for the workshop and confirmed, without sharing the detail, that we had our own Plan B. She responded later that evening.

Wednesday 6:27pm

Thx Mike. Good approach. FYI I've told Christiaan that I disagree with Rudy's approach here. Plse do your best to be ready for next Tues. Di

When I called Emily that night, I told her about some of the shenanigans of the past few days and let her know that I wouldn't be home for the long weekend. She was sad for me that I would miss yet another holiday weekend with the family, and one that I looked forward to every year, but she understood that I needed to do what I needed to do. She did ask me whether this was yet again a case of me doing others' work for them to save them, as usual; but I reassured her that I was simply trying to ensure that The Company went into the workshop at least partially prepared, so that we could avoid complete and utter embarrassment.

She said, 'I trust your judgement on this, Michael. Just please don't be a hero to save someone else's butt on this, and don't think that Brad will think any less of you if your Company chooses to do some stupid things on this deal.'

Then without waiting for me to acknowledge this statement, she shifted the conversation. 'Have you had any update yet on those outstanding bonus payments The Company owes you?'

'No, not this year. Good point. I'll send another follow-up note.'

## Chapter Forty-Nine

# Fallback Foresight

IT HAD BEEN A LONG and lonely long weekend away from the family. Even when you are under the pump with lots to get done, time away from those you love seems to drag even more, especially when you know that most normal people are off work. Clyde, Mario and I spent most of Saturday and Sunday in a conference room on a different floor than the deal war room. We made some pretty good progress and by late Saturday afternoon we'd pretty much nailed down a shortlist of six solid clarification questions that we would submit for the session on Tuesday. These questions were made up of three that would have high value to us in framing our response to Transport Co, two that were 'Dorothy Dixers' to just show that we'd thoroughly digested the requirements, and one that was designed to send our competitors off on a tangent. It was all part of the games-manship that went with high stakes business deals of this magnitude.

Clyde and I spent Sunday drafting our initial POV, or at least our emergency fallback version of it, in case it was needed in the likely event that Consulting had done fuck-all on it by Tuesday. We kept it as generic and high level as we could, but with enough substance to show that we'd started and had it as a work in progress. We also made sure it tied back to some of our clarification questions. Then we headed across to Crown Casino for a feed and a couple of whiskeys.

I then spent the holiday Monday holed up in my apartment, updating the Stakeholder Assessment with some better insights based on what I knew and what I could research online. I also did some checking on our competitors and their work in the Transport sector. From the publicly accessible information on their websites it seemed that both had a very strong client base in the transport sector, which didn't bode well for our chances of success. I sent these off to Mario on Monday evening along with a smart-arse note saying what a ripping time I'd had on my holiday Monday and I wouldn't have swapped it for the beach or a barbie somewhere else at any cost.

By Tuesday morning I was well over the disappointment of a wasted long weekend and I actually felt slightly smug and self-righteous that I'd done the right thing by The Company. Not that The Company ever seemed to reciprocate when you'd gone above and beyond, but in a personal and professional sense I always felt much better with myself when I was properly prepared for the battle ahead. My next priority was to get hold of Stefano to confirm the attendees at the workshop that afternoon. He hadn't bothered returning my calls from last Thursday and Friday, so I camped outside the war room so that I could collar him on his way in.

Stefano swept in at around 9:15 clutching his coffee keep cup in one hand and today's *Age* newspaper in the other, with his Crumpler messenger bag slung over his shoulder. Thankfully he'd gone a bit conservative today and was actually wearing a navy-blue jacket, which was probably a wise choice for the client session that afternoon.

He greeted me and apologised for not returning my calls, because he'd been so busy catching up with his friends in Sydney over the weekend. When I broached the question about our team for the workshop, he said that he'd already agreed that with Rudy. Much to my relief he'd included Clyde and myself in the group to be present. I guess he wasn't completely stupid and knew that he really needed us to be in the room, and had managed to convince Rudy of this too. He was also coming, along with some other stooge from Consulting. The fifth and final member of our team was a bit of a surprise. It was to be Jenni-Lee. When I asked why we needed her there, he said that he and Rudy had agreed that she should be there to get a first-hand feel for the client and their culture as she built out our marketing strategy for the deal.

Given that I'd already got what I wanted, which was for Clyde and myself to be there and preferably for Rudy to not be there, I wasn't about to argue the toss on her attending or not. As long as she shut the fuck up in the session, I really didn't care if she was there or not. The way I'd thought it through, I figured she might well be a distraction for the competition and at least would ensure that we were not represented by an all-male crew. I messaged Clyde and Mario to let them know ahead of the team meeting that we'd had a small win on this one.

In the team meeting that morning it quickly became clear that our colleagues had made sweet fuck-all progress on their deliverables for the workshop. In some ways this news was almost a welcome relief because if they had actually blindsided us and done some stellar work on the Point Of View response, it would have meant that I really had wasted my long weekend. In actuality, their POV response had not progressed beyond the series of headings they developed mid last week. What the fuck had these guys been doing? Obviously, nothing beyond refreshing themselves over the long weekend, as they had been instructed by Rudy, who was also noticeably absent this morning. They also confessed that they had not heard back from the offshore team that was meant to be developing the prototype application.

As Stefano became increasingly flustered and panic started to ripple through the meeting, Mario piped up with, 'Well, at least we've got the questions ready for the workshop, thanks to Michael and Clyde. And I believe they may have done some other good work over the weekend that might help dig us out of the shit before the workshop this arvo.'

Clyde, cool as always, calmed things down and suggested that the five-member core team attending the workshop break off separately to prepare for the session, while Mario worked with the rest of the team taking stock of where they were against the schedule on their allocated tasks.

Mario grinned like a maniac at this suggestion. As an old-school bid manager who regarded the schedule as sacrosanct, he was going to enjoy ripping some people a few new ones. Since it was clear that most people on this deal team had regarded the schedule as merely providing a rough guideline that didn't really apply to them and their tasks.

## Chapter Fifty

# The Workshop

THE FIRST WORKSHOP WAS BEING held at Transport Co's offices in the Docklands, and at the insistence of Clyde and myself, our representative party of five had arrived a good fifteen minutes ahead of the scheduled start time. Even Stefano, who would no doubt be late to his own funeral, didn't argue the toss on this. Since he had become aware of our fallback preparation on the POV, he'd adopted a very agreeable approach to any suggestions by Clyde or me. In fact, we'd effectively now scripted the entire Company component of this first workshop, trying to salvage as much value - and save as much face - as we possibly could. We'd also set down the rules of engagement for the session for our team.

It's fair to say that Jenni-Lee, clearly used to being the centre of attention, wasn't impressed that she was to have no speaking role in this session. She was even less impressed when told that she was not to use her mobile phone during the session either.

'But I need to use it to take pictures and video for my live blog of the event,' she exclaimed, before Clyde helpfully explained that we were under a strict non-disclosure agreement on this deal that would see her employment terminated immediately if she did any such thing.

On arrival we were ushered into a very large conference room, where we found the team from Indirev Systems already seated. As we said hello and exchanged pleasantries with them, it was apparent that several of their all-male team members were just a little bit distracted by the glamorous presence of Jenni-Lee on our team.

The Program Director from Transport Co made his way over to us and explained the running sheet for the workshop. There would be introductory remarks by Transport Co, followed by each team having 45 minutes to present their POV response, provide an update on the prototype application, and ask their clarification questions. Indirev Systems would be up first, we were to be second, and MultiCo would go last.

The start of the session had to be pushed back 15 minutes, thanks to the team from MultiCo who were disrespectfully late in arriving. Once it got underway it quickly became apparent that Indirev Systems would be formidable competition for this business and they were clearly far better prepared than we were. They presented a comprehensive and well thought out POV on Transport Co's requirements, highlighting its strengths and pointing out several areas where they suggested alternative approaches would be beneficial.

Shit, I thought as they continued to lay out their reasoned response, we are going to look very underdone following them. Thank Christ we'd done our fallback preparation though, otherwise we really would have been screwed.

Indirev then moved on to provide an update on their progress on the prototype application. They did this by actually showing several mocked-up screenshots of their proposed prototype rather than just providing a verbal update on progress. Holy shit, we really are screwed, I thought this time.

When it came to our turn, Clyde and I did our best to showcase the work we had done on the POV in as positive a way as possible, but we were nowhere near the depth and slickness of our competitors from Indirev Systems. And from the body language of the Transport Co evaluation team, it showed. We spun a bit of a story around our progress on the prototype application, and stated confidently that Transport Co would be extremely impressed when they saw our work at the next workshop. We recovered a little in the clarification question section, and I noticed some positive nodding from the Transport Co people, as well as some note taking by both of our competitors' teams. We'd obviously picked up a couple of threads here that they hadn't, which was good.

It was with quite some relief that we wrapped up our component and handed over to MultiCo for their turn. That feeling of relief grew considerably stronger with what happened next.

Right at the outset, the MultiCo team leader stated that they would not be following the Transport Co agenda and said that they had no intention of sharing their POV feedback and prototype progress in such a session, where there were competitors present. They would instead move straight into the clarification questions and would then like to share a presentation on their global transportation industry credentials.

The Program Director from Transport Co was clearly not impressed or amused by this. He told MultiCo in no uncertain terms that they could ask their clarification questions now, but stated that there would be no presentation from them unless it was directly related to the POV or prototype.

Following this little altercation, the mood in the workshop remained dark and almost confrontational for the rest of the session. At least MultiCo, by choosing not to play by the client's rules, had made us look way better than we really were. In these contests sometimes you just needed to be ahead of the worst placed competitor to remain in the game. At least, that was what we hoped as we debriefed after the session.

After the debrief I called Dianne to update her that things didn't go great for us at the session, but that we'd fared better than MultiCo. She would normally be really interested in this sort of discussion and would ask lots of questions in order to be prepared for any brief she had to give Christiaan or to counter any other feedback he may have heard from other sources. However, she seemed distracted and wasn't really engaging in the conversation as she usually would.

She did give me some advice to keep my nose clean on this one though, adding: 'Michael, if this one looks like going totally pear-shaped, stay out of the way, and don't, whatever you do, compromise your relationship with Brad.'

Hmmm, I thought. There must be something significant going on in the background here that Di knows about. I was more than just a little bit intrigued.

## Chapter Fifty-One

# The Billing Code

W E FOUND OUT LATER THAT week that we were now in a race of two. MultiCo had been dropped out of the process by Transport Co because they were not willing to enter into the workshops in the cooperative manner required. At least, that was what the formal notification from Transport Co said, confirming that we were invited to the second and third round of workshops. So, despite our early slip-ups and our somewhat poor showing in Workshop One, it was to be a battle between us and Indirev Systems.

We knew that we needed to lift our game significantly if we were to offer some stiff competition for Indirev Systems, not that Rudy seemed too concerned. Whilst he had become significantly more engaged on the deal, he remained dismissive of the competition. Apparently, he'd been given a real rocket by Christiaan when he heard that the first workshop hadn't gone spectacularly well. Naturally, Rudy tried to deflect the blame away from his team onto Clyde and myself, but Clyde wasn't putting up with the that and he got hold of Christiaan to let him know the real story. Christiaan wasn't the least bit interested in the truth, however, and instead he pulled Rudy into the room with Clyde and told the two of them to '… stop their fucken petty little-girly squabbling and get on with the business of winning him the fucken business!' Or something along those lines.

So Rudy had begun to take much more of a hands-on interest in the pursuit, but it was quite obvious from his commentary (he loves to share his wisdom and perspective with the rest of us mere plebs at every opportunity), that he simply didn't rate Indirev Systems as serious competition. Now that MultiCo were out of the game, Rudy seemed to think that the business was simply ours for the taking. Every time we tried to explain how well credentialled, competitive and downright good at this Indirev Systems were, he just dismissed these opinions. He disparagingly called them a 'Ganesh come lately organisation' that just went around buying business to gain market share. He didn't rate their capabilities and downplayed their recent successful expansion into our region as simply the by-product of a cost-conscious market hell bent on offshoring everything.

This was a problem as it meant, in spite of Christiaan's spray at him, that Rudy still wasn't demanding the level of effort and maniacal focus from his part of the team that was necessary to get us back in the game against Indirev Systems. Especially when they still owned the two main streams of work that were required for the next workshop - the presentation of our more detailed POV along with feedback on their requirements and the demonstration of the application prototype.

At least we'd had one distraction removed from the deal team. Jenni-Lee had self-selected herself off the team on Wednesday, since she didn't actually understand all this technology stuff and what it was exactly that we were trying to sell to Transport Co. Plus the fact that, as she confided with Liam the Graduate, the three-hour workshop on Tuesday was the longest, most boring three hours of her life, and she simply couldn't imagine being without access to her phone and social channels for that long ever again. Apparently, she described the direction from Clyde of no phone use in the workshop as 'a clear violation of her human rights' and a 'form of workplace bullying'. Even quiet young Liam broke into a broad smile when he told us this. He then asked if he could still stick around on the team because he felt that he was learning heaps and could maybe help with a few things.

Despite several days of consistent goading from Mario, Clyde and myself to ensure that we got back on track for Workshop Two, we were becoming more and more worried about our overall state of preparedness. By Friday we were nearly at the end of our tether at the perceived lack of progress, and Clyde demanded that Stefano hold a further status update meeting that afternoon, specifically to review the current status of the two key deliverables before we all broke off for the weekend.

Once Stefano arrived back from what must have been a long and luxurious lunch - given that he vanished at noon and arrived back at around 3 pm - we could finally get to the bottom of the true status of the two work streams. Except that Rudy had now taken personal ownership of the POV deliverable, since he apparently had decided to take Jenni-Lee's spot and attend the second workshop to personally present the POV response. And Rudy was indisposed that afternoon.

'Fucker is probably off playing golf,' whispered Mario none too subtly.

So we'd have to wait for an update over the weekend (as if) or next Monday.

'OK, so let's focus on the prototype, then,' said Clyde, exhaling deeply with frustration. 'Stefano, what have you got so far from the offshore technical team that we can look at?' he asked.

'Well, that one's been a teensy bit frustrating, really,' said Stefano. 'I've been emailing back and forth to the offshore guys, but all I seem to keep getting from them is more questions, and they still haven't sent me the prototype that I requested yet,' he said, obviously irritated that they hadn't just given him what he wanted without fuss.

'Well, Stefano, what did the last email from the Technical Leader over there say?' enquired Clyde.

'Let me see,' said Stefano as he fussed over his iPad. 'It says something about them confirming that they are ready to start once I send them the billing code and the clarification responses,' he answered matter-of-factly.

'You mean they don't have a fucken billing code yet?' blurted Mario. 'You do know that the offshore team can't and won't lift a fucken finger until you give them the fucken time billing code for this deal don't you, Stefano?' said Mario, shaking his head in disbelief and muttering about being two weeks in and no f'n code.

'Thanks, Mario,' said Clyde, quickly intervening to shush him from delivering any further expletives. 'Stefano, Mario is right,' said Clyde. 'The offshore team operates under a cost-recovery model, and they will absolutely not engage on this until we give them the time billing code, so I suggest that you do that pronto. Now, what was that you said about the clarification responses? Did the offshore team have some questions about the prototype requirements?'

Stefano stared intently at his iPad, not looking up, scrolling away in search of something. 'Ah yes, there is a spreadsheet they sent in an earlier note that has some questions about the prototype that they want to clarify before they can start work on it,' he responded helpfully.

'Stefano,' I said, as I came to grips with the impending disaster here, 'I need you to forward those questions to me straight away. I'll take a look at them with Clyde and we'll see what we can get back to the offshore guys today to get them started immediately.'

Then, turning to Clyde, I said, 'I think we now all know exactly where we stand on these deliverables.'

I opened the spreadsheet as soon as Stefano's email hit. It contained a long list of questions from the offshore technical team, probably about forty or so all up. Some looked pretty straightforward, others more detailed. They at least showed that they had looked at the ask from Transport Co. However, with three and bit days to go before Workshop Two and a weekend in between, with nothing effectively done we were going to be under the pump big time. And from a personal perspective, I could see my planned quick dash home to Adelaide for the weekend now spiralling away before my very eyes.

Clyde and I huddled around the screen and young Liam wandered over and asked if he could assist. The cheeky bugger said something about being able to touch type much quicker than me, so maybe he could put the answers together as Clyde and I went through the questions.

'Awesome. That would be great thanks, Liam,' I said as I moved out of the way. I turned to Clyde and said, 'You know, I was planning on going home this weekend, but with this…'

He cut me off and said, 'Now, Mike lad, once we've sent these off there's not much you can actually do here. It's over to the Consulting and offshore guys to dig us out of this friggin' hole. So I suggest that you catch your flight tonight and just be ready to take any calls from the team in India if needed.'

'Thanks, Clyde, much appreciated,' was my response.

Over the next hour and a half we worked our way through the questions, giving the offshore team the answers or assumptions that they needed to get cracking on the application prototype. Clyde or I would dictate the response to a question and Liam, who really was very quick on the keyboard, banged it all into a nicely formatted response spreadsheet.

Once we'd finished collating the answers, I sent the email with all the responses to the Technical Leader in India, cc'ing Clyde, Stefano and Liam and asking the Tech Lead to call me tonight or on the weekend if they had any further questions, given the now red-hot urgency of this.

I then bade some quick goodbyes to the team, noting that Stefano had already left for the weekend, and dashed to grab a cab for the journey up the Tullamarine Freeway to the airport.

## Chapter Fifty-Two

# Saved from the Brink

I'D KEPT MY MOBILE PHONE handy and had been monitoring my emails all weekend, but by Sunday lunchtime I hadn't heard anything from the offshore team in India on the responses we'd sent to them on Friday. So there had been no indication of progress which was making me extremely nervous. Or it could mean, I reassured myself, that they were simply head down and getting on with producing the prototype application that we needed for next Tuesday.

I sent yet another follow-up email to the offshore Technical Leader, and this time he actually responded, and quite quickly. He politely thanked me for providing the responses to the questions, and informed me that they were still awaiting the time billing code to be provided before they could start work on the design of the prototype application.

Shit!!!!!! Fucken Stefano still hadn't sent them the billing code, so the team in India still hadn't actually started work on the prototype application and we were now about 48 hours away from having to present it to Transport Co. Shit, fuck and bollocks!

I walked out into the backyard so that the family couldn't hear me, and I called Clyde. As soon as he answered I blurted out, 'Mate, I just confirmed that complete waste of fucken space Stefano never sent them the motherfucking billing code, so they've not started work on the prototype over in India, and we are royally fucked on this deal now!'

'Hello, Michael,' he slowly and sarcastically said. 'Are you not having a good weekend? You should learn to relax a bit more'.

'Seriously, Clyde? When we are working with fucken numpties like these idiots, I'm telling you we are fucked. Dianne and Christiaan will both go berserk when they hear about this, and I'm not taking the fall for that fuckwit Rudy this time.'

'Michael, seriously, take a deep breath, lad. All is not lost,' said Clyde.

'What do you mean, Clyde?' I enquired.

'Well lad, did you see the email from young Liam this morning?'

'I saw it come through but I haven't opened it yet'.

Clyde said, 'Well, I suggest you do. I've just been looking at what he sent through, Mikey, and I think the little bugger may have saved our bacon'.

'Why? What's he done, Clyde?' I asked quizzically, wondering what the hell Clyde was on about.

'Well, it seems that he's quite the technical boffin, this lad. He's only gone and sent us a very bloody nice looking and what appears to be a fully working prototype application! Seriously, it looks way better than the screenshots that Indirev Systems showed off last week, and I suspect that it would be way better than anything that our offshore team could come up with between now and Tuesday,' stated Clyde.

'Holy crap, Clyde!' I exclaimed, as I headed back indoors to grab the laptop and take a look. 'How the hell did he do that?' I asked, more rhetorically than anything.

'I don't know, laddie. But he's friggin well done it and it's a beauty,' said Clyde. 'Why don't you take a thorough look at it and call me back when you're done, and we can compare notes? I'm sending Liam a thank you message right now and I'll ask him to meet us in the office tomorrow morning to fill us in on how he's managed to do this.'

'Sure thing, Clyde, no worries,' I said. 'Isn't it amazing how often it's the quiet ones that come through when the going gets tough, eh?' I wondered out loud.

I took a good look over the prototype application that Liam had designed and saw that Clyde was right. It was brilliant! He'd done an amazing job and had essentially put together a fully functioning prototype app which included multiple screen layers to click through. It was all designed using Transport Co's logos and their colour scheme, and it looked a treat on my laptop. Now I couldn't wait to thank him. If this went down as well as I hoped with Transport Co, I'd be putting Liam forward for the best possible Company award that I could.

I rang Clyde and confirmed that his view was spot on - this prototype would fit the bill very nicely indeed for Tuesday. We quietly asked the offshore Technical Leader to stand down his team on this requirement for now, and we gave him the time billing code for the time that his team had already put into researching the requirements for the proto-type up until now.

I couldn't wait for Monday, firstly to thank Liam and also to ask him how the fuck he put together, seemingly in a day or so, what our Consulting and offshore Technical teams couldn't do in over two weeks. And also, of course, to absolutely stir the pot on Stefano and the Consulting crew yet again fucking up and letting the team down.

Emily wandered in and asked, 'What's up with the sudden mood swing, Michael? Thirty minutes ago you were ready to throttle someone, judging from the language bouncing around the back yard, and now you're grinning like the cat that just got the cream.'

I explained to Emily what had transpired, and she was relieved and very happy for me, not just because I had a way forward for next Tuesday, but also because this time around it was someone else doing the saving for a change.

## Chapter Fifty-Three

# Liam the Magnificent

I FLEW BACK INTO MELBOURNE ON Sunday night so that I could be in the office bright and early Monday morning, and to avoid an hour stuck in traffic on the Tullamarine. Clyde and I caught up with Mario first thing and shared the story of how Liam had saved our bacon on the prototype. God only knew what shape we were in on the POV response, but the Consulting guys were supposedly progressing that ready for Tuesday. I guess we'll soon know, I thought. Mario was beside himself with schadenfreude when he found out that Stefano didn't know about Liam's prototype application yet, and that Stefano hadn't, as he had clearly been asked to do last Friday, provided the billing code to the offshore team as yet.

Liam came and joined us right on 8:30 am, as per the message of thanks that Clyde sent to him yesterday. He was clearly very embarrassed and a bit overwhelmed at all the handshakes and backslaps we were giving him as we thanked him for what he'd done, so we needed to tone it back a bit. The key question we wanted him to answer was: how the bloody hell did you do it?

'Well,' said Liam, 'It was actually pretty simple. I had some spare time over the weekend and I've been wanting to take a look at this new low-code platform that is, you know, like really lit in the market just now. I thought I'd have a bit of a play using the prototype application as a test bed. You know, to see how easy it was to punch out the screens. So, I downloaded the free trial version and messed around working out how to use it. I'd already spent some time last week after Jenni-Lee disappeared, analysing the requirements from Transport Co. So I think I understood pretty much what they were looking for. Then after all that drama on Friday, I took into account the clarifications you guys provided, and really it wasn't that much trouble. So I just hope it's useful,' he finished, shrugging his shoulders.

'Liam, mate,' I said, 'useful is a massive understatement. I've looked at it on the laptop and it's a thing of beauty that will be of great value tomorrow in the workshop. We can't thank you enough, mate'. Liam was again embarrassed by this attention so we paused and let him find his breath.

'I'm glad you like it. It was fun to do. Maybe you'd like to take a look at the mobile and tablet versions that I ported across last night?' he asked.

We all looked at each other incredulously as Liam fumbled in his backpack for his tablet computer.

'Liam, do you mean that you've got versions of the prototype application for mobile phones and tablets?' asked Clyde cautiously.

'Sure have,' shrugged Liam. 'It was no bother as the platform has features that let you easily do that. After you sent me that message yesterday saying that you liked it, I just spent another five minutes or so porting them over. They work on both Android and Apple and look pretty good, actually.'

'Liam, you are a fucken legend,' said Clyde, beaming warmly and putting his arm across his shoulder and leaning in to see what Liam was pulling up on his tablet.

'Amen to that,' said both Mario and I. 'Amen'.

Before we headed in to the deal war room for the daily status meeting that morning, Clyde ensured that we had our scripts lined up. This was going to be fun, and being the scheming bastards that we were, we were not about to miss a chance to get one back at these Consulting pricks - really get one back!

Stefano the flamboyant walked in to the room looking extremely flustered and not his usual debonair, flashy self. Instead he was as white as a ghost and looked a bit ill.

Clyde led off with, 'Stefano, are you OK? You look like you've seen a ghost, lad.'

Stefano put down his bag and his coffee, and turned to face where we were sitting. He clasped his hands together in front of his chest, and drew in a deep breath. 'Clyde and team, I have a big confession to make. I'm terribly, terribly sorry, but I forgot to send the billing code to the offshore team on Friday as I promised.' He bowed his head in shame, or at least mock shame, as Clyde stood up.

Everyone in the room, apart from Mario, Liam and myself, held their breath waiting for Clyde to launch a full-blown tirade at Stefano. Instead, Clyde walked calmly around the table over to Stefano, who by now appeared to actually be crying, and he put his arm gently around Stefano and paused again before speaking.

'Stefano. We know you royally fucked up, son. The offshore team leader told us yesterday. They've not done a single thing to develop the prototype, thanks to you.' He paused again for effect and continued, 'But, thanks to that highly intelligent, diligent and unassuming young man sitting down over there,' - he pointed over to Liam - 'we have a way out of this mess. Indeed, thanks to the magnificent Liam we now have a very good way forward and a wonderful working prototype application.'

By now everyone had turned their eyes on to Liam and the poor bugger retreated into his seat and bowed his head in the face of all this embarrassing attention.

Stefano continued to sob gently as Clyde continued. 'So the person that you need to thank for saving your pathetic arse this time around is young Liam. And Stefano, don't you ever fuck up like that again on one of my deals,' he said, and he removed his arm and calmly walked back around to his seat next to the sheepish young hero, now dubbed 'Liam the Magnificent'.

## Chapter Fifty-Four

# The Rudy Problem

LATER THAT DAY RUDY BRIEFLY stopped in at the deal war room while Clyde and I were out grabbing a quick sandwich. Stefano proceeded to give him the full download on what had transpired around the prototype, and Mario was there in the room to hear the whole exchange. Although Stefano said how wonderful what Liam had done was and tried to show the prototype to Rudy on his screen, Rudy was clearly uninterested and unimpressed.

Rudy said to Stefano, 'This is all just a storm in a teacup. I'm sure our offshore team would have built it just fine, and they would have produced an even better prototype if they hadn't pulled the plug on them.'

Mario was furious and walked out rather than confront Rudy yet again. We bumped into Mario on our way back into the building and he relayed the story and his disgust that Rudy would just wipe it away as he inhaled deeply on his ciggie.

The Consulting guys, who seemed to come and go from the deal war room at random, continued to play their cards very close to their chests on the status of the POV response. We hadn't bothered progressing with our original fallback draft once we had handed that over to Consulting after the first workshop. Every time any of us raised questions or offered some assistance, we got pushback saying they had it and it was all under control. One of Rudy's feistier henchmen even had the audacity to tell me it was none of my business since Rudy would be presenting that part in the workshop; so as they were being so guarded and shedding no light on progress, we strongly suspected that they were way behind the eight ball on this.

There really was little we could do if they wouldn't accept our help, so once we'd spent a few hours scripting the presentation of the prototype application that I was going to do in Workshop Two tomorrow, we turned our attention to other response tasks. After all, once we got Workshop Two out of the way, we still had Workshop Three to prepare for along with comprehensive written submissions and a fully priced solution. Of course, we needed the POV solution response from Consulting before we could progress too far on that...

We had scheduled a workshop team rehearsal session for Tuesday morning in place of the usual array of status and workstream meetings. Not surprisingly, Rudy didn't show up despite having anointed himself to a key role in Workshop Two. Clyde rang him and left a suitably blunt voice message, and soon after Rudy messaged Stefano and told him that he'd meet us down at Transport Co in time for the workshop. So much for team work and thorough preparation ahead of a key client workshop. Even Stefano couldn't hide his annoyance. We knew we couldn't let Rudy's lack of cohesion and his game playing put us off ahead of this workshop, so we prepared as best we could around the gaping hole in the POV component.

Our team for the workshop (minus Rudy) ended up signing in and heading up to the conference room, because by five minutes before start time Rudy hadn't shown up or responded to Stefano's increasingly frantic messaging. The run sheet for this workshop had us kicking off before Indirev Systems this time around, which was fine by me as I was looking forward to leading off with our prototype application.

Rudy rocked into the room right on the session start time, and after chastising Stefano for not waiting and then completely ignoring the Indirev Systems team, he went straight around to introduce himself to the Transport Co evaluation team as the Executive Leader of this initiative for The Company. Rudy then started to blather on about how pleased he was to be working with them before the Program Director politely asked him to take a seat with his team, as it was after all time to start.

I kicked us off with a nicely structured demonstration of the prototype that Liam had built and it's fair to say that the Transport Co team seemed very captivated with what they saw. Even the Indirev Systems guys were taking notes and seemed quite impressed. The high point came when one of the Transport Co team asked me about whether, in theory, this could be extended to operate on other platforms. I was able to answer this by handing them a tablet and a smart phone on which they could play with the prototype as I continued to showcase its features. It was an awesome start to the session for us, and I was warmly thanked by the Program Director when I finished to hand over to Rudy.

Well, from there onwards things went downhill rapidly for us.

Rudy took to the floor to present our updated POV response to their requirements. As he began his extended introductory comments, a feeling of dread came across me. Stefano brought up the first slide from the USB stick that Rudy had given him and the feeling deepened. Essentially, it was the same fallback material that we'd shown them a week earlier with just a few minor alterations, and I sure as hell hoped that he had something more substantial to show them as he progressed. About four slides in, it was apparent to us and the Transport Co team that he didn't. He was really just regurgitating the material from last week with a small addition here or there, and padding the whole thing out with gibberish about digital innovation, joint venture possibilities and global reach.

Internally, I was contemplating just how it was even possible to go from such a great start to such a train smash so quickly.

The Transport Co Program Director interrupted Rudy and politely but firmly asked him if we had any new material in our POV to share with them, since they had seen all of this previously in Workshop One.

Rudy, clearly thinking that attack was the best form of defence, decided to respond by having a go at Transport Co's process and saying that we'd be able to provide a much better POV once they had down selected The Company as their preferred partner and we were 'fully in the tent so to speak'.

Holy shit! Clyde cut in and tried to defuse the situation by apologising and clarifying that we'd been so focused on the prototype that we hadn't progressed the POV part nearly as far as we'd hoped, and that Rudy was just trying to emphasise the strengths in our thinking so far, and we looked forward to continuing to collaborate, and presenting a much better response and perspective on their needs next week.

While Clyde was speaking Rudy just stood with his arms folded looking upwards like a pompous, unimpressed and petulant twat. Business as usual for him!

The Program Director thanked Rudy and Clyde and suggested that, despite showing off a very impressive prototype application, we needed to be much, much better prepared for the final workshop next week, and if there were no further questions from his team to The Company, then Rudy could take his seat and we'd move on to hear what Indirev Systems had to share.

Phew, it was a miracle that they didn't kick us out of the process right then and there. However, at least for now it seemed that in spite of Rudy and Consulting letting us down yet again, we remained in the contest... albeit, I suspected, running a very distant second and falling further back with every passing moment.

Indirev Systems presented their prototype which, whilst comprehensive, lacked the slick look and feel of Liam's. They also didn't have a mobile platform version of it ready to show today but indicated it was in the works, which of course they had to say now that they'd seen ours was already a multi-platform prototype. They offered some impressive thinking in the POV part and were quite obviously weeks ahead of us in that regard. As they wrapped up their session, our man Rudy couldn't quite help himself and decided to offer the room some commentary.

'You know, they don't have any *real* Consulting capability here. They just fly people in and out of India when needed...' he offered.

He was immediately told, by a now clearly irritated Program Director, to: 'Please refrain from commentary on your competitors and give them the same polite respect that they offered your team, thank you, Rudy.'

Clyde and I looked at each other in despair. Couldn't this dickhead just for once hide his innate stupidity by not opening his mouth? To be a prick to the competition in front of them and the client was just next level dumb.

As soon as the workshop finished, Rudy got up and left the room, not even thanking or saying goodbye to the Transport Co and Indirev Systems teams that he'd managed to offend.

Clyde and I went straight over to the Indirev Systems team leader and apologised on behalf of The Company. He accepted and responded with a bit of a smile, saying that he suspected that every company has a few 'nasty, rotten people' and that he believed in karma, so our colleague and people like him would eventually face consequences for their actions.

Clyde and I walked across the footbridge over the Yarra River and reconvened to count the cost of the damage at the Boatbuilders Yard bar at South Wharf. We both felt in need of a drink to make sense of what just happened and to plan our next steps. I was quite down in the dumps and didn't think that at this stage we could really recover from the self-harm that Rudy had inflicted on our campaign.

Clyde agreed that we'd been severely wounded, but he stressed that we were still in the game and that Transport Co themselves had indicated that we'd have a chance to redeem ourselves in Workshop Three next week. Clyde thought that we needed a truly massive effort from the entire team to pull ourselves back into contention, and I agreed.

But in addition, we really had to deal with the Rudy problem. We simply couldn't allow him to cause any more destruction, and Clyde was going to escalate directly to Christiaan to try and have him removed from the deal pursuit.

I wasn't convinced that this full-frontal approach to Christiaan would get us the outcome we wanted, as Christiaan had a habit of taking Rudy's side, so I implored Clyde to at least sound out Dianne for her advice before confronting Christiaan.

Clyde was talking to Dianne when I returned with the second round of beers. He had given Di the short version of the horror story that was Workshop Two, and after a couple of minutes of conversation Clyde ended the call.

'Very interesting, Michael,' he said. 'Dianne was in some meeting she'd stepped out of to talk to me, and her mind was clearly on other things. However, she did give me some firm advice.'

'What did she say, Clyde'?

'Well, lad, she understood we were in dire straits, and said that we should keep trying to do the best we could in the circumstances and that we shouldn't escalate to Christiaan. She even said we should let Rudy go about his way on this one'.

'Clyde, that is fucken bizarre coming from Di,' I said, and added, 'but she said something similar to me last week when we last spoke'.

'Hmmm,' pondered Clyde. 'There's something cooking here, laddie. I think we should actually take Di's advice and not confront Rudy head on, as much as I want to take the wind of out that miserable prick's sails. Let's scramble from tomorrow and see if we can impose our help on these Consulting fuckwits to give it the best shot that we can.'

'No worries, Clyde. Cheers to that,' I said, raising my glass.

'Cheers, lad, and thanks for everything. You've been a saving grace on this deal and we'd no doubt be completely and utterly fucked without you.'

## Chapter Fifty-Five

# The Recovery

First thing on Wednesday morning we had a war council-type gathering with Stefano and a few of the more sensible Consulting team members, to agree an action plan to rescue the situation. We purposely kept Rudy out of the discussions since he was unlikely to accept our help, and we really had no time to argue the toss if we were to recover this deal for The Company.

Our advice and assistance were warmly welcomed by Stefano, who was still smarting from both his personal stuff-up on the billing code and the embarrassment he'd felt at Workshop Two. It seemed that he was very rapidly falling out of love with Rudy as he saw more of him in action. The other Consulting guys remained a bit guarded, but as we outlined a plan for the coming days to get our solution and an evolved POV for Transport Co together, they seemed more willing to buy in and play their part. Perhaps they had made little or no progress, since they just didn't know exactly what needed to be done and in what order. With that and a lack of real leadership from either Stefano or Rudy, it was no wonder we were where we were.

It was an ambitious plan but it simply had to be. We were at least two weeks behind Indirev Systems in pulling together our comprehensive response to Transport Co's requirements, and developing the 10-year roadmap of IT initiatives would take longer than we had before the third and final workshop next Tuesday. So we assigned out individual workstreams to owners and took a divide-and-conquer approach. I took on two of the more complex workstreams since I'd had experience in these areas that the Consulting guys simply didn't have. I roped Mario, Liam and a couple of other resources into my sub-team and put them all to work, with some tough deadlines in place to give me sufficient time to pull their work together with what I had to prepare myself.

I spent all day Wednesday reaching out for inputs from some of my contacts as well as gathering some raw content. I worked until the early hours of Thursday morning trying to turn it into a cohesive story for Transport Co, skipping out of my regular Wednesday night Global conference call. To me, not having to sit on that for a change was a bit of a bonus, really.

We then regrouped quickly on Thursday morning and I fed the inputs generated so far into Clyde and Stefano, who were the joint coordination point for all content. Clyde was tasked with getting it all formatted into a presentable form, and in parallel getting the Solution team to provide enough substance behind our thinking for the Pricers to develop our pricing. Stefano was tasked with keeping Rudy informed but away from the team so that we could keep cracking on without his distractions. As soon as I'd passed over Wednesday's content to Clyde and his work team, I reconvened with my sub-team and we repeated the cycle on the next set of requirements we had to tackle.

So, by my calculations I thought we could probably knock off my first workstream by late Friday, leaving the weekend to do the second; and if we finished the second one by Sunday night, that gave us Monday to tie it all together with all the other workstreams and get it through an offline approval process ready to present on Tuesday.

Phew! I was really tired just thinking about it, but somehow I was also re-energised at the prospect of helping pull this one from the fire.

Thursday flew by in a torrent of phone calls, emails and conversations with team members. I'd also realised that I needed to call in a couple of reinforcements to deal with some specific requirements, so had been busy brokering in a few new short-term team members to inject the required talent. I was so flat out all day that I didn't get to spend any time at all on my inputs until that evening, so I scoffed some take away food back at the apartment, messaged Emily that I was sorry I couldn't talk but would call in the morning, and got stuck into it. It was some time after 3 am when I realised that I was writing incoherent crap and head-bobbing above the laptop keyboard, so I went to bed.

On Friday we made some further positive progress as my reinforcements landed and started to get productive. Clyde was almost being overwhelmed now by the amount of input coming in and was working frantically with a small team to distil it down and hand over the salient parts to Solutioning, and there was a real buzz around the team now. Things quietened down at around 3 pm when most of the Consulting guys headed off to attend some mandatory internal meeting that they had all been instructed to attend, despite Clyde and I pleading that we couldn't really afford to lose that hour of productive time. While they were out, Clyde and I had a quick chat in which we agreed that we were nearly back on track, but still with a mountain to climb. However, we were getting there.

The Consulting guys came back in and the whole mood seemed to change again. They ushered themselves back in and got busy, but there was something strange going on.

Stefano wandered over and asked if he could speak with me in private. We got up and walked to the lunch room down the hallway and I said, 'What's up, Stefano? You don't seem too comfortable about something.'

'We just had a meeting with Rudy, Chloe and the senior Consulting team. They believe that we've got this submission under control now, and they asked me to thank you for your efforts and to get you to hand over the work you've done on this so far,' he said very sheepishly. He finished with, 'And we won't be needing you to attend Workshop Three next week either'.

'But we've just got this bloody thing back on some sort of track,' I said incredulously. 'It's crazy to even think this is under control, and sheer insanity to stop the momentum now. Rudy is even more fucken deluded than I thought possible if he thinks this is under control,' I continued, still trying to really comprehend what exactly was going on here.

'It wasn't my idea, sorry, Michael,' said Stefano. He continued to say, 'I argued against it, telling them what great progress you were making, but they pushed back'.

'I know it's not you making the call on this, Stefano; but Rudy has no right to do this and fuck it, I'm taking it up with

Clyde and Dianne. I've got too much invested in this to let it fail now,' I said as I stormed off in search of Clyde.

I was furious at these dickheads. Just because Rudy was the Executive Sponsor for the deal, it didn't make him lord and master in all things. It was Clyde's client, after all, and I wasn't taking this lying down, as I felt there was still life for us in this game-changing deal if I was a part of it and we continued gaining momentum as we had for the past few days.

I found Clyde and once he got off the phone I took him into a room to have this chat in private. As angry as I was, I didn't want the Consulting guys to hear me ranting about this, since in their meeting they'd already heard Rudy's perspective, which was clearly bullshit.

Clyde had in fact been on the phone with Rudy, so he knew what I was angry about. He was mildly agitated himself but had quite a calm air as I downloaded in all my fury.

Once I'd finished, he told me that he knew that we were completely stuffed on this deal if I didn't play a key role in getting us to Workshop Three. In fact, he'd told Rudy that. He had also told Rudy that it wasn't his decision to make, so if I wanted to keep engaged with the team on getting this done, Clyde would absolutely welcome that and would run interference for me to do so.

I was quite relieved to hear Clyde say this. My pride had been dented by being told to step away, and in spite of the hiccups along the way, I was by now very personally vested in this one.

After speaking with Clyde I decided it best to clear off from the deal war room, and I headed back to my apartment to continue working. Despite Clyde's support for me, I was still fuming inside when I called Emily, whom I'd not spoken to for three days now given how busy I'd been. I told her what had gone on and vented my frustration about Rudy and some of these other idiots in Consulting, saying how they were jeopardising any chance we had of recovering this deal, along with the good work that people like Liam, Clyde and myself had already put in.

She listened politely to my ravings and took it all in. Then as I caught myself thinking this is the last thing she wants to hear about, and changed tack to ask her about her and her plans for the weekend, she took aim.

'You know, Michael, these people don't deserve to have you working on this. You are committed, yet again, to saving a bunch of people who will not thank you. And from how you've described them and based on the track record at your Company, they will likely take all the credit if, in fact, the damn Company does win the business. Maybe it's high time for you to step back and actually let them struggle through on this. Perhaps it's best if they do fail sometimes. You know, they might actually learn something'.

'But I can't, Emily. I'd be letting down Clyde, Dianne and myself if we lose this deal. And I'd be letting down Brad too,' I said.

'Would you?' Emily responded softly but firmly. 'Would you really?'

## Chapter Fifty-Six

# Taking a Stand

DESPITE BEING DOG TIRED AFTER back-to-back seventeen-plus-hour days, I slept very restlessly on Friday night. But when I woke up on Saturday morning, I found that I had more clarity and resolve than ever.

I ate some breakfast and waited until after 9 am before I rang Dianne, just in case she'd been out as usual on a Friday night.

'Good morning, Michael,' she answered. 'To what do I owe the pleasure of an early Saturday call? It must be something pretty important, I assume.'

'Sorry to disturb you, Di, but it is important. Have you heard about Rudy's latest directive on the Transport deal from yesterday afternoon?' I asked.

'Yes,' said Dianne. 'Clyde called me last night and told me what had happened. He said that you were pretty upset by it all, but as usual you were determined to double down and show them a thing or two.'

'Well, here's the thing, Di,' I said. 'I wanted to let you know that I've actually decided to accept Rudy's suggestion and step away from the deal. I've decided that I simply can't keep saving dickheads like him from their own stupidity. And whilst this deal means a lot to me, and I don't want in any way to let you and Clyde down, I really do need to make a personal stand this time.' I stopped there, feeling a huge weight come off my chest, and waited for her reaction.

'Well, Michael, that's a very big call. But you have my full and complete support in this decision and I'm sure Clyde will feel the same way when you tell him, if you haven't already. You are a really resilient guy and I always value your contributions and your judgement,' she said. 'For a while now I've actually been pondering how long it might take you to crack and take a stand like this, especially with all that's been thrown at you in the past year or so. I also know how important this particular deal is to you because of Brad.'

Dianne's words were very reassuring and I breathed a huge sigh of relief as a wave of positive, almost euphoric emotion came over me.

Dianne added, 'Your timing on this might turn out to be quite impeccable too. I can't tell you why yet, but you'll see what I mean in a few weeks.'

'Thanks, Di. I really do appreciate your support on this. I haven't told Clyde yet but I'll call him now. I'm then planning to fly home for the rest of the weekend. It's been a very tough few weeks, as you know.'

'That's great, Mike. I'm sure Emily will appreciate having you home for a change, too.'

I called Clyde straight after finishing the call with Dianne. He too told me that he was fully supportive of my decision. He expressed some disappointment that I wouldn't be there with him to see this one through, but from the way he spoke I figured that was more because it left him with no one except Mario as a trusted ally on the deal. He also knew that the slight chance he had of keeping The Company in the game on this deal was probably over now. Well, that's what I told myself, and he understood my call on this and told me he'd walk away from it too if he could. He also probed me to see if Dianne had told me anything about what she'd been up to lately as, like me, he was as curious as hell about what was going on.

Next up I called the Travel Booking Agency to get on a flight home that day and cut short my serviced apartment rental. There was no point in hanging around in Melbourne anymore and I was very keen to get home to Emily and the kids.

I sent a message to Mario so that he was in the loop on my decision. Then I dropped an urgent email to those I'd recruited on to the sub-team over the past couple of days, and told them there had been a change in approach on the deal, and asked them to stand down. I also asked them to continue to support Clyde and Mario where they needed it. Then I cleaned out the remnants in my fridge, packed up my things and headed to the airport.

On the way back through Adelaide Airport I stopped by Cocolat to pick up Emily's favourite dessert, an extravagant chocolate mousse cake called a Wild Thing. I figured if I was going to surprise her with my presence, I may as well thank her for her sage advice with one of her favourite treats.

## Chapter Fifty-Seven

# The Final Nail

After a great half of a weekend back home with the family, the initial feeling of euphoria of freeing myself from the swamp that was the Transport Co deal was subsiding quite rapidly. By Monday morning I'd started to feel a bit down and had begun to question myself about whether this was the right call. Who was I letting down in taking this stand? What would Brad make of all of this once the dust settled?

My self-doubt began to evaporate quickly, though, when Mario called me with an update on the circus that the deal had become. Apparently, we'd received formal notice from Transport Co advising that The Company had breached their probity requirements twice in the last week, and warning us that one more probity strike would see us eliminated immediately from the selection process. The detail of the two breaches had been set out in the notification letter we'd been emailed. The first one occurred the day after Workshop Two when Rudy had apparently approached one of their evaluation team and tried to discuss Indirev Systems with them. The notice stipulated that 'attempts such as this to influence the process and to demean your competition will absolutely not be tolerated'. The second breach occurred when Rudy called the office of the CEO and tried to make an appointment to meet with the CEO, with the stated intention of 'discussing their Generational IT Change Initiative'.

Wow! Rudy is even more completely deluded than I ever thought, as well as being a first-class idiot. Anyone with the slightest ounce of business acumen knows how seriously probity is treated on major initiatives such as this. As part of the protocol of ensuring fairness, the CEO's office would be regularly issued with a watchlist of companies involved in major tender opportunities like this program, and asked to report back on any attempted contact. What the fuck was Rudy thinking? Did he really believe that he could just waltz in to see Brad and tell him to give us the business because we were better than Indirev?

Well, at least the news of these probity strikes had helped turn my downward mood spiral around, as they removed absolutely any doubt from my mind that The Company still had a chance of winning this business. If I had stayed the course and worked my arse off all weekend trying to save this opportunity, it wouldn't have mattered a squat. We were already way behind Indirev and these black marks against The Company were almost the final nail in the coffin in our pursuit of this business.

I tried my best to tune out completely from the deal over the next day or so. I kept myself occupied on catching up with some of the myriad of tasks that I'd been ignoring for weeks now. I worked through confirming the revised sales targets for my team for the year, pumped through a big backlog of expense reports, completed overdue compulsory training, and started to compile some reports that Global had requested about three weeks ago. I was still receiving all of the Transport Co deal team emails but I ignored those completely, despite the temptation to see what the latest disaster was.

I'd just left the office and was in the car on the way home when Clyde called me. He sounded like a broken man and obviously needed someone to console him. They'd finished the third and final workshop a couple of hours ago, and unsurprisingly it did not go well. The Consulting guys had of course panicked on Monday when they finally realised that there wasn't enough time to respond properly with our POV on the Transport Co requirements. In their wisdom they discarded all of the work that had been done on our POV, and they came up with an alternative plan where they would present their own '2030 Vision for Transport Co', based not on their stated requirements, but on what Consulting thought the IT and Transportation markets would look like then. No substance, no solution, no pricing, just visionary motherhood-type statements about 'continued market disruption' that offered no value to Transport Co, and were quite possibly what Transport Co could easily have put together for themselves in about a two-hour think-tank type of workshop. It certainly wasn't what they were looking for as part of a robust go-to-market tender program that would be pivotal to their future business success over the next decade.

Clyde said that this time around they politely listened to the spiel from our colleagues, but he thought that their body language was extremely negative and he said that there was virtually no engagement from the Transport Co team at all. This indicated, to me at least, that they'd finally lost patience and given up on us. The Transport Co Program Director ended the session by thanking us for our work to date and commenting on our 'unorthodox' approach to the last workshop.

'So Clyde, that was the final nail, then?' I enquired.

'Well, Mike, if that wasn't it, then I'm afraid that the final nail came just after we finished our workshop,' he responded.

Clyde then told me how Rudy had clearly not had the emotional intelligence to read the room properly and had come out of the workshop quite cock-a-hoop, thinking that they'd put The Company into a winning position with their 'disruptive approach showing our thought leadership'. As Rudy had wandered through the foyer with some of his Consulting team, congratulating each other on their intellectual superiority, Rudy had spotted the Indirev Systems team, who were waiting to be signed in for their turn at Workshop Three. As Clyde told it, Rudy made a bee-line for them and then proceeded to loudly goad them as a bunch of losers who were no doubt now a distant second to his team, so they may as well not even bother going in to the workshop!

Neither the Indirev Systems team nor the Transport Co Program Director who had come down to sign them in through security were evidently very impressed with this arrogant, unprofessional and downright pathetic tirade from Rudy, who was high-fiving with his team as they exited the building.

'That,' said Clyde, 'was the final nail, lad.'

## Chapter Fifty-Eight

# Counting Chickens

Now that this deal had almost certainly been lost for The Company, it weighed quite heavily on my mind. I guess that was mainly because of my friendship with Brad, as I really wanted us to put in a good, positive showing; but I was very comfortable with my decision to withdraw and to not try to save these fools from themselves. Indeed, I doubted if anything I could have humanly done would have overcome such abject stupidity. However, that wasn't the point for me. For me it was all about reconciling myself that I couldn't and shouldn't constantly try to be the saviour, and I certainly had no intention of being the fall guy anymore, especially on this deal.

I talked it over at dinner that night with Emily, looking for some further confirmation to erase the last shred of self-doubt.

Emily listened carefully and closed out the conversation by simply saying, 'Michael, you've finally made the hard decision to put yourself first for a change and I'm proud of you.'

My phone rang bright and early the next morning, and unexpectedly it was Brad.

'Hey, Brad, how's it going, mate?' I answered.

'Hi, Mike. I'm great thanks, buddy. The family is all well and we are getting right into the swing of the new year. How's Emily and the kids?'

'Doing real well thanks, Brad. I'm actually back in Adelaide with them at the moment, which makes for a really pleasant change,' I said.

'That's great, Mike. Hey listen, I just wanted to give you a personal, off-the-record heads-up on the Generational IT deal, because I know you've been across it a bit from your side.'

'Sure, Brad. I appreciate the call. What's the news?' I asked with more than a little trepidation, fearing the feedback that was about to come.

'Well, Mike, I'm sure that you probably know this already, but your mob didn't exactly cover themselves in glory on this one. Our Program Director was extremely upset and critical over some of the behaviour from your reps. Apparently they didn't listen to directions or our requirements, and made up their own approach as the process progressed. There were also a couple of probity issues. Now please don't take any of this personally Mike as, knowing you as well as I do, I know that nothing like this would have happened if they'd put you in control on this.'

'No offence taken at all, Brad. I actually had to pull back from this deal myself for the sake of my own sanity and to make a bit of a stand against some of the really dumb stuff that was going on,' I stated.

Brad continued on, 'That's good, Mike. The Program Director did tell me that you were easily the best guy on your team when you were engaged in the early workshops, but as for your Exec leader on the deal, this Rudy guy... Well, from the feedback I've been given it seems he's a real knob and not a very nice person at all. He's been rude to our team and also treated your competitors very unprofessionally. I'd say that he is the primary reason that your Company lost this deal, since we have decided to go with Indirev Systems moving forward. But please keep that under your hat until we announce it in a couple of days. And can you please do your best to make sure that this Rudy character never sets foot in my business again, Mike?'

'I'll do my absolute best, Brad,' I said with a grin as I processed his feedback.

'Cool. Thanks, Mike. Say hi to Emily for me and tell her we'll catch up again soon, mate,' he said, and he closed out the brief, and very informative, call.

Well, well, well. These insights from Brad were very interesting, and they must have made their final decision very quickly yesterday after the third workshop. This conversation had removed all doubt about where we stood. Clyde and I were right. We'd been nowhere near Indirev Systems in this race. And it wasn't just us - evidently everyone thought that Rudy was an arrogant prat!

Boy, I'd love to use Brad's insights on Rudy to send that bastard down in flames. It was an incredibly tempting urge, mostly because it would be so satisfying after all that that prick had put us through, not just on this, but over the past year or so. As much fun as that would be, I knew that I had to be the bigger man and just sit back and let this take its course. I was hopeful that for once the truth might actually prevail on this deal.

I was slightly relieved that Brad hadn't thought poorly of me at all on this. Emily was proven right yet again on that count. What Brad had shared with me was gold in terms of information, and if there was to be any finger pointing or blamestorming after the decision became known, I now had direct, first class information on Transport Co's real perspective. There was no way on earth that I was going to be copping any negative heat on this one. I now just needed to sit on this until the fallout began, since there was no way I was going to compromise Brad's personal trust of me and share this with anyone yet. Not even Dianne and Clyde.

I did my best to lie low for the next couple of days. I was keen to minimise any contact with Dianne, Clyde or anyone associated with the deal. Not that I was going to share anything I knew, but I thought it best to avoid any temptation as much as possible. So I continued with my busy work, catching up on my personal backlog of admin, attempting to follow up with Sales Admin yet again on the status of my outstanding bonuses, preparing reports and ensuring that my team was on top of all of their deals and their quotas for the year ahead. The ever-awesome Amy in the Adelaide office had also been helping me get some errors in the Sales Record System fixed. Strangely, I found all of this usually dull admin work - that I always put off until it absolutely had to happen, to avoid serious repercussions - quite therapeutic this time around.

Mario did manage to get hold of me on Thursday morning while he was out on one of his ciggie breaks. He phoned me to give me the lowdown on the past couple of days, so I let him go on with it rather than avoid the conversation.

He confirmed what Clyde had indicated when we last spoke, that Rudy came out of the third workshop proclaiming himself as the hero that had saved the deal for The Company. He carried on in a form of full-blown self-worship, saying that he alone was taking full responsibility for the impending victory, and grandstanding about how his team 'changed the game completely' and beat out the 'so-called competition from that Indian mob'.

I had to go on mute for a moment when Mario was telling me this, as I'd started to chuckle to myself.

Mario then told me that Rudy had repeated all of this in an email he sent to the Executive Leadership Team and had cc'd the deal team, blowing his own trumpet in much detail. I took a mental note to take a look for that email as I thought it could turn out to be an absolute keeper - you know, one to file away for future mirth.

Mario finished his ranting download to me by saying, 'You know what else this fuckwit has done, Mike? This wanker is that fucken cocky that he's gone and arranged for celebration drinks for his team tonight, and of course we don't even get the final decision from Transport Co until tomorrow morning! I'm telling you, Mikey, I'm never working with that fucken arrogant, selfish arsehole ever again.'

'I hear you, Mario. We'd all love to not have to deal with him again. Talk about counting your chickens before they hatch,' I said, knowing full well that these chickens would never hatch. Not that I was telling Mario that. Hopefully, however, they would all come home to roost very shortly.

## Chapter Fifty-Nine

# The Call

I DIDN'T HEAR A PEEP ABOUT the Transport Co deal all the next morning, so I was actually starting to get a bit edgy to hear the formal news. Once that news dropped, I felt that I could actually share my off-the-record insights with Dianne and Clyde as the shit no doubt hit the fan. It had all been a bit like the calm before the storm, so by mid-afternoon it was all a little unnerving. My mind started to wander. What if they changed their mind? What if the personal fallout for me was so bad that no one wanted to even associate with me? Really crazy thoughts, knowing what I did; but I'd long ago learnt to occasionally expect the absolutely unexpected in the corporate bubble of big business.

I was jolted back to reality by a call on my mobile phone. It was a Sydney number that I didn't recognise. Usually I didn't answer calls from people I don't have programmed into my contacts, but for some strange reason in this case I felt compelled to make an exception.

'Good afternoon, Michael Mansfield speaking,' I answered.

'Michael, it's Christiaan,' blasted the voice down the line to me. 'Why the fuck don't you have my number in your phone? Or is that how you greet everyone?' he stammered at me.

I was completely taken aback. I knew that this wasn't a question, but I felt that I needed to respond and not just let him push me around from the outset.

'Hello, Christiaan. Well, I don't have your number in my phone because I'm pretty sure that this is the first time we've ever actually spoken directly,' I said, not quite believing what was actually coming out of my mouth.

After a moment of silence, his initial response was, 'Hmmpf.' So I thought it best to wait for him to continue, as I was pretty sure I knew what was coming.

He started his rant with, 'This bloody Transport deal, what a complete and utter cock-up it's been. I've just got a letter from them telling me that we came a very distant second and it includes some very blunt and not very good feedback on our team's performance, which has really fucking pissed me off.'

Holy shit! He was starting to really wind up now, but I didn't want to interrupt, and I thought it best to just let him vent his spleen. Unless, of course, he started talking bullshit and blaming me, because I was resolved to have none of that. Not even from this arsehole of a CEO.

Christiaan carried on. 'If it wasn't for some other major changes about to happen in The Company, I'd have some fucking people's heads on sticks over this,' he said. 'Because I'm sure you are well aware, Michael, that I fucking hate losing business. Especially big deals like this.'

'Yes, Christiaan, I understand. I can assure you that I'm devastated to hear that we've lost this opportunity, too,' I said when he paused for breath, trying to rapidly think through exactly what he was saying and where this might be going.

Christiaan then said, 'It's very clear, from the letter and from what else I've found out, who the culprits that fucked this one up for us are.'

Here we go, I thought, time to buckle up as this shit gets real.

'It was bloody Rudy and some of his overpaid fucken Consultants that completely fucked this one up for us, Michael. I know that for a fact, not that it's going to bother me soon, as you'll find out. However, I've actually had some really positive feedback about you and Clyde, and I think that we'd have been thrown out of this race even quicker if it wasn't for some of your hard work,' Christiaan stated, sounding rather matter-of-fact. And of course, it was a compliment of the highest order coming from him.

'But I didn't call you just to blow smoke up your arse. Clearly Dianne rates you, as do most of the Executive Leadership Team. And your results last year were solid too. We are about to make some major announcements about some acquisitions and divestitures to our business, and I'd like you to take on a key role in a business we are acquiring.'

I tried to speak, but Christiaan just rolled right along across the top of me. 'Now, Dianne will call you with some details, and I'm keen for you to take this on, OK?' he said, again as a statement not a question.

'Thank you, Christiaan,' I finally managed to say. 'I'll give this new role my full consideration,' I added, somewhat excited and with my head spinning, but not wanting to fully commit to something I didn't yet understand.

'You do that, Michael. Oh, and you should be aware that I've approved the release of your full bonus payments for that Telco deal and the other ones you did last year. Sales Admin will be processing them now,' he finished.

'Thanks, Chr...' was about all I got out as he hung up on me.

## Chapter Sixty

# Opportunity Knocks

I MESSAGED DIANNE WITHIN 30 SECONDS of finishing my call with Christiaan.

Thursday 3:48pm

> Di, I've just has a very strange call from Christiaan. He said you would fill me in. Please call me as soon as you can. thx Mike

> Will do. Just tied up finishing something critical and related to what CJ likely discussed. D

Dianne's response shed absolutely no light on the situation at all, apart of course from the reassurance that she seemed to be in on whatever the fuck it was that was happening within the business.

I tried to unpack the conversation with Christiaan in my head, searching for clues, but there really weren't any apart from the fact that he wanted me to take on a new and important role to do with some business The Company was acquiring. Well, at least that was what I think he said. After all, I'd still been getting over the 'Rudy fucked up but you did OK' part of the conversation, and was feeling immense relief from that. I was not expecting it to suddenly head off down some other rabbit hole about new roles.

And the bonus bit. Sweet! It looked like that longstanding saga might finally be resolved, and in my favour too. I was pretty sure that was no coincidence of timing, and the fact that The Company now wanted something else from me probably forced their hand a little. Almost like a pre-emptive goodwill gesture to take on this role. Shit, I hoped that didn't mean that it was going to be a terrible opportunity for me.

The next couple of hours dragged by as my thoughts whirled around and I waited for Dianne to call. I'd had a few calls from people around the Transport Co deal, but I wasn't taking them lest I missed Dianne's call. No doubt the fallout around the deal was starting to hit and I just hoped that these Consulting guys were held to account for screwing this up, which was a very distinct possibility now that Christiaan clearly had them in his sights.

Before I headed home, I remembered to put Christiaan's name against his number in my phone. Once bitten twice shy.

Dianne called me at about 6:30 that evening, just moments after I'd arrived home, and immediately apologised that she'd not had the chance to get to me with some background before Christiaan called me.

'No worries, Dianne. I know you've been completely consumed on something. Whilst he was pissed off about losing the deal, I think it was quite a positive chat I had with Christiaan. However, he was short on detail on this new role he wants me to take. What can you tell me about it?' I asked.

'Well, Mike, tomorrow we are announcing some major changes to The Company. We are acquiring two new businesses as well as selling off quite a significant part of The Company business. One of the acquisitions is a rapidly growing services business based in Adelaide, and we would like you to take on the role of General Manager for that business, essentially heading it up, making sure that it continues to grow, and ensuring that we properly integrate it with The Company over the next few years,' said Dianne.

'Wow, Di. That sounds pretty intriguing. Can I ask if it was you that put me up for this opportunity?' I queried.

'Well, I certainly had some say, but it was actually Christiaan who threw your hat into the ring. He'd never tell you this, but he thinks you are quite a dedicated exec, who gets on with doing the right things, without being distracted by all of the political nonsense in The Company.' Dianne continued, 'In any case, Mike, myself and the Executive Leadership Team think you'd be perfect for this role, even if it means that I lose a gun Sales leader from my team.'

'Thanks, Di. That's really nice to know,' I said.

Dianne then added, 'It's not only a good career opportunity for you Mike, but it will also be a great opportunity for you to spend a whole lot more time at home, as there'd be almost no travel required. Think about it, Mike, please. I really need to know by first thing in the morning so that we can finalise the announcements.'

'No need, Di,' I said as I wandered into the edge of the dining room, where Emily and the kids were just finishing dinner. Emily looked over to me quizzically as I nodded to her. 'I've made my decision and I'll take it on,' I said as I broke into a broad smile.

'That's great news, Michael. Thank you. We'll work on some of the finer details tomorrow, after the announcement comes out,' said Dianne. 'Oh, and by the way, there are some other announcements coming out tomorrow that I think you'll really enjoy,' she added.

## Chapter Sixty-One

# The Announcement

EMILY AND THE KIDS HAD been ecstatic when I told them that I was moving over to a new job with The Company that would see me based in Adelaide full time. I had been worried about telling them straight away, as sometimes these things can take a last-minute twist and turn or two, but I felt it was worth the risk though, and I owed it to them that they be the first to know after Di. After all, they'd been the ones to maintain some semblance of sanity in my life as I gallivanted around the country and the world for many years doing this mysterious business stuff.

I waited until Emily and I were alone to tell her about the bonus payments being approved by Christiaan. These would more than cover a great holiday with the kids somewhere really nice once I'd settled in to this new role. Besides, I might actually look forward to travelling again for pleasure now that it wouldn't be a weekly grind.

I was also looking forward to stepping into a role that wasn't just pure sales, too. The idea of managing other aspects of the business and people beyond hard core sales targets and numbers had some great appeal, as well as the very nice thought of stepping back from late-night global conference calls several times a week. So at this stage I could see nothing but upside, and I had the chance to make of it what I wanted. I just couldn't wait to see the announcement now.

The announcement finally came through to my inbox mid-morning the following day and it did not disappoint.

---

**From:** Christiaan Joubert – 06/02/2020 10:17am

**To:** All Staff

**Subject:** Announcement – Significant Company Restructuring

---

As a modern IT Services organisation, we are continuously looking for opportunities to expand our business in areas of growth and to also move away from those areas of the business that are in decline or showing limited opportunities for growth and profitability.

Over recent months, a special Team within my broader Executive Leadership Team has been evaluating some specific acquisition and divestiture opportunities for The Company and our business.

Yesterday we signed binding memorandums to commit fully to these significant changes, and as we start this new decade, I am very pleased to share with you the details of these changes.

On the acquisition front we have acquired two new companies that extend the breadth of our service offerings, and allow us to expand our market footprint further.

The first of these is PGFY Solutions, an Adelaide based IT Services company with a rapidly growing business. Mr Michael Mansfield, a Director within our Sales Leadership team, will take up the role of General Manager of this new division of our business.

The second acquisition is Macro Tech Investments, which is an innovative Technology Start Up and Incubation organisation based in Sydney. We have asked Ms Chloe Lovett, former Director of our Strategic Consulting business, to lead this organisation.

Please join me in congratulating Michael and Chloe on their new roles.

In restructuring our business model, we have also made the difficult decision to divest ourselves of the troubled Consulting division, led by Rudy Beaumont. This part of our business has been challenged for some time and has comprehensively failed to deliver the return on investment that we require.

We have therefore sold this business in its entirety to Indirev Systems, one of the world's fastest growing Indian headquartered IT companies. As part of this sale, Rudy and the Consulting team will all transfer across to become employees of Indirev Systems.

Please join me in wishing Rudy and the Consulting team all the best in their new home at Indirev Systems.

Christiaan Joubert
**Managing Director**

# Epilogue

WHATEVER YOU DO, DON'T GIVE in to the corporate arseholes and start to play the game by their rules.

Don't try and out-prick the pricks.

Work diligently and with integrity to do the right thing by the business, its clients, and its people.

Most importantly, put your family first in this fast-changing, always on, and highly demanding business environment.

Finally, always call out corporate stupidity wherever and whenever you see it.

# Acronyms

PEOPLE IN BUSINESS OR PROFESSIONS love to make up acronyms, creating their own self-important insiders' language that makes their world seem mysterious, and more difficult for those outside to fully comprehend. Nowhere is this more evident than in the world of Information Technology (IT) big business.

In the story, I've tried to keep the use of these acronyms to a minimum, to allow anyone not completely fluent with the world of big business, IT or geek speak to read and understand this work. However, by necessity some have crept in and/or been used to add some flavour. So I have made the table below, which gives **descriptions**, *definitions* and some commentary of these, in case they weren't already self-evident when I used them. I hope that it's helpful.

| | |
|---|---|
| **BAFO** | **Best and Final Offer** |
| | *Term used in bids to indicate that no further negotiation on the amount or terms is possible.*[1] |
| | Often a desperate attempt by a client to play two or more equally desperate organisations off against each other, to ascertain who is willing to completely drop their pants on the price in order to win the business. |
| **BS** | **Bullshit** |
| | *A slang term and a profanity which means 'nonsense'.* [2] |
| | Pretty self-explanatory, I think. |
| **CPI** | **Consumer Price Index** |
| | *Measures changes in the price level of a weighted average market basket of consumer goods and services purchased by households. The CPI is a statistical estimate constructed using the prices of a sample of representative items whose prices are collected periodically.*[2] |
| | CPI increases are often built in to IT Services contracts as a contract clause, enabling the service provider to adjust the price annually (in line with government-set CPI figures) to cover the increased costs of providing the services. Such clauses actually had some merit back in the days when companies used to provide regular pay increases as their employees upskilled and became more productive, but now it just helps the company providing the services to claw back or pad out their profit margin. |
| **ELM** | **Executive Leadership Meeting** |
| | *The weekly meeting of The Company Executive Leadership Team.* |
| | The regular gathering of the designated geniuses in charge of a company, to guide that company onwards and upwards to greatness. Or potentially to make stupid decisions which completely destroy the fabric and value of said company. |

| GICI | **Generational IT Change Initiative** |
|------|----------------------------------------|
|      | No definition necessary, since this is a made-up acronym to give a cool and plausible sounding name to the initiative behind the Transport Co deal. Similar to but not the same as making up a kooky project codename such as Project Gravity. |
| **HQ** | **Headquarters** |
|      | *The designated company head office location.* |
|      | In the case of a global organisation, the overall company Headquarters is sometimes referred to as Intergalactic HQ. |
| **HR** | **Human Resources** |
|      | *This is the department within a business that is responsible for all things worker-related. That includes recruiting, vetting, selecting, hiring, onboarding, training, promoting, paying, and firing employees and independent contractors.*[3] |
|      | Sometimes referred to as the 'Human Remains' department, given that in modern business this function doesn't seem to exist to support the people or the managers in the business. Rather, it exists as a promoter of the latest corporate social responsibility policies (so that the company and its Executives can devote plenty of their time to virtue-signalling on social media) and as a policing function to administer the latest oppressive personnel-related policies implemented by the business in the quest for greater profits. |

| IP | **Intellectual Property** (No it's not 'Internet Protocol' - for all the nerds out there.) |
| --- | --- |
| | *A category of property that includes intangible creations of the human intellect.*[2] |
| | In the IT services business world, it often refers to investments in creating software, code, applications or systems that have some potential value across multiple clients. Hence businesses get very excited at the prospect of reselling the same piece of IP multiple times over. |
| IT | **Please refer to the top paragraph at the beginning of this section.** |
| | If you got to this stage of the book without knowing what this meant, then you've done very well. |
| KPIs | **Key Performance Indicators** |
| | *A type of performance measurement. KPIs evaluate the success of an organisation or of a particular activity in which it engages.*[2] |
| | In the world of IT Services sales, or in fact any business with a sales function, these are normally set as unachievable stretch targets for individual employees or sections of the business to minimise the payment of any potential bonuses. |
| MD | **Managing Director** |
| | *A Chief Executive.* |
| | In the case of this story, there would be a picture of an arsehole named Christiaan next to this definition. |

| PISS | **Performance Indicator Sales System** |
|------|----------------------------------------|
|      | *No definition needed as this is a made-up term.* |
|      | This was the system created by Sales Admin to help them collate all of the measures around individual sales targets and performance. It was included to take the piss out of the Sales Admin function, and also people who don't think through acronym implications clearly enough at the beginning of a project. |
| **PMP** | **Performance Management Process** |
|      | *In the context of this story it's a formal process used to manage and hopefully improve the performance of an individual who is not currently meeting the requirements of their job role.* |
|      | This really is code for the process of managing a poorly performing employee out of the organisation. In the US it's not really required as you can just fire people, but in many countries around the world there are tight guidelines to be followed which have been put in place to help protect an employee's rights. |
| **POV** | **Point of View** |
|      | *An opinion or perspective.* |
|      | In this story it was a requirement to provide an informed service provider's perspective on whether Transport Co were on the right track. Sometimes clients will seek broad points of view from the market in order to obtain some free consulting, and hopefully a few good ideas that they can then implement themselves. |

| Q1, Q2 etc | **Quarter 1, Quarter 2, etc.** |
|---|---|
| | *A quarter is a three-month period on a company's financial calendar that acts as a basis for periodic financial reports and the paying of dividends. A quarter refers to one-fourth of a year and is typically expressed as 'Q1' for the first quarter, 'Q2' for the second quarter, and so forth.*[4] |
| | These are the increasingly short-term and narrow timeframes on which 'strategic' business decisions are being made. |
| **RFP** | **Request for Proposal** |
| | *A business document that announces and provides details about a project, as well as soliciting bids from contractors who will help complete the project.* [4] |
| | RFPs are closely related to, but not exactly the same as RFIs, RFTs and RFQs. And they are all pains in the arse to respond to. Often put together by people from Procurement who really have no idea or any care about what the business really wants. |
| **SLAs** | **Service Level Agreements** |
| | *A service-level agreement (SLA) is a commitment between a service provider and a client. Particular aspects of the service – quality, availability, responsibilities – are agreed between the service provider and the service user.* [2] |
| | I'm not going to add any further flavour to the definition of SLAs, since I have previously witnessed passionate, near-violent debates about the merits of particular SLA measures that would make most long-standing religious conflicts look like minor schoolyard scuffles. |

| SOW | **Statement of Work** |
|---|---|
| | *A document routinely employed in the field of project management. ... It defines project-specific activities, deliverables and timelines for a vendor providing services to the client.* [2] |
| | A Statement of Work is one of those totally necessary but painful evils in life. It exists in order to ensure that the scope of work is documented in enough detail to hopefully prevent having lawyers at twenty paces when the wheels inevitably fall off the project. I will leave this earth a happy man if I never have to participate in the creation of another SOW ever again. |
| **WTF** | **WTF?!** I can't believe you don't know what that means! Google it... |

[1] Source: www.businessdictionary.com
[2] Source: Wikipedia
[3] Source: www.shopify.com.au
[4] Source: www.investopedia.com

**STEVE EATTS** has worked in the field of Information Technology for more than 30 years, in a wide range of roles in both public and private sector organisations. Throughout his career he has taken on business assignments in the United Kingdom, USA, India, Japan, New Zealand, the Philippines and all states of Australia.

Steve is a widower who lives in Adelaide, South Australia with his two sons, and he once purchased a Harley Davidson with his sales bonus from clinching a deal.

Lightning Source UK Ltd.
Milton Keynes UK
UKHW010924031221
394997UK00004B/1261